NO REMEDY

BOUNTY - BOOK TWO

CHRISTINE D'ABO

RIPTIDE
PUBLISHING

Riptide Publishing
PO Box 1537
Burnsville, NC 28714
www.riptidepublishing.com

No Remedy

Cover art: Lou Harper, louharper.com/design.html
Editor: Delphine Dryden, delphinedryden.com/editing
Layout: L.C. Chase, lcchase.com/design.htm

ISBN: 978-1-62649-402-2

Second edition
May, 2016

Also available in ebook:
ISBN: 978-1-62649-401-5

NO REMEDY

BOUNTY - BOOK TWO

CHRISTINE
D'ABO

RIPTIDE
PUBLISHING

TABLE OF
CONTENTS

CHAPTER

ONE

Mace Simms tugged uncomfortably on her lab coat before slipping into the console chair to initiate the latest in her series of tests. *Gods, please let it work this time.* Her fingernails bit into the flesh of her palms as the scanner whirled up to full power, pulling the sample into its innards.

It had taken Mace the better part of three months to become familiar with the procedures Alec insisted she use in his lab. It was only when she could complete them to his satisfaction that he left her alone for more than five minutes at a time. *Gods, he was so stubborn.* The last thing she wanted was him hanging over her shoulder, questioning her every move.

The computer hummed pleasantly as it ran the latest chemical analysis of their continued attempts at an antidote for the *ryana* poison. Gritting her teeth, Mace tried to ignore the persistent memory of her most recent communication with her brother, Gar. She couldn't bear to recall the look of worry coloring his normally impassive face. Gar's husband, Faolan—Mace's captain, mentor, friend—had taken a turn for the worse in recent months. *Ryana* poison was now attacking his nervous system, turning him from a vivacious man who laughed with everyone into a shell of his former self. They'd hoped for ten years of good health before the poison got to this stage—they'd barely gotten three.

The computer beeped mournfully, announcing the end of its analysis. Huffing out a breath and shoving her short hair behind her ears, Mace triggered the readout and mentally rattled off the one and only prayer she knew. Numbers and compounds filled the screen, revealing a complex chemical breakdown of the interaction results. She leaned forward, pressing her fingertip to the screen as she followed the lines of text, trying to work out exactly what it meant. It was close—the compound had torn down the poison's structure, but also destroyed the surrounding cells.

"Shit." She fell back into her seat with a groan, pressing the heels of her hands to her eyes. *This will kill Faolan faster than the poison.*

"That doesn't sound good."

Mace turned her head and watched Alec stride into the room. She shivered as he scratched the back of his neck; her eyes were drawn to the flex of muscles across his arms and chest, barely concealed by his black, short-sleeved shirt. Gods, he was a temptation she hadn't anticipated when she'd set out to find Faolan's cure. Having lived on a ship full of men since she was twelve years old, she had learned to control her impulses long before now.

There was something about Alec, though. He wasn't loud and boisterous like the pirates on Faolan's ship, the *Belle Kurve*. Alec had a quiet strength about him, making him more of a mystery to her than any other person she'd met. And while she wished he would relax enough to let her past the walls he'd erected, she enjoyed the flashes of his sarcastic humor. Slowly he was starting to trust her, even if he still refused to talk about his past.

Honestly, who was she to criticize him for keeping secrets?

Crossing her arms, she snorted. "Oh, it worked. It ripped the infected cells to shreds . . . along with the uninfected ones."

Alec stood behind her chair, leaning forward until the back of her head pressed against his chest. She glanced up in time to watch him slide his glasses up the bridge of his nose, wondering again why he hadn't undergone the operation to repair his corneas. He had the resources and credits available to have it done legally. Hell, he could probably perform the bloody operation on himself if he were so inclined.

Mace looked back at the screen as Alec reached ahead to advance the report. He seemed completely oblivious to how much of his body was pressed against hers. Hell, most of the time he didn't show any awareness of her except as another functional piece of equipment in his lab. She wasn't used to being ignored or blending into the background. That was more her brother's style.

Gar had been the best and most infamous operative in the Bounty Hunters' Guild. If he was on the trail of a mark, nobody would know it until he was right on top of them—and then it was too late to do anything but give the hell up. Mace had some of those instincts too. On the other hand, Faolan had taught her the benefits of seizing life by the throat and living it to its full extent, which usually meant being the center of attention.

"You're right. Shit." Alec's voice rumbled in his chest. "We're closer this time, so that's promising."

Mace rolled her eyes. "Sure, if killing the patient is forward progress."

"Depends on the patient. If a Sayton happens to ingest the *ryana*, then we'll have an antidote ready to go."

"Too bad *ryana* only seems to affect humans."

Alec stiffened and pulled back. "Be thankful it isn't more races."

The loss of his contact was as unnerving as his reaction. He always withdrew whenever she tried to talk about the origins of the poison they were studying, and for the life of her, Mace couldn't figure out why. Sliding her hands over the tops of her thighs, she turned and glanced at him.

His cropped black hair looked as though he'd been running his hands through it compulsively. He did that when he was stressed about something. He wasn't wearing his lab coat, but as civilian or scientist, Alec always appealed to her in a way he shouldn't.

Damn it. The last thing she needed was to get tangled up in feelings for a man she would inevitably leave when she returned to the *Belle Kurve*. She would use Alec to get the antidote for Faolan and then she'd get the hell off this stupid planet. She'd deal with her emotions once she knew Faolan was better.

Allowing herself a final admiring glance at his mussed appearance, she said, "Good old Rusty trying to press you for credits again?" She leaned her elbow against the top of the chair and propped her chin in her hand. "I'm surprised he hasn't stopped playing bully yet."

Mace didn't know the security officer's real name and frankly didn't give a shit. She'd dubbed him "Rusty" based solely on the massive amounts of rust covering the UVA he drove. Planet Naveeo clearly wasn't high on the Loyalist list of priorities when it came to new equipment. Hell, it was lucky to get the few castoffs it did, given the reputation of most of the colony's inhabitants.

Alec's gaze dropped to her cleavage before quickly snapping back to her face. Those little slips were the only reason she knew he was attracted to her, although he was too professional to ever make a move. And she was too guarded to let him.

But it felt . . . good.

Maybe she *should* let him.

"Our *friend* wanted me to pay extra for my not-so-new colleague. Again." Alec smirked as he nodded his chin in her direction. "Seems it's hard work to keep the brutes from stealing you away. I set him straight, but if he gives you any trouble, let me know. I'm not going to let him get away with this bullshit any longer."

Mace rolled her eyes but sat up straighter. "Next time invite him over for a little sparring. I'd be more than happy to show him how little protection I need."

"Not necessary. I showed him the imprint of your foot on my back and told him it was from a month ago."

"Liar." She grinned. "Though it really was a good kick."

Alec didn't respond. His brown gaze slipped again, this time to the side of her neck. Gods, she could almost feel it like a touch on her skin, sending a shiver through her body. He hadn't shaved yet today, giving him an uncharacteristic ruggedness. Alec stepped closer, and Mace's breath hitched.

"How long have you been at this?" He reached out and tapped the tip of his finger against the chair's top. "I don't remember seeing you come in this morning."

She watched, transfixed, as his light tapping continued. If Alec knew how many hours she'd been working, he would no doubt try to enforce the restrictions he'd previously put in place "for her own good." His last lecture about overworking herself still stung.

His tapping increased in speed, but the rhythm remained constant. Mace couldn't look away as her body relaxed. Something in the back of her mind tickled. Her mouth began to move before she could stop herself.

"I didn't go home last night."

The words slipped from her without conscious thought. The moment she'd spoken, Alec stopped the tapping, and Mace shook off the spell she'd slipped under. The sudden fog on her brain lifted, and she glared at Alec.

Alec reached forward and caught her chin in his hand. "Mace, you promised me you weren't going to bury yourself in this work."

What the hell? "I didn't mean to say that."

"Stop trying to deflect. You'll kill yourself if you continue at this pace. I know, because I've seen it happen to enough of my colleagues."

"Why did I tell you—"

"I refuse to sit by and watch you burn yourself out." Alec sighed as he shifted his hold and brushed his fingers against her jaw. "I'm taking you out to eat."

She snapped her mouth shut, frowned, and pulled away from his touch. "What?"

"Come on, up."

"Alec—"

"Move, Mace. If you expect to keep working for me, you'll need to learn when to take some time and unwind. Flashes of brilliance can't happen when you're exhausted."

It was pointless to argue the point, and she got to her feet in defeat. "Says the man who slept here every night for two weeks straight last month."

He snorted as he slipped an arm around her waist. "Completely different. And if I remember correctly, you gave me hell for doing that."

"As I should have."

"Well, consider this payment in kind."

Alec towered over Mace as he guided her toward the exit. The last of her argument slipped away. Warmth from his body bled through the thin material of his shirt and her body soaked it in. His tactile nature reminded her so much of Faolan. The pirate captain needed physical contact as a reminder that the ones he loved were still present—still safe. Mace wondered what motivated Alec's need for touch.

"I've been told," Alec whispered against her ear as they stepped out into the heat of the twin suns, "that Dail has come up with a new concoction he claims tastes exactly like Hydraxian ale. I suggest we go get a couple of mugs and a plate of *narn*. Both of us can relax for a change."

Mace let Alec lead her through the square comprising the colony center, ignoring her natural impulses to pull away from his protective stance and show him she was more than capable of looking after herself. Despite their occasional sparring rounds, she had managed to maintain her cover as a relatively harmless scientist. As far as Alec was concerned, Mace's sharp tongue was her deadliest weapon.

Besides, the bounty on Mace's head was too big to risk drawing attention to herself.

"Drinks and *narn*. Sounds good to me." She leaned a bit closer as they approached the bar. "But you can keep the ale. I swear Dail slipped something into mine the last time."

Laughter greeted them as the door slid open, revealing darkness and the stench of unwashed bodies. Mace cringed but kept moving forward until she found an empty booth to the side of the room. The surface of the seat was pitted and sticky with a residue she thought it best not to examine too closely. If it weren't for the fact this was the best place in the settlement to get food, she'd never have set foot in here twice.

Alec dropped into the seat opposite her, and with a quick push of his glasses, leaned across the table. "No arguments. We eat, drink, and then I'm escorting you back to your apartment so you can get some rest."

The look of absolute seriousness immediately reminded Mace of her brother, how Gar would get when trying to convince Faolan to lie down or take his medication. Despite her deception, she appreciated Alec's genuine concern. It was touching. Screw that, it was downright sexy.

Rolling her eyes, she leaned back and crossed her arms. "Are you going to tuck me in too?"

They'd done this dance before without it going anywhere. Alec was too much of a gentleman to be anything but the proper boss, but Mace had spent too many years as one of a very few women in a ship full of men to *not* instigate a little flirting. It wasn't natural to avoid risqué banter.

Although with Alec it was different. She knew he wouldn't take her up on it. He was safe.

This time, though, something flashed in his eyes. "Is that an invitation?"

Mace tucked the hair that had fallen forward behind her ear again, cocking her head. "Does it matter?"

"Yes." His voice sounded rough.

"You've never agreed before." She caught herself fidgeting and quickly sat on her hands. "Why would this time be different?"

"You weren't serious before."

Oh. Shit.

She wasn't serious now. Was she?

"Alec! You bastard."

Mace's gaze snapped to Dail as the short Cybrax waddled in their direction.

She smiled at Alec's sigh and silently thanked the obnoxious bar owner for saving her from confronting her rising attraction to Alec. Now wasn't the time to give in to her lust. She was still too far away from getting her hands on a cure.

"Dail, I thought you were off-world." Alec seemed amused enough to almost sound friendly.

The Cybrax made a high-pitched squeak that Mace recognized as his equivalent of a snort. "Is that why I find you gracing my establishment?" Dail reached over and lifted Mace's hand to his lips. "And you brought your beautiful assistant as well. I am truly honored."

Slimy lips smeared across her skin, sending a shiver of disgust through her. "I've been told you have new ale," she managed to say with a smile. "The temptation was too much for me to resist."

Dail let loose another squeak. "You need to improve your dissembling abilities, my dear. You've far too honest a face for anyone to believe your lies."

Mace found it hard not to laugh. Instead she simply shrugged and gave him a small smile. "What can I say? My parents raised me to always tell the truth."

Never mind that both her parents had been murdered and she'd been taught to lie by the best pirate in the sector.

Alec growled softly as he liberated Mace's hand from Dail. "If you think you can tear yourself away from molesting my assistant, we could stand to have some food and drink. But if you can't provide us with any, we can try over at Dominars." Alec smirked.

Mace's skin tingled as he methodically rubbed her pulse point with his thumb. She knew she should move away. She was finding it increasingly hard to resist his pull.

Alec looked back to Mace as Dail shouted out an order to one of the waitresses. Lifting an eyebrow, he increased the pressure of the contact but slowed the pace. He was waiting for her to respond, withdraw her hand, make a snarky comment, or one of the other million things she normally did to keep him at bay.

"You've never agreed before."

"You weren't serious before."

Seemingly oblivious to the silent dance before him, Dail turned back and squeaked again. "Hard to find good help out here on the fringe. I assume you'll want the same thing you always eat. Shalaya will bring your order soon enough."

"Thanks, Dail." Alec finally released Mace and leaned back in the chair. "Just make sure it isn't drugged this time. I'd hate to have to slip a diarrheic into your water supply again."

"You bastard! That was you?"

"They'll never be able to trace it back to me. It was due to a sudden bout of spoiled food resulting from improper storage. My tests will confirm this, naturally." Alec tapped his finger against his lips.

Mace giggled at the look of horror on the Cybrax's face. "Know thy enemy, Dail."

"Shalaya! Hold that order." Dail scurried away, shouting orders in his native language.

Alec's grin told Mace how much he'd enjoyed his little rebellion. She relished these brief moments where she saw the flashes of the man he must have been before coming to Naveeo. She didn't think Alec was necessarily in exile, but people didn't choose to live in a dung hole like this voluntarily. Something must have happened to have brought him here.

Tucking her hair behind her ear once again, Mace leaned closer. "Did you really put something in the water?"

"Would you think any less of me if I had?"

"Not at all." Licking her lips, she dipped her head closer. "In fact, I might have to give you a proper thank-you."

"Then I most certainly did. Twice the dose of what Dail reported, in fact." Alec reached forward to brush her forearm where it rested on the table. "So, about that thank-you."

Biting her lower lip, she slid her arm so it pressed against his. Lust flared low in her gut, making her pussy clench and her breath hitch. It had been so long since she'd been with a man, even longer since she'd been with someone who could satisfy her particular needs. She pulled away enough to break the contact, reduce the temptation. Mace could speculate all she liked about what Alec would be like in bed, but she couldn't risk finding out.

She kept her voice low. "Alec, while I've known you for a few months now, I can't say I know much *about* you."

"Not much to say." Alec traced a pattern on the skin of her arm. "Just trying to help people where I can."

"Without taking anything in return?" She cocked an eyebrow. "I know this will sound jaded, but people don't do the types of things you do without wanting something back."

"I'm a selfless kind of guy."

"While I'm not arguing your point, I also know there's more to it than that."

Alec lifted his hand but didn't quite pull away. She could tell from his expression that he was fighting some sort of internal battle. "I don't think you would like me very much if you heard the full story."

"Everyone has secrets."

"Even you?"

Mace wasn't sure how to respond. She somehow knew the words she chose would shape their relationship going forward. "Yes, even me. I've always said it's not the secret itself so much as how we choose to live with its consequences."

Before Alec could respond, the front door was pushed open and light flooded the bar. Silence spread across the room as everyone took in the newcomers—three men, dressed head to toe in brown *drax* leather. The hairs on the back of Mace's neck stood up.

Bounty hunters. *Shit.*

Turning to face Alec, she tried coming up with an excuse to leave. She was shocked to see a flash of panic on his face, followed by bleak determination. Why the hell would he care that bounty hunters had just walked into the bar? Many of the colony's inhabitants weren't high-class citizens, and any of them could have bounties on their heads. Unless Alec's secret went deeper than she could imagine, there wasn't any reason for him to panic.

Me, on the other hand . . .

Alec grabbed her hand and squeezed hard. "Mind if we get out of here?"

Her pirate instincts roared back to her in a heartbeat, despite having lived the life of a meek researcher these past few months. She was particularly good at avoiding bounty hunters. Reaching out to snag two mugs of ale from the passing waitress, she thrust one into Alec's grip.

"Follow my lead," she whispered, then slugged back half the mug.

"Mace, what the hell?"

Standing up quickly, she made sure to throw in an exaggerated wobble as she laughed. Strategically keeping her back to the trio, she slammed the mug down on the table and started to sing.

"Oh, *carna*, the things you do to meeeeee." She pulled Alec's arm, urging him to his feet. "Oh, *carna*, you can never leave me beeeeeee."

"Mace," he hissed.

Get up, she mouthed, stumbling backward to bump into the table behind her. The action allowed her to turn her head and get a glimpse of the hunters. Her little drunken act seemed to be of no interest to them, just as she had hoped. For an intelligent man, Alec's lack of understanding was frustrating as hell.

She grabbed his hand and twirled in a drunken circle in an abysmal attempt at a dance spin. "Take me home, *carna*. Take meeeee home."

Not wanting to push her luck, she tugged Alec with her, leading him toward the toilets and the back door. She tripped over her feet, sending Alec's body crashing into hers as they stumbled into the dark hallway. Ignoring the feel of his thighs against her ass and the warmth of his chest seeping through her thin shirt, Mace bit back a groan and forced herself to continue on.

The second they were far enough down the hall to be hidden in shadow, she stopped moving. She pressed her hand to Alec's mouth when he tried to speak, pushing him backward until he was against the wall. From this vantage point, she could look out into the bar without being noticed.

A minute passed, and she thought their luck would hold out. Of course, Dail's high-pitched squeak echoed above the normal bar noise and disabused her of that notion. *Shit.* Of course the slimy little Cybrax would turn her over in a heartbeat if he knew how large a bounty she currently wore around her neck.

Mace ignored how hot Alec looked with her hand gagging him. "We need to get out of here."

He nodded, cautiously reaching up to pull her hand from his mouth. "I'm pretty sure Dail keeps this door locked."

"Not a problem." She grinned as she patted Alec's cheek. "I have a bit of experience in that area."

"Why do I get the feeling you haven't told me everything about your work history?"

"It wasn't relevant at the time, but let's say my credentials are a bit more robust than I let on. Come on."

She dropped to her knees in front of the door panel, quickly prying it open with the knife she kept tucked into her boot. She could feel Alec watching every flick of her hands as she rewired the controls. A few taps on the keys and the door slid silently open.

"I'd appreciate an updated résumé when we get back to your place."

Looking up at him in surprise, she stood, not bothering to cover her handiwork. "Why my place?" *Gods, it'll be the first place they check.*

Alec wrapped his fingers around her biceps and pulled her out the door. "Trust me when I say they are after me. I'll get you safely to your apartment, and then I'll disappear."

Why the hell are bounty hunters after Alec? "Even if that were true, if you think I'm going to let you scurry off into the sunset without an explanation, you're insane."

"Later. Just move."

She gritted her teeth against her annoyance as he yanked her out the door. She hated playing the hapless Loyalist woman with no skills to defend herself. She hadn't been raised to believe the government was there to protect and keep her safe. She knew firsthand how little the corrupt men in power would do to help those in their care.

Alec wasn't a man like that, but she still . . .

The colony was on the fringe of society, full of colonists who were trying to evade the law for one reason or another; the sudden appearance of bounty hunters seemed to have scared off the crowd in the square outside the bar. Mace felt too exposed in the empty, open space, and Alec seemed of the same mind. Keeping their heads down, they skirted the perimeter until they reached one of the cross alleys.

Alec released her arm and laced his hand with hers as they increased their pace. Mace's living quarters were in one of the newer buildings near the outskirts of the colony. She had specifically chosen it in the event she needed to make a quick escape. At the rate her day was going, that would be sooner rather than later.

She wasn't sure if it was her paranoia kicking in, but as they rounded the corner, her building's front door in sight, a prickle of awareness raised every tiny hair on her skin. Someone was watching. She jerked her hand free from Alec, sidestepping his attempt to hold her back as she jogged ahead. The security scanner was cool under her palm, the flash of light bright in the rapidly approaching evening.

"I shouldn't come in." Alec's voice sounded tight. "I'll put you in more danger."

"The only danger you're in right now is of me killing you if you think about leaving without giving me some answers first."

The door clicked open, giving Mace room to yank Alec in behind her. Neither of them spoke until they were safely on the other side of her apartment door.

Alec went immediately to the window, looking out the one-way glass. "I don't think anyone followed us."

"It won't take those hunters long to figure out where we went."

"I'm sorry you got mixed up in this." Scrubbing a hand down his face, he turned to lean against the wall. "I didn't think they'd find me."

"What the hell is going on?" She marched to the safe where she kept her weapon hidden. "Why would bounty hunters come after a scientist?"

The low whine of a blaster being activated filled the momentary pause. Shit, she'd made a rookie mistake: not checking the room for intruders the moment she got in. Not wanting to distract herself by looking at Alec, she turned her head toward the origin of the noise.

Standing in the doorway to her bedchamber was a tall man dressed head to toe in black. His eyes were hidden behind a fitted pair of radiation goggles. He'd shaved his head down to stubble. His attention was fixed completely on Alec, who stared back as if he were seeing a ghost.

"The lady has asked an excellent question." The stranger had a gravelly voice, as if he were suffering the aftereffects of shouting for hours. He lifted the blaster an inch higher, his aim fixed somewhere near the middle of Alec's chest. "One I'd like an answer to myself."

It was obvious the bounty hunter didn't consider her a threat. She might have enough time before he realized his mistake to get her own blaster free of the safe. She was about to make her move when Alec stepped forward away from the wall. She couldn't tear her eyes from him.

"Answer the question, Alec." The man thumbed the energy setting up a notch. "Why the hell did a bounty order come in to the guild to bring you in dead?"

"My gods." Alec staggered two steps closer to the stranger, a look of pained remorse fixed firmly on his face. "Byron?"

The man nodded and smirked. "Miss me?"

CHAPTER

TWO

I t was as if the last ten years of Alec's life had suddenly evaporated. Byron couldn't be here, not after Alec had been so careful to cover his trail. Gods, he'd managed to stay five steps ahead of his ex-lover for so long, he had started to believe this day would never come.

Wrong again, Roiten.

He'd gotten complacent since Mace's arrival. And now, if Byron was here, it meant the Loyalist brutes wouldn't be far behind. Gods help him if he'd spent the past seven years on his own, only to fail before finding an antidote for the last of his mistakes. It would be worse if Mace or Byron got killed in the crossfire. Byron knew he was taking that risk, though; if he died, Alec would find a way to resurrect him, just for the chance to kill him again. Stupid bounty hunter.

But Mace was an innocent in this mess. He needed to get her out of here, especially now that he was an even bigger target.

Byron's aim didn't waver, though he flexed his fingers around the grip of his blaster. "You ran from the Loyalists. Why? And why do they want you out of the way *now*? What have you done?"

Alec clenched his teeth together. He wasn't going to give in, not when he was so close to his goal. "Get out of here, hunter."

"Hunter? *Hunter*? Now isn't that charming?" Byron narrowed his gaze as a muscle twitched in his jaw. "Not happening. Not without you in tow at least."

"Alec." Alec jerked at the sound of Mace's voice, turning toward her as she spoke to him. "You didn't tell me company was coming. Kind of rude, you know."

She was still crouched low in front of her safe, but her gaze was locked on Byron. *Shit, stupid ass.* He'd put her in danger without even trying. Knowing Byron, if Mace so much as flinched in the wrong direction, he'd shoot her in her leg to make a point.

"You don't worry about a thing, sweetie." Byron's easy drawl sent a shudder through Alec. Gods, he'd missed the sound of that low timbre. "I'm just an old friend catching up with our boy. I'll take the good doctor here, and we'll get out of your hair. You stay there and keep looking pretty."

The damn asshole hadn't changed from the last time Alec had seen him. Blue eyes so light they looked silver peeked from behind Byron's goggles. The familiar steel was in his stance, even as he shot a glance full of unspoken questions Alec's way. Questions Alec had no intention of answering. Not here at least. How the hell had Byron found him? The high-pitched whine of another blaster powering up made Alec twist to follow the sound.

Mace was on her feet, a short-barreled weapon pointed half a foot from Byron's head. "Well, pardon me if I can't agree to that."

Gods, he hadn't seen her move, she'd been so fast.

"Mace, what are you doing?" He swallowed hard, inching closer to her.

Byron turned, finally paying proper attention to her. His aim stayed fixed on Alec, meaning he would catch the brunt of Byron's attack when it came. *That's good at least.*

"She appears to be trying to save your sorry ass, Alec. And holding a piece of equipment she shouldn't have access to. That's guild issue."

"Oh, you'd be surprised what I have access to." Mace cocked an eyebrow. "Now there are several ways this can play out. Few of them work out in your favor . . . Byron, is it?"

"Yes, sweetie." Byron cocked his head, letting his gaze travel down Mace's body. "Proper attack stance. Well-developed forearms and thighs. I bet you have a nice ass too. Seems you're not a typical lab *strat*. Alec, I see you still have a type. Young, pretty, and dangerous."

"Fuck off, Byron. Leave Mace out of this."

"It doesn't appear she is *interested* in being left out of the party." Byron chuckled. "So either you're an ex-hunter or know someone who is. Could be a pirate, I guess. Easier to steal what you need rather than earn it."

Mace thumbed up the blaster's power. "You're going to slowly disengage your weapon."

"Not going to answer me?"

"Then you'll hold it out from your body by your finger so I can retrieve it. If you try to stop me, I'll kill you. Understand?"

Alec ignored the way his chest tightened at the thought of Byron dying. It hurt as much as the idea that Mace was capable of blasting a hole in his ex-lover's chest. He'd known there was more to her than she had let on. A green researcher on her first assignment didn't show the level of skepticism or tacit determination she had from the moment of her arrival. Even Alec had carried a sheen of wide-eyed optimism on his first case, and he was from one of the nastiest planets in the sector. Seeing Mace now, the way she held the weapon and the unwavering resolve on her face, Alec knew there was so much more to her story than he'd suspected.

Yet another person he'd been fooled by.

He didn't like to think he was gullible, but he did have a blind spot for certain people. A plea said in a particular way and Alec knew he could be swayed. It was that element of desperation he hated to see reflected in another person. He needed to help them.

His gaze bounced between Mace and Byron as he stepped forward. As inappropriate as it was, his heart was beating faster at the whole situation—and not solely because of fear. It might have been the power struggle between the three of them, a dynamic he had come to associate so strongly with sex that he was conditioned to react with arousal. Or it might have been that he'd had so few relationships since he'd left Byron, so little time for sex at all. His cock twitched at the memory of the things they'd done. And Mace? Gods, so many fantasies threatened to pop to life, his body shook from the strain of holding them back.

He'd wanted her from the moment she'd walked into his life. He'd never *stopped* wanting Byron. But it was hardly the time to ponder his sex life.

"Byron, I think you should listen to her." He inched forward. "You won't get any answers if you're dead. I know how much you hate not knowing what's going on."

Byron snorted. "Death does put a kink in my information-gathering technique." On the word *kink* his gaze flicked toward Alec.

Mace cocked an eyebrow and nodded toward Byron. "You know what I need you to do, then."

For a moment, Alec didn't think Byron would listen. The stubborn bastard always liked to do things the hard way and refused to take orders from others. It went against his nature. So when Byron let the weight of the blaster swing down, hooking his finger around the trigger to hold it out from his body, relief swept through him. Apparently, no one was dying today.

Mace adjusted her stance, taking a half step backward. "On second thought, keep holding it like that and drop to your knees. Put your free hand behind your head."

Alec wanted to groan at the grin on Byron's face.

"Ah, sweetheart, if I'd known you were into that kind of game, this evening could have started on a far more pleasant note." Byron sank to his knees, winking as he braced his hand against his neck. "I should warn you, I'm normally the one giving the commands."

"Any other time, I might be tempted to take you up on the offer." Mace's cool grin sent a shiver through Alec. "For now I'll have to settle for you placing the blaster on the floor and pushing it toward me."

As Byron followed her directions, Mace reached behind her back, tossing a set of electro-cuffs to Alec. The metal was cool in his hands . . . and the shape was so familiar he nearly whimpered as all the inappropriate thoughts surged back into his mind.

"Alec, secure his hands behind his back."

"Mace, listen—"

"I'll listen when I know he's secure and your life isn't in danger anymore. So shut up and do what I tell you to."

"Yeah, Alec, do what the lady says," Byron taunted. "I know how much you love to follow orders."

Ignoring him as best he could, Alec skirted around to his back to yank Byron's hands down and fix the heavy electro-cuffs on properly. He couldn't stop from swaying close to his former lover, taking in the scent of sweat and leather as he jerked on the metal.

"All done," he whispered against Byron's ear.

The small act of rebellion felt good. He had been beneath Byron more times than he could count. He'd succumbed to the other man's will so often he'd forgotten he had a mind of his own. Hell, surviving their reunion without ending up naked was a miracle, enough to make his blood sing through his veins.

His feelings for Byron had always been confused, but their parting had complicated matters to the point that Alec didn't know his own heart any longer. Gods, he had never thought he'd be in this position again.

Byron turned his head so Alec's nose brushed his cheek. "Don't think we're done here. We need to talk."

"You're not in a position to be giving orders."

"I'm *always* in a position to give orders. It was one of the things you loved about me."

A hand tugged Alec back. His gaze locked onto Mace's as he turned.

"You need to step away." She gave him a gentle squeeze. "I want to make sure he's been secured properly so we can talk."

Byron's breath hitched, but he didn't comment. Gods, Alec wanted nothing more than to forget everything and convince Byron to come to bed with him. Hell, if he could get Mace to come as well, he could cross a major fantasy off his list.

Not now.

He kept his back to the pair of them, instead looking out the window. He already knew the questions Mace would ask Byron, as much as he knew what the answers would be. His carefully constructed world was about to come crashing down around him, and surprisingly he wasn't as upset as he should have been.

"You're a bounty hunter." Mace's voice was strong and confident. "You mentioned the guild. Are you with them or freelance?"

Byron's silence filled the room, making Alec want to turn back and shout at him, demanding an answer. He curled his fingers around the edge of the table in front of him and locked his gaze on the people on the street outside.

Thankfully Mace wasn't deterred by Byron's stubborn refusal to cooperate. "I have connections inside the guild, so it won't take me any time to find out exactly who you are."

This time Byron chuckled. "I figured you did."

"Then there's no point in holding back."

"Sweetheart, there is always a point. I'll learn as much about you as you learn about me during this little interrogation."

"While that may be true, I'm currently the one with the blaster and the key to your electro-cuffs. So let's start again. Why is the guild after Alec?"

"I think that's a question for your boy."

"I asked *you*." Mace leaned closer to Byron, who didn't react to her apparent attempt to loom over him in a menacing way. Even on his knees, Byron was nearly as tall as Mace.

Alec turned, leaning his weight against the table. "When did the bounty come through?" He didn't really want to ask Byron anything, but he had to know how much time they had before more hunters came.

For once, the cocky expression on Byron's face slipped. Mace might not have recognized the look as one of concern, but Alec did. Byron's chin dipped down toward his chest as he let out a soft huff.

"Orders came across my desk three months ago. You did well, Alec. I wasn't sure I was ever going to be able to find you in time."

Alec couldn't keep from rolling his eyes. "Like you would have bothered if there weren't credits involved."

Byron jerked forward and only stopped when Mace pressed the muzzle of the blaster against his temple.

"Down, boy."

"I bothered, you jackass!" Byron growled up at Alec, settling back again. "I searched for you after your little disappearing act. I couldn't pick up your trail after the Centarin outpost. Guess you were paying attention during my bitching sessions. But you must have gotten sloppy recently, making my job a hell of a lot easier. Really? Alec Randall? Too close to your real name, *Roiten*."

"Guess so." Alec ignored the sudden tightening of his throat. Byron had looked for him. Alec honestly hadn't thought he would.

"Enough!" Mace leaned against the wall. "Three months isn't a long time. How big is the bounty?"

Byron grimaced, turning to Mace. "Five million."

"Shit."

"Big enough for me to worry. I delayed the information getting out as long as possible so I could try to locate you first." Byron jerked on the bindings. "Not that I'm much good to you trussed up like this. Let me go, Alec, so we can talk."

Alec shook his head. "No. What do they want me for?" He knew the real reason, but while he assumed the Loyalist government was behind the bounty, they weren't going to be stupid enough to broadcast their true motivation.

Byron narrowed his gaze on Alec. "Multiple murders of Loyalist officials. I'd ask if you did it, but I made discreet inquiries at the facility after you left and there was never any murders. So they lied to hide the real reason."

Alec was across the room, Byron's neck between his hands. He wanted to shout at him to leave well enough alone, to let them find him, to go away and save himself rather than condemning them both. But he could only glare into Byron's face. His heart ached for how things could have been. If he hadn't learned the truth. If he hadn't realized just how bad . . .

"I could have helped you," Byron managed to squeeze out. "You didn't give me a chance."

"I had my reasons." Alec pushed Byron away, letting the other man suck in a gulp of air. "You shouldn't have come after me."

Mace stepped forward and smashed the butt of her blaster against the back of Byron's head. Alec watched his ex-lover's eyes roll up into his head before he fell unconscious to the floor.

"What the hell are you doing?" He straightened as Mace stepped over Byron's prone body. "He's not the only one who'll be looking for me."

"Exactly. We need to get out of here as quickly as possible. Sorry, but we won't have time to go back to your apartment. We'll have to pick up whatever you'll need once we get out of this system. Might take a while to find an outpost, but I have a few contacts."

Mace disappeared for a few minutes, banging around loudly in the next room. Alec couldn't move. Byron was here, despite the efforts Alec had taken to keep him away. Protect him. A sickening realization settled in the pit of his stomach—maybe things could have been different had Alec stayed. But trusting Byron would have meant putting him in danger, something Alec had no intention of doing then or now.

Mace returned with a large black bag slung over her shoulder. "We'll be able to use the back streets to get to the lowlands. I have my ship stashed there." She'd thrown on a pair of black pants and a dark-blue leather vest, and held a strange stone necklace in her hand. She no longer appeared to be the meek assistant he'd come to know over the recent months.

In fact, she looked a lot like Byron.

"Wait." He shook his head. "You have a ship?"

She cocked an eyebrow. "You didn't think I walked here, did you?"

"I assumed public transport, actually. How can you afford a private ship?"

"The less you know about that, the better."

Something else he'd have to pursue with her once they were far from here. "Where are we going?"

"We have a few options available to us." She nudged Byron with the toe of her boot. "What do you want to do with this one?"

Gods, that was a question he had asked himself more times than he could count. "We can't leave him here. I doubt he's changed much, which means he has more than his fair share of enemies who would take advantage if they found him like this."

"I don't think dragging him along is the best idea."

Alec crouched beside Byron, close but not touching. Unconscious, he'd lost the harsh edge in his face. Alec wanted nothing more than to reach out and touch the warm skin of Byron's neck. They'd only been together a year before he'd run, but he regretted ending things the way he had.

People had died as a result of Alec's actions. He needed to put things right if he was ever going to allow himself to be with another person. He couldn't live in peace and harmony knowing he'd murdered innocents.

But seeing Byron again . . .

"We have to take him. Now that he knows for sure I'm alive, he won't stop until he's found me again."

"He'll just cause problems for us when we want them the least." Mace sighed as she pulled a bio syringe from her pack and jabbed it into Byron's neck. "That will keep him unconscious until we can get him secured on my ship. You'll have to carry him, though. I'll grab what gear I can. We leave now."

Alec's back and shoulders were screaming as they breached the top of the latest hill. He wouldn't be able to take much more of this—Mace was more of a slave driver than he was. Thankfully she'd stopped a few meters away, giving him a chance to catch up.

Byron was bloody heavy.

Mace glanced over her shoulder at his approach. There was a twinkle in her eye as she checked him out. Gods, he must look as tired as he felt.

"There she is." Mace nodded toward the valley. "She might not seem like a lot on the outside, but the *Geilt* is one of the toughest ships I know."

Alec sucked in a breath when his gaze landed on the hulking mass settled by the tree line. The ship must have been sleek and gleaming when it was new, but now its hull was mottled with blaster burns and pockmarked with countless dents and scratches. "It's spaceworthy, right?"

Mace snorted. "If my brother heard you insult his ship, he'd kill you."

"Remind me never to meet your brother."

"If you're hanging around me long enough, it's inevitable. Just remember your manners and you'll survive the privilege."

Byron made a soft moaning noise, his arm twitching in Alec's grip.

"Let's get on board. I forgot how heavy this bastard is."

To her credit, Mace hadn't asked any questions about his obvious relationship with Byron. Whether it was out of some perverse sense of respect or if she was simply practical enough to know this wasn't the time for an interrogation, Alec was thankful.

As they approached the ship, Mace pulled out a slim control pad and typed a code. The loud hiss of a hydraulic lock disengaging caused a flock of *tyranian* beasts to shoot into the sky from the surrounding treetops. The ominous sound of their squawks sent a shiver through him.

"I've come to check on my baby every week since arriving here, so it won't take me long to get us ready once we get inside. It looks like no one has bothered her."

Mace paused at the still-closed door to press her hand to a bio scanner. Another beep and the door whooshed open for them. "You can set him down here and—"

The echo of shouting rolled down the hill to them. As soon as Alec turned, he recognized the men from the bar running full-tilt toward the *Geilt*. Bounty hunters.

Fuck.

"Go, go, go!" Mace pushed him into the ship, sending him staggering under Byron's weight.

Alec managed to keep his feet long enough to set Byron down on a padded bench off to the side of what appeared to be the main cabin. Mace slapped her hand against the internal bio scanner, sending the hatch door snapping shut.

"Secure him and then yourself. I'll get us into the sky."

"How the hell did they find us?" he shouted as she disappeared into what he assumed was the cockpit.

"The same way your lover boy did." A set of keys flew through the air, landing half a meter from where he knelt. "Undo his cuffs and secure him to the bench. There's a bar underneath you can use."

The ship shuddered as blaster fire painted the side of the hull. Alec's fingers shook as he released one side of Byron's electro-cuffs. Gods, how could he have let this happen? His normally tight emotional control was slipping, which would lead to bad things if he didn't get a handle on them shortly. The ship rocked again, but this time he recognized the familiar rattle of an engine starting up.

As quickly as he could, he snapped the cuff to the bar, making sure Byron was positioned as comfortably as possible. Despite their differences, Alec never wanted to see Byron hurt. With any luck, he wouldn't wake up until they'd gotten into space.

He'd have to ask Mace if there was somewhere else they could move him. Alec might not wish Byron any harm, but he also didn't want to spend the duration of the trip—however long it would be—in either a staring contest or a verbal chess match with the man he'd run out on.

"Alec?" There was a note of urgency in Mace's voice he couldn't ignore.

"Coming."

The cockpit was small, but there was a copilot chair; he fell into it and did up the restraints. "I hope this thing is fast."

Mace snorted. "I've seen my brother pull maneuvers with this bucket that would make your head spin. She'll have enough to get us out of here. Hold on."

The jerk of takeoff forced him back into the seat. He looked at the scanners to see the bounty hunters from the bar scrambling back to avoid the heat of the engine's thrusters. Alec prayed all the hunters' resources were on the ground, not in orbit, and Mace had managed a clean escape. As his gaze slid over to her, he grew fascinated by the movement of her hands over the controls. Her precision with the commands indicated she was an expert pilot, as did her practiced ascent into the atmosphere.

His moment of admiration at her skill was replaced with sudden, deep-burning anger. Mace was just another person who'd lied to him. And like an idiot, he'd been taken in by her. "Who the hell *are* you?"

She jerked but kept her gaze averted. "Not now, Alec."

"I've worked with you, side by side, for months now." Fury bubbled up through his chest, suddenly making it hard to breathe. "Was anything you told me true?"

"Not. *Now.*"

He knew he should resist the urge to use his ability. They were on the run with bounty hunters breathing down their neck. Shit, she was flying their damn escape vessel—he needed to leave it alone. At the last moment, he realized he'd started tapping his finger on the side of the computer panel anyway, and forced himself to stop. Now was not the time to play with people's minds.

"We're breaching the upper atmosphere. Hold on."

The ship shook violently for a few seconds before instantly calming. The dark blanket of space felt like a cool balm on his pounding heart. He let out a huff of air and tried to relax.

"We made it," he said softly.

"Not exactly."

He froze at the sound of Byron's voice directly behind him. The low whine of a blaster told him how badly he had screwed up.

THREE

Mace sighed heavily. "Great, Alec."

Byron wanted to laugh at the look of utter annoyance on the woman's face. When it came to his ex-lover, he'd felt the same thing on more than one occasion. "Not his fault, darling. He thought I was still out of it, and you didn't exactly have time to check me for spare keys. Now if you'd be so kind as to fly us to the gate, I'll get us to a guild outpost."

"No!" Alec tried to move away, but Byron pressed the blaster to his side.

"I don't fucking think so." Mace twisted in her seat to meet his gaze directly. "I'm not going anywhere near the guild."

"Don't like bounty hunters? I can't imagine why." Byron knew he was being an asshole, but there was something about the hellion in front of him that made him want to fight. "I bet if I placed a few communications I'd learn some interesting things about you. Who did you say you were again?"

"Fuck you."

"Unfortunate name. Your parents must be fun."

"My parents are dead, jackass."

He winced internally. He may not have had the best home in the universe, but at least he still had his father around to share in the misery. "Sorry."

Mace snorted. "I doubt it."

"I hate to break up this little argument, but I think we may still have a problem." Alec stepped away from the blaster and pressed the display. "It looks like our friends on the ground weren't alone. We have at least two ships on an intercept vector."

Mace glared at Byron, looking more irritated than scared. "Mind if I take care of them? I'd hate to have a hole blown in my head before I get us to the dimension gate."

"I don't think the gate is a good—" Alec snapped his mouth shut.

Byron almost forgave Mace for knocking him out when he saw the look of concern on her face. "What?"

"Nothing."

"It's not nothing," Mace growled. "We're running out of time to make decisions. Is there a problem we need to be aware of, Alec?"

There was something in her manner, the way she said certain words or looked at him in a particular way that tugged on Byron's memory. He was sure he'd never met this woman before, but he couldn't quite shake the feeling of familiarity. It didn't sit right, and nothing bothered him more than not having all the information he needed.

It was clear she wasn't out to collect the bounty on Alec. The way she'd spoken to him when they'd thought Byron was still unconscious told him as much. For certain, she had an agenda, something he'd need to discover as quickly as possible.

For the time being, she was useful.

"Get us out of here," Alec said in a resigned voice.

Mace nodded, turning to face the computer. "Alec, ever fly a ship before?"

"Not one like this."

"What about you, bounty hunter? Ever fly a ship?"

Byron resisted the urge to roll his eyes. "Move, Alec."

The space was confined, making it nearly impossible for him to avoid contact with the other man as they shifted around each other. Byron thought he'd long gotten over his lust for Alec, but the way his cock stiffened at the brush of his hip against Alec's proved otherwise.

Catching Alec's gaze, he looked for any sign the other man had noticed, or perhaps even still reciprocated the long-smoldering attraction. What he read in Alec's face was confusion and something remotely akin to dread. Not the reaction he'd been hoping for.

"Sorry." Alec dropped eye contact before sliding out of the way.

As far as Byron was concerned, it was going to take more than a simple apology to make up for the past seven years.

Forcing his concentration to the matter at hand, he took up position in the copilot seat and familiarized himself with the controls.

"These commands are programmed in Zeten common language. Are you from there?"

Mace pointedly ignored the question. "Bring up the scanner and tell me how quickly they're approaching. I don't think we'll have enough time to make a gate jump."

"If you can distract them long enough, I'll get the ship ready to go." Byron quickly scanned the area. "There's no one in the queue. I'll start the process using a signal repeater. Just be ready to fly us in when I say to go."

"If you damage this ship, I'll kill you." Mace pressed the throttle to full, jerking them forward at a mad speed. "Alec, you better strap yourself in. The other room has a chair."

"I don't think—" He froze as Mace and Byron turned at the same time to glare at him. "Okay, fuck. I'm going."

Neither of them moved until he left the doorway, allowing Mace to secure the door before swinging back into her seat. Her fingers flew over the controls. "Was he always that stubborn?"

"Worse. At least he's listening to reason this time. You must be a good influence, sweetheart." He looked over to see a small smile on her lips.

"Maybe he's matured since you knew him."

"It would take more than seven years for me to believe that." The computer beeped. "You need to stall them for ten minutes. That's the soonest I can get us through."

"Time to dance."

He braced himself against the inertia pull. Mace threw the ship into a spiral dive as both hostile ships pulled into weapons range. The computer shouted at them, announcing the approaching laser fire. Mace easily shifted the ship to the side, avoiding the blasts.

He was surprised when she took them directly toward the dimension gate but shot past it at a super speed. To their pursuers it would look as if they were heading deeper into the quadrant.

"There's an asteroid field not far from here. With any luck, they'll think I'm heading there."

"And where are we really heading?"

She shot him a full-blown, slightly evil grin. "Just wait and see."

Just you wait and see, Byron.

He shivered as the male voice echoed in his head. One he hadn't heard for a very long time. It had to be a coincidence.

Mace held her course, speeding forward for what felt like an eternity, then jammed on the reverse thrusters as she yanked on their pitch controls. The nose of the ship jerked up, pulling them into a loop. The two ships chasing them shot past their location as she rolled the ship back to an even keel and headed directly toward the gate.

"You better get it up now, hunter, or you'll have totally ruined the best escape ever."

"You have self-esteem issues, don't you?"

She chuckled. "I wasn't raised to be modest."

He had just enough time to activate the coordinates and open the dimension gate. Mace flew them through, dead center.

The world around him stretched thin, only to open up and fold over on itself. He loved the sensation of the universe invading his body, bleeding under his skin until he felt like tiny particles of the world were embedded within his soul.

Gods, he'd missed this. He'd been behind a desk for too long.

Space snapped back to normal as they cleared the gate.

Mace wasted no time maneuvering the ship away from the opening. "Where are we?"

"Somewhere they won't easily be able to follow. I used a guild scrambler to mask our destination. It will take them days to sort through the useless code and work out where we ended up."

"Good."

Whether it was instinct or simply amazing insight, they both moved at the same time, drawing their weapons on each other. Byron admired the speed and accuracy with which she could point a blaster. He could only imagine her training extended to firing.

Lucky for him, he was just as good with a weapon.

Mace cocked her head as she looked him in the eye. "So."

"So."

"You're the ex?"

"Yup. You the current?"

"No."

Damn, Byron wasn't sure if he was disappointed or not. "No, or not yet?"

She smirked and shrugged. "That a problem?"

"Not particularly. Though Alec does have a tendency to take off without notice."

"That couldn't be because you did something requiring him to run for his life? With you being a bounty hunter and all?"

Byron stiffened. "I never did anything to put him in danger. I . . . Things weren't like that seven years ago. And for the record, I was only freelance back then. I mostly worked security for the Loyalists."

Mace seemed to consider his words before nodding slowly. "He's quiet but not weak. I can't see him letting anyone take advantage."

Advantage, no. Control, yes. There had been many nights when Alec had willingly dropped to his knees in front of Byron, begging him to give the orders, take charge. He'd worked Alec's submission until Byron could anticipate every one of Alec's needs. Byron had known when he needed a firm hand and when he'd simply needed guidance. Their relationship had gotten to a point where Byron was considering making it a permanent arrangement. He'd intended to formalize what they had together.

Alec left before he could.

"There is nothing weak about Alec." He licked his lips. "But he sometimes can't see friend from foe. I'm not about to let anything happen to him now that I've finally tracked him down."

"I have no intention of hurting Alec. I need his help."

"With what?" He wasn't expecting honesty, so Byron was surprised when he got exactly that.

"A friend of mine is sick. Alec's research is the only thing that might come close to saving his life." Mace sighed and released her iron grip on the trigger. She pulled the muzzle of her blaster up so it no longer pointed at him. "Look, I'm not here to hurt anyone. I've had more than enough chances to do something to Alec if I'd wanted to."

Byron believed her, but he needed to make sure. "It's an awful lot of credits."

"I don't need them."

"Everyone needs credits."

"Not me."

Replacing his blaster into his holster, Byron let his gaze rake down her body. A leather vest covered her breasts and stomach, leaving her arms and throat exposed. She wore the look well. He could almost picture her on her knees beside Alec, sucking his cock until he came on both their faces. It wasn't what he needed to be thinking about when trying to negotiate with somebody who was most likely a pirate.

Ignoring his swelling cock, he held out his hand. "Let's do this proper. Byron."

She stared at him for a second before accepting his offer of peace. "Mace. Pleasure."

When their hands clasped, Mace shivered with the contact, but she didn't acknowledge her reaction. She broke away first and stood. "We better check on Alec. He'll be thinking we've killed each other."

"Poor boy would be stuck out here with no one to fly him home. Where are you from again? I can't place your accent."

The door automatically opened when Mace approached. "Zeten, but I haven't been on planet since I was a kid."

He would have questioned her further, but she'd stopped dead in her tracks.

"What are you—"

"Alec!"

Mace raced to Alec's prone body. Byron was a split second behind her. He began to check his ex-lover's body for injuries, moving down Alec's sides and across his stomach. No obvious wounds. Mace cupped Alec's face as she leaned over him.

"Alec? Hon, are you okay?"

Byron's breath hitched when he realized Alec's cock was rock-hard in his pants. Alec moaned loudly and bucked up, thrusting into the air. He half rolled on his side and pressed his face into Mace's lap.

She looked up at Byron as she gripped Alec's shoulders. "What the hell is wrong with him?"

"He's fucking horny," Byron muttered. "Boy, what is going on?"

Alec moaned again, and his eyes fluttered open. "Dimension . . . jump."

Byron's brain took a moment before he realized what must have happened. "Fuck. You *idiot*."

"What?" Mace fought to keep Alec on the ground but was overpowered when he rolled and shoved his face against her pussy.

"Have you ever heard of Brasillian syndrome?"

She looked up at him and blinked. "Bullshit."

"There have been a number of documented cases noted in the Loyalist record banks."

"Alec is *not* aroused because of a dimension jump. He would need to be Syrilian, and unless I'm blind, he doesn't have green skin or a beak."

She was right, but Byron knew Alec had a habit of tinkering with his genetic code, giving him more than a few quirks and additional abilities he didn't advertise to others. "Trust me on this one. We need to get him to a bed."

Mace jerked her head toward a door. "There's one in the stateroom."

"Help me get him there."

"Let me program a course for the ship to follow." She pressed her palm to yet another bio scanner, unlocking the inner door to reveal a short corridor. "Down the hall, cabin's on the left."

Mace jumped back into the cockpit, leaving Byron to manage his former lover. He yanked Alec to his feet and fought off a groan when Alec ground his hard cock against his hip.

"Bry, I missed you."

"Not yet. We need to get you someplace safe." He looped his arm under Alec's, pulling his body close. "I need you to walk."

"I want you to fuck me." Alec leaned in too quickly, bumping his nose against Byron's neck. "Remember how you liked to fuck me? Telling me what to do and how to do it?"

The air in the corridor was stale yet cool—a blessing given how hot Alec's skin currently burned. Despite his active libido, Byron had rarely found time in the past year to give in to his baser desires. He'd been too busy with his new job. And he hadn't met a man or woman who'd caught his attention the way Alec had.

Gods, he was already stiff as stone just thinking about some of the nights they'd spent together.

Alec's cool fingers worked their way beneath his shirt, and Byron shivered, a contrast to the heat roaring through his body. Alec bit down on Byron's pulse point, while his tongue lapped sloppily at his skin.

"Bry, I want you to fuck me while I fuck Mace. So good."

"I think your little spitfire would have something to say about playing one of your games."

"She wouldn't. I can tell. Can smell her arousal. She just needs the right man. Men. Us."

Thankfully they didn't have far to go. Byron pushed Alec up against the wall, holding him in place with a single hand to his chest. For the first time since this whole nightmare began, he was able to really look at Alec, at the man he'd become after leaving Byron.

After running away.

He was thinner, the lines around his eyes and mouth were more pronounced, giving him the appearance of being older than thirty-four years old. It wasn't simply aging, though—Alec had fundamentally changed. His skin was darker than before, his hair nearly black instead of darkish brown. It could be nothing more than Byron's memories not quite living up to reality. Or it could mean Alec had been tinkering again. Somewhere his glasses had fallen off. Byron would have to find those for him later.

The glazed look in Alec's brown eyes drove home how far gone he was.

"I'm coming." Mace raced down the corridor to them, opening the door the second she arrived. "The bed is straight ahead."

"Mace . . . come with me." Alec tried to grab hold of her as Byron pushed him into the room. "I need . . . Stay with me."

Whether it was to keep Alec calm or out of a morbid sense of curiosity, Mace followed them into the room. Byron unceremoniously pushed him onto the bed, watching as Alec moaned and thrashed on the covers.

"Now what?" Mace ran her hands up and down her arms. "Is there something we can give him to settle the symptoms? I don't have a lot in the way of meds on the ship, but I can check the reserves."

"Darling, there are only two things we can do for our boy." Byron held up his forefinger. "Lock him in here to suffer for a few days and pray he doesn't kill himself. You got any lotion on board? Might help him out."

Mace's eyes popped wide open. "And option number two?"

Instead of holding up two fingers, he shrugged. "We can give him exactly what he wants."

She stared at him, her mouth opening briefly before she snapped it shut. Byron couldn't be sure if fucking Alec into the mattress would work beyond taking the edge off. He'd only ever heard of the rare case of Brasillian syndrome, and the prognosis for those who didn't get the fire out of their system wasn't good. There was a reason the Syrilians rarely left their quadrant now. A decade earlier, a fluke mining incident had caused a deadly toxin to leach into the water supply reservoir for the capital city, killing millions within days. Shortly afterward, the virus resulting in Brasillian syndrome had swept over their planet, infecting most of the remaining population. The two disasters had crashed the Syrili system's economy. Now, dimension gate travel was all but impossible for them without the proper treatment—and few Syrilians could afford it.

While the Syrilians' chemical makeup allowed them to survive in thin atmosphere and environments that would have been toxic to most species, the same genetic markers had triggered the seemingly mild intestinal virus to mutate and cause subtle but permanent changes in hormone and enzyme production. When those who'd been infected attempted gate travel, the dimensional shift activated the Brasillian syndrome; the victim's hormone production raged out of control for days, accompanied by a potentially fatal fever, and only a potent cocktail of endorphins, dopamine, oxytocin, and specific antibodies could ease the condition. The first few unfortunate sufferers had quickly discovered that when medicine wasn't available, fucking could help them survive until it was. That was where Alec was.

Byron pulled his goggles from around his neck and tossed them to the side. He quickly yanked off his shirt and threw it on top of them. He had started to work on his belt buckle when he looked back at Mace.

"What?" The clink of metal on metal rattled in the room. "Unless you have the drugs in your stash, this is the best way to help him."

"You're going to fuck him?"

"Until he's too sore, then I might have to let him fuck me." It had been a long time since he'd had anything shoved up his ass.

He figured it was only proper Alec be the one to reclaim that privilege. "It's more efficient. More brain chemicals that way or something. It's a much better bet than letting him try to jack off for days, anyway. Plus if he's done what I think he has to his DNA, he might have that crazy Syrilian sense of smell now. It'll drive him crazy being able to smell if we're turned on and not be able to get at us, and that could make his condition even worse."

Most men and women of Byron's acquaintance weren't comfortable with his dominant nature, and he'd often had to hold back with his casual lovers. But Alec had thrived under that attention. Mace had a way about her—the way she held her body, the tilt to her head, and the way her gaze bounced between his strip show and Alec's writhing form.

I wonder.

"He wants you too." He let the artificial gravity do its job and allowed his pants to fall to the floor with a *thud*. "I believe you'd be useful."

Mace snorted and braced her hands on her hips. "And what would you know about something like that?"

Despite her cocky outward appearance, he could tell she was intrigued. Now completely naked, he stood directly in front of her with his cock already hard and bobbing close to his belly. He knew exactly how he appeared. Mace didn't blush, nor did she look directly at his erection or into his eyes.

Interesting. "I know more than a few things about usefulness. Alec likes to be useful. Don't you, Alec?"

The lewd groan was all the answer he needed. Mace glanced at the bed. She bit her bottom lip and her fingers dug into her hips. Byron moved half a step closer, so his breath would tickle the side of her face.

"See, I like to help people be useful. Before he turned tail and ran, Alec enjoyed me telling him what to do. And I have a feeling you might appreciate someone else taking the lead in your life for a change. Help you work out all those problems piling up before your eyes and resting on your shoulders. I can help you, Mace. If you let me."

Another groan from Alec, and Byron knew he couldn't waste any more time trying to convince Mace to join them. His boy needed him now.

He knelt on the side of the mattress, giving himself enough room to pull the hem of Alec's shirt over his head.

"Let's get you naked. I promise I'll make you feel better."

"I don't deserve your help." Alec sobbed, pressing his cheek against the sheet and bucking his hips into the air. "It burns, Bry."

"I know it does."

"I need . . . No. Let me suffer."

Byron couldn't help running his hand across Alec's bare chest, teasing his nipples as he went. "Don't ask me to do that. You know I looked after you whenever you had a problem."

"*N-n-n-no.*"

"Sorry, not listening. Pants next."

"Let me help." Mace moved to Alec's feet and started to pull off his boots.

"Change your mind?" Byron fumbled over Alec's belt, fighting against his overeager lover. "I'm not going to have time to coddle you if we do this. Alec is my priority."

"I want to help him." She reached out and ran her hand along his bare arm. "I just . . . Tell me what to do."

The knot of apprehension he'd felt was chased away by the rush of anticipation. Byron exhaled slowly, waiting until Mace dropped Alec's second boot to the floor before taking the final plunge.

"Good girl. Now strip."

CHAPTER

FOUR

Mace didn't think it was possible for her heart to beat any faster. But when Byron looked up at her with that silver-blue gaze, she thought it was going to pound through the muscle and bone. He was more commanding naked than he'd been fully clothed and armed to the teeth. Unlike other men, Byron really was as dangerous as he let on—with or without weapons.

Gods, she couldn't believe she was going to do this—with a stranger.

She would do everything in her power to help Alec, never mind that he didn't seem to want the help. His research was the best chance Faolan had. She would make sure Alec was healthy enough to see it through to its conclusion. If that meant succumbing to the sexual desires of a handsome stranger and a man she'd lusted after since nearly the moment she'd met him—well, it really wasn't much of a hardship.

With a single step backward, she popped the buttons holding her vest together. Her breasts sprang free of their binding, making her nipples instantly hard. Byron let his gaze run slowly down her front, his eyes widening slightly at the sight. Alec's face was now turned toward her. He licked his lips and his cock twitched against his bare stomach. His eyes looked almost black; she knew if she got close enough, she'd see that his pupils were fully dilated.

She could have slipped off the vest, but something kept her from removing it completely. While she wasn't ashamed of her body, the tease was proving to be as enticing as the main event. A rare occurrence in her experience.

Biting down on her lip again, she hooked her finger around the button of her pants and popped it free. Shivering from the intensity of their gazes, she kicked off her boots before she shimmied out of the hot leather to let it fall to the floor.

"Very nice." Byron shifted to stretch out beside Alec on the bed. "Leave the vest on. Get rid of the rest."

With a little effort, she managed to pull her feet free and kick the pants away. If someone had asked her to dress like this, she would have laughed in their face. But in her current state of seminakedness, she felt like a sexual goddess.

"Alec, you were a smart man to let this one work for you. However, I don't think you fully appreciated the siren you had hiding beneath that stubborn nose of yours."

Alec let out a sob. "It burns."

"I know. Mace and I will make it all better." When Byron ran his hand through Alec's hair, Mace knew that whatever rift had driven the men apart in the past, there was still something between them—at least on Byron's side. "Come join us, Mace. You're no good to me on the other side of the room."

Ignoring the nervous twitter in her stomach, she did as he said. She sat on the edge of the bed at first, leaning back to put her weight on her arms. Alec immediately rolled and covered her with his body, forcing her flat to the bed. He pressed his face to her neck; the first swipe of his tongue across her skin drew a soft sigh from her. She'd wanted him for so long, denied her own pleasure knowing that Gar and Faolan were suffering. She'd forgotten how devastating a simple touch could be.

Mace hadn't realized her eyes had slipped shut until she felt a hand force its way into her hair, cupping the back of her head. Opening them, she looked over at Byron. Gone was the cocky bounty hunter and jilted lover. In his place spoke a man who knew what he wanted and rarely took no for an answer.

"Alec, you're lucky you're not in a good way at the moment. Otherwise I'd have to ignore you in favor of this luscious creature."

She shivered.

"Want to watch." Alec bit down softly on her shoulder. "I want to watch you fuck her."

"Not now. Maybe next time I'll tie you up so you won't have a choice. I'll pound into her across your lap until you're begging me to let you come. Would you like that?"

Alec stiffened against her and groaned. Her pussy clenched as a rush of wet trickled down and dampened her thighs. In the next breath, Alec was pulled away from her and was once more laid out flat before her. Byron didn't hesitate, covering Alec's mouth in a deep kiss. Alec responded immediately, reaching up to lock his arms around Byron's neck.

With them occupied, Mace took in the sight of the men, the strength of their bodies as they rubbed against each other. Sweat and the scent of male arousal washed over her, filling her senses and making her head spin.

She groaned and let her fingers find their way to her cunt. Brushing the soft curls, she sought out her clit and pressed down. With her free hand, she reached over to caress the top of Alec's thigh, teasing the coarse hair as she approached his cock.

Avoiding more intimate contact, she dug her nails into his skin as she swiped the pubic hair on her way up to his stomach. With his eyes closed and without breaking their kiss, Byron reached over and captured her hand. Sightless, he guided her back down to Alec's cock. Instinctively she wrapped her fingers around the hot, engorged flesh, and her stomach flipped at the strangled noise Alec made in the back of his throat.

Byron pulled back, panting, turning his head enough to look at her. "Lick his nipples. He likes that, and it will help make him come faster. And stop touching yourself. I haven't given you permission to do that yet."

Bastard.

To decrease the temptation, she shifted her position on the bed so she required both hands to keep her balance to do what Byron instructed. While she was no shy virgin, her recent experiences with men had been relegated to the boring variety. The few times she'd had more adventurous encounters, she'd been forced to move on too quickly. There were few chances at repeat performances as a pirate if you didn't have a lover among the crew. Which was why something as mundane as licking a nipple somehow seemed thrilling. Her mouth watered, forcing her to swallow before leaning fully over Alec, flattening her tongue and lapping at the tight bud. The reaction was near instantaneous.

Alec's spine bowed so severely, Byron was forced to press him back into the mattress. Mace used her body weight to hold him down as well, but continued her attack. Alec latched on to her shoulder, squeezing hard.

"Yes, yes, yes, yes," he chanted steadily. "More. Give me more now."

"You can't wait, can you?" Byron muttered. "Mace, do you have any lube?"

Her brain didn't want to cooperate. She had to think hard. "This is my brother's ship. I think he has some in the table."

"Get it."

She never thought she'd jump to follow any man's command—other than her captain's—but something in Byron's voice had her obeying before she even considered doing otherwise. A quick search of Gar's possessions turned up a mostly full bottle of lube. Pushing away images she never wanted to have of her brother, she went back to the bed.

She was in time to see Byron shift Alec's legs to either side of his shoulders and lie between them. Climbing onto the bed to kneel beside the two men, she watched Byron lick a long path from Alec's asshole to the tip of his cock. The sight almost made her come on the spot.

Without looking directly at her, Byron extended two fingers. Mace cursed her nervousness as she squeezed lube onto them. Making sure to get in between the digits, she used as much as she thought necessary before pulling back.

Byron moaned his appreciation as he set out to stretch Alec's ass. Fascinated, she watched him prepare his lover, stretching Alec wide and getting him ready to accept Byron's cock. Mace didn't know what to do with herself, and finally decided to explore Alec's chest once again.

With tongue, teeth, and fingers, she teased Alec. The sweat on his skin tasted unusually sweet, an addiction she could quickly acquire. She wondered if Byron was right, and Alec had been experimenting on his own DNA. In this case she liked the result, but she worried about what other features might be lurking inside him.

Alec's arms wrapped around her to pull her up for a kiss. Every brush of his lips against hers was a fantasy come true. A mix of hard and soft bodies. She knew she could either melt completely against him or burst into flames. Alec suddenly turned his head to groan.

"*F-f-f-fuck.*"

Byron had gotten to his knees and was pushing his cock into Alec's ass. The angry red tip of Alec's cock deepened in color as Byron filled him. Mace stopped breathing until the two of them settled.

"Gods," she breathed.

"Don't worry, sweetheart. I'm just getting started." Byron smirked, thrusting forward shallowly. "We'll have some real fun in a moment. For now I want you to jerk him off until he comes."

Alec's eyes rolled back. "*Yes.*"

Mace knew enough about Brasillian syndrome to know Alec would need as many orgasms as they could give him. They'd all be sore and tired long before he built up enough natural defenses to stave off the worst of the symptoms.

Wrapping her hand around Alec's cock, she looked at Byron to set the pace. Taking the counterpoint to his thrust, together they worked Alec's body until he was panting furiously. Byron pounded into him harder and faster until Mace felt Alec tense beneath her.

With no warning, Alec's face contorted into a mask of pleasure as cum shot from his cock in white ropes that covered both her hand and his stomach. Byron rode him through the aftershocks, slowing his pace until Alec was no longer moving.

Looking over at Byron, Mace was fascinated by the sweat soaking his skin. He clearly hadn't orgasmed with Alec. Running his fingers through Alec's cum, Byron scooped up as much of the fluid as he could before holding his hand out to her.

"Lick it off." The deep, gravelly quality had returned to his voice.

She hesitated. Locking her gaze with Byron's, she leaned forward and sucked both his fingers into her mouth, swirling her tongue around and between them. Byron gritted his teeth but didn't look away. Only once she was done did she release him with a *pop*.

"Now what?" She was pleased her voice didn't shake.

Byron chuckled, giving his hips a lazy thrust forward. "He's still nice and hard. I know he has one or two good orgasms still in him. Are you on the standard precautions?"

Mace nodded. Faolan allowed his crew to take no chances with "one in every port" diseases—or with pregnancy, as the condition made interdimensional travel unfeasible. Everybody on the *Belle Kurve* received military-grade inoculations and birth control.

"Good." Byron flicked the base of Alec's erection, eliciting a whimper from him. "Get on top and ride his cock. Face him, not me."

Her breath caught, but she complied without argument. Not sure of the best way to approach things, she knelt up before turning to face Alec. While he didn't look unhappy to have her climbing onto his lap, there was still a sense of urgency reflected in his eyes. Not sure exactly how quickly the Brasillian symptoms would start to wear him down, she swung her leg over his body and settled over his cock. It would be best to drive him over the edge as quickly as possible.

Looking Alec in the face proved to be a bit harder than she'd anticipated. While she had no doubt he was aware of her churning emotions, this wasn't exactly how she'd envisioned their relationship starting out—though in a way, it was exactly how she should have figured things would go. Fast and unpredictable.

Alec reached up as she settled him at her opening, giving herself room to sink down the length of his shaft. When she fell forward, he cupped her breasts, pinching her nipples between his fingers.

"Gods, you're fucking beautiful. Just like I'd dreamed."

She closed her eyes but didn't stop her smile. "Thank you."

Hands cupped her ass from behind, reminding her of Byron's presence. "No coming until I say. Alec gets to go before us."

"Hardly seems fair," she said on a sigh as she swiveled her hips to grind down. "I think we've earned a treat."

A hard slap to her ass drove a cry from her. "Not until I say."

"Trust Byron, Mace. He'll look after you. He makes things *so* good."

Leaning forward to brace her weight on her forearms, Mace knew Alec was right. She pressed her mouth to his ear and sucked the lobe into her mouth as Byron began to thrust once more in earnest.

After a few moments, they fell into a new rhythm. Byron would thrust deep into Alec, pushing him into her cunt with each snap forward. Moaning, grunting, and groaning filled the room, making Mace's skin tingle. Alec's thick cock filled her, setting her nerve endings on fire. The drag of skin on skin burned into her memory. Alec wrapped his arms around her, his knees bracketing either side of her hips while Byron drove them closer to completion.

Her body began to shake, the muscles tightening and relaxing as she drew closer to her release. It was far harder than she thought it would be to fight against the promise of bliss, but somehow she managed to hold her own.

"Byron." Alec bucked up hard into her. "I need to come."

A soft groan behind her preceded Byron leaning forward to press his forehead to Mace's back. His sweat-soaked skin slid across hers. "Gods, yes."

Alec thrashed beneath her, in no way resembling the formal and professional man who had never once acted in an inappropriate manner toward her. He squeezed her tight with his legs and arms, bucking up hard and coming with a shout.

Behind her, Byron cursed and shifted, pulling her back against his chest. He buried his fingers in the short curls of her hair, licking at her shoulders.

"Can you feel him? His cum deep inside your pussy? He's wanted to fuck you for a long time. Do you like his cock inside you? Alec, I want you to touch her clit. Make her come hard."

Mace didn't have time to catch her breath before Alec did as he was told. Both their juices soaked her cunt and covered his shaft and pubic hair. Alec caught as much of it as he could from their joined bodies, pressing his thumb against her clit. It took only the barest of contacts for her to seize up. A scream ripped from her chest. Waves of pleasure crashed through her until she could no longer form coherent thought.

Muscles weak, she fell forward onto Alec's chest. Byron continued to thrust, then his hips stuttered before he finally cried out and slumped over her back.

They lay together in a massive heap, panting desperately to catch their breath. A hand stroked her hair, tucking the loose strands behind her ear. She didn't quite care who it was, though she had the uneasy impression Byron was laying a claim over her.

When she couldn't take the weighty silence any longer, Mace rolled off Alec, displacing Byron in the process. "How are you feeling?"

"Tired," Alec muttered. "My skin . . . is still . . . burning."

"That's the particles from the dimension gate swirling around inside that thick skull of yours." Byron slapped Alec's thigh. "What the hell were you doing to get stuck with Brasillian syndrome? More importantly, why didn't you say something?"

"I tried." Alec stiffened and turned away from both of them. At least with Byron there, Mace had an ally to get him to talk. They reached at the same time, stopping him from his retreat.

Alec stared at them both, and she didn't like the serious expression he now wore. He looked angry and frustrated, both emotions she'd rarely seen from him.

"I was trying to find a way to help." His jaw clenched. "I was fixing a mistake."

"Help who?" Mace shook her head, baffled. "Brasillian syndrome isn't very common in this part of the galaxy. We're not even in the same quadrant as the Syrili system." She ran her hand along his arm, hoping the little reassurance she could offer would be accepted. "Though I'm sure they would thank you if you managed to find a more accessible cure."

Alec sat up straight, his gaze never dropping from hers. She'd seen the look on his face before—from a pirate who'd been convicted of a crime. One he'd been guilty of.

"I killed them."

Mace stiffened in Byron's embrace, not believing what she'd heard. "What? Who?"

"All of them. I killed them all."

CHAPTER
FIVE

Alec was strangely relieved to finally tell someone. His blood still burned from the dimension jump, distracting him. It would be easier for him to give in to the pain and brush his words aside as a delusion. He couldn't—*wouldn't* do that. He owed it to the people he'd wronged to let the truth come out. Closing his eyes for the briefest of moments, he swallowed past the growing tightness of his throat. There was only one final wrong for him to right. Shit, he should have gotten further with his research given all the time he'd had to fix things. Facing Byron again, letting Mace know exactly the type of monster he really was, would have been far easier if he could show them his penance.

"What happened?" Byron asked, but Alec felt Mace's smaller hand brush across the back of his shoulder.

He tensed, yet somehow managed to keep from pulling away. Gods, he was an idiot for saying anything at all. Byron's tenacity aside, Mace would never let him drop it without further explanation. It had already occurred to him that Mace wasn't interested in the science of his work and she wasn't looking to turn him in for the credits. She was only after the *ryana* poison's antidote, probably for a loved one.

"Alec?" Mace's voice pulled him out of his darkening thoughts.

Alec swallowed, ignoring the growing burn in his blood. "Before I ran away from those Loyalist bastards, I was one of them. I worked in chemical research and development. Not for the military. I was tasked with developing a toxin to kill a particular pest that had overrun one of the outlying colonies and was ruining crops. In the pictures they sent—which I later learned were faked, of course—this thing looked like some unholy hybrid of a lizard, a cockroach, and a *strat*.

Features of mammal, reptile, and insect. They gave me a number of blood samples to test. It only took me a few months to find a combination of chemicals they could use to eradicate the pests."

Mace's fingers dug harder into his skin. "Shit."

He couldn't stop his dark chuckle. "The Syrilians started dying off shortly thereafter. It didn't take me long to figure out who the *pests* were the Loyalist government wanted dead. When the Loyalists started strip-mining on Syrili Prime, there had been the threat of an uprising. That quickly stopped once everyone started dying. By the time the miners were blamed for the *accidental* poisoning, half the population was gone or near death. Nobody was in any kind of shape for a revolution."

Mace rolled against him. Her breasts were cool against the hot skin of his back. "You didn't know what they were going to use it for. Surely you could have said something to the Syrilians?"

"And admit to everyone I was a mass murderer? I would have been shot on the spot. As selfless as you may think I am, suicide was never on my list of ways to die. The only thing I could do was try to come up with a cure. It helped knowing what had gone into the poison. The problem was how I'd engineered the bloody thing. It had already started to transform in response to the environment. It took a long time to come up with a cure, to figure out how to spread it virally, and there are lasting effects in their society."

"Brasillian syndrome," Byron said softly.

He nodded, not caring if either of them saw him. "I made . . . some modifications, and injected myself with the poison so I could test the virus. I wasn't about to infect another Syrilian if I could help it. When the council found out, let's just say the Loyalists' motivation to find a cure increased tenfold. Apparently I'm valuable."

Anger twisted Byron's face. "Why the hell would you do this?" Grabbing Alec's chin, Byron forced Alec to look into his eyes. "Are you punishing yourself? Think this will make up for what you'd done? Why the hell didn't you tell me anything?"

No. Alec wasn't about to let Byron make him feel any worse than he did already. Jerking out of Byron's grasp, he rolled onto his back, letting his anger keep him focused on what he had to say.

"You remember what it was like. How they manipulated the truth, kept information from me. How many other times before Syrili did I think I was making a pesticide or an herbicide, when I was really making a weapon?" It had taken Alec years to realize how naïve he'd been. His inexperience with the universe outside the lab, his belief that the Loyalist government was a benign leadership, had blinded him to common sense. Byron had been one of the guards keeping the Loyalists' commodity—*him*—safe from harm. They'd learned the real nature of their employer together. "I have to make amends."

Byron punched the mattress with his fist. "Not this way. How the hell can you travel like this, Alec? We need you healthy if you want to continue the work you were doing on the planet."

It had broken his heart to leave Byron, but Alec had decided he wouldn't be responsible for another life being cut short. He was already living every day in terror that his work on the curative virus would be discovered. Then his superiors had threatened to have Byron killed if Alec revealed the truth about the attempted Syrilian genocide to anyone.

Instead of staying in place with his head down, waiting for the axe to fall, Alec had disappeared into the black of space, leaving a message for his government keepers. If they so much as looked at Byron or anyone else he cared about, he would reveal them as the party responsible for the poisoning . . . and ultimately the ones to blame for the Brasillian syndrome as well. And a host of other biological warfare agents. Surprisingly, they'd let him go without giving chase.

What they hadn't counted on was him working on cures for everything they'd had him create. He made them look like fools with every successful antidote or treatment he discovered. But he'd hidden himself well, made no overt attacks on the government, and had made no attempt to reach anyone he cared for.

"I don't understand why they waited this long, then put a bounty on me *now*." He groaned as another wave of lust reared up, stealing his breath away. "And I was so close to a cure for the *ryana* poison."

Mace gasped and stiffened before she rolled away. He missed her heat but understood why she wouldn't want to be near him. *Not any longer.* The cool air of the room replaced her body heat, and the blood beneath Alec's skin burned. Byron looked over him, and Alec knew he was watching her dress. The rustle of clothing filled him with lonely dread. The near-silent opening of the door was the final break in his relationship with her—she was gone.

"She's not coming back." He closed his eyes against the unexpected tears threatening to break. He *never* cried. But knowing Mace could no longer be near him broke his heart. *Gods, I don't even know who she was trying to help.*

"*I'm* here." Byron dropped back down to fill his field of vision. "I'm not going anywhere, and I'm going to look after you."

"I don't want you to. I figured out how to look after myself a long time ago."

Byron growled. "I *want* to, you stupid idiot."

Alec shook his head, biting the inside of his cheek. The pain helped him focus some, but the burning inside him was growing. "It hurts."

Byron didn't say anything else as he leaned in for a kiss. It was the first time since the start of his seven-year nightmare that Alec felt the cold weight in his chest start to crack. Reaching for Byron, he lost himself in the sweet weight of that familiar mouth.

The pressure in his cock was a mix of pleasure and pain, merging as it fired the cells in his blood. He shuddered, his body screaming for chemicals it couldn't produce in sufficient quantities. The more aroused his body grew, the more brutal the attack. He needed to come to stem the pain.

Byron bit down on Alec's lower lip. "I'm going to look after you. I'm going to make you scream my name. Then you're going to sleep while I get something to make you feel better."

Alec pulled away, rolling onto his back.

Byron followed him as he went, hovering several inches above. "You are not the monster you think you are, Alec. I know you well enough to realize you would never have consented to making anything that would hurt a sentient being."

The unwanted tears finally escaped, falling in a gentle trail down Alec's cheeks to pool behind his ears. Gods, he didn't want Byron to think he was weak. "You always told me I was too trusting and naïve for my own good. I think you were being kind. I was a complete mindless idiot who jumped when my Loyalist masters said to do so. I never questioned. Not once, Bry."

Knowing the smallest dose of logical skepticism on his part would have saved hundreds of thousands of lives over the years, Alec had long since come to the conclusion that he didn't deserve to live . . . except as a form of penance. Byron would have argued with him about experimenting on himself, tried to convince him to do something else to make up for what he'd done. But it wouldn't have been enough.

"Enough thinking." Byron reached down and grabbed Alec's still-hard cock. "Right now I'm going to fuck you into oblivion. We'll worry about the rest of this later."

Nodding, Alec closed his eyes and gave himself over to the sensations. Byron's sure hands teased him, fingers tugging his balls and pressing against his perineum. Moaning, he ground his body into Byron's touch, trying to increase the pressure.

"Yeah, you like that," Byron cooed in his ear. He bit down on the fleshy lobe, flicking the tip with his tongue. "You've always been such a slut for my cock, Alec. I've fucked you and you've come twice and you're still panting for more. You want my cock up your ass again? Do you?"

Alec couldn't pull in breath fast enough to keep up with the pounding of his heart. "Yes. *Fuck*, I need you, Bry."

Byron fell on him, pressing his body down hard so every inch of him covered Alec. Feet, fingers, shoulders, everything protected by Byron. It felt amazing.

"We're going to do this like old times," Byron whispered.

Without any further warning, Byron curled his hands under Alec's shoulders, rolling them so Alec was on top. Alec's stomach flipped when he realized what Byron wanted him to do. He'd dreamed of this so many nights, the look on Byron's face as he rode him. It had fueled his fantasies as he masturbated alone in the dark.

Alec was already slick from cum and lube. He shifted his body so his ass was directly above Byron's cock. Waiting for the nod, he stared deep into Byron's eyes while his body vibrated from need.

Swallowing hard, Byron barely moved his chin, but it was enough. *Permission*. Alec held a breath and slowly let it out as he sank down on Byron's shaft, inch by blessed inch. Unlike their earlier session, he was coherent enough to fully appreciate how amazing it felt to have Byron once again. They'd always fit perfectly, but there was something different this time. The reconnection sparked something inside him he'd long thought gone.

He felt alive.

"That's it," Byron encouraged. "Fuck down on me hard. Come when you can."

Bracing his hands on Byron's shoulders, he pushed down until he could swivel his hips and press against Byron's balls. Byron had always loved when he'd done that—the pressure against the sensitive skin. He wasn't disappointed when Byron let out a low moan and his eyes clamped shut.

As quickly as the thoughts came, Alec's mind emptied out. The sickness running through his blood demanded satisfaction. Using his legs, he began to ride Byron in earnest, slamming down as quickly as he could. The tip of Byron's cock rubbed against his prostate as he moved, making every thrust more pleasurable. Sweat broke out across his skin, trying to cool the heat raging inside but accomplishing little.

Byron's fingers wrapped around Alec's cock, and he squeezed hard. The smooth brush of his thumb across the tip, smearing pre-cum across the skin, made Alec sigh and increase the pace.

"That's it," Byron encouraged. "You're so close, aren't you? I can feel your ass squeezing me tight. I forgot how big your cock is, Alec. Once you get your energy back, I'll have to get you to fuck me. You'd like to feel me clamping around you, wouldn't you? I bet you'd come so hard I'd taste it."

He continued to jerk Alec in time with the rhythm of his words. The constant onslaught pushed Alec to the edge. But it wasn't enough.

"Look at me."

Alec's eyes reluctantly shifted to Byron. He knew what was coming—it had always been like this between them.

"Alec." Byron increased the tempo of his hand. "Come for me. Now."

Alec's back arched at the familiar trigger, cum exploding from his cock and a scream ripping from his throat. His blood filled with what he needed, and the burning ebbed as his mind blanked with pleasure.

A vague realization that Byron was tensing below him brought him back to the present. Byron's hands squeezed his hips, holding him still as he thrust up into his waiting body. There was a slight pause and loss of rhythm before Byron groaned and hot cum filled him.

Alec relaxed and leaned forward to cover Byron's chest. The ache in his bones was fading into the background, though not disappearing entirely. Byron's hands held him in a loose embrace, fingers tracing lazy patterns on his back.

"I'm sorry," Alec whispered after the minutes of silence stretched on.

Byron's fingers paused midpath before continuing. "You didn't mean it. We'll find a way to make this better."

"I've tried, Bry. There are so many people . . . I've hurt. I need to put things right."

A soft kiss to his cheek and Byron reached around him to pull up a blanket. "Sleep now. We'll worry about fixing the universe later. Okay?"

"Yup."

Whether he deserved it or not, Alec was selfish enough to take the comfort.

Mace sat in the cockpit and stared out into space. She'd spent months in Alec's company, had spent so many more researching him in her search to find an antidote for Faolan's condition. Not once was there any indication he'd been responsible for the creation of the poison they were trying to counteract. Or for the Syrilian poison, or anything like the virus that had caused the Brasillian syndrome. It just didn't match up with the man who she'd come to know.

She'd been conned.

Alec had been on the run from the Loyalist government. He was the creator of poisons and viruses so vicious only a monster could have engineered them. But she'd always considered herself to be an excellent judge of character. It was one of the things Faolan had always commented on, how she'd always been able to just *know* a person.

Alec had never struck her as a man capable of killing. She'd known he was intense, always focused. Sure, he had a few weird quirks, some she had yet to completely figure out. But he wasn't an uncaring, heartless bastard out to murder innocents—she would stake her life on it.

Alec wanted to *save* people—she'd been with him long enough to know that. Nothing he did had been for profit or fame. He hadn't once charged any of the colony's inhabitants, or any of his mysterious off-world clients, for any of the cures he offered. Which made things worse. She'd never considered that his motivations for finding the remedies were a result of his own active participation in making them necessary. It was simply inconceivable.

Pushing those thoughts aside, she pulled up the scan of the sector Byron had brought them to. There wasn't a whole lot in the area, but something about the location was bugging her. Something familiar she couldn't quite put her finger on. She'd have asked Byron, but it was clear he was going to be looking after Alec's needs for the next little while.

And you walked out of the room.

She'd been moving before her brain fully registered what she was doing. The last thing she wanted to do now was dwell on the dark thoughts circling the outskirts of her brain.

Alec and the *ryana* poison.

Enough!

It had been two weeks since she'd had an opportunity to talk to Gar and find out how Faolan was doing.

Wanting to ensure privacy, Mace flicked the lock to the cockpit door before sending out the call over a secure channel to the *Belle Kurve*. There was no immediate response, so she set the communicator to repeat. Gods only knew where the ship was. Maybe they were in the middle of an attack. While Faolan had gone low profile over the past few years, there were still many enemies out there who would gladly slit his throat if they crossed his path.

Not that Gar would give them the opportunity to do so.

Mace stared into the depths of space, enjoying the peace of the stars for the first time in months. While her life may have begun on ground, she had always been a child of space. She'd been reborn the day Faolan hauled her from Zeten and gave her a life on his ship. That was where she belonged.

Someday she hoped to find a person she could spend her life with, maybe even on a ship of her own. Not that she was anxious to leave the *Belle Kurve*, especially now that she had the opportunity to live with her brother and learn about his life and the man he'd become.

The double beep of the computer announced the incoming communications signal. Sitting up straighter, she tucked her hair behind her ears and grinned as she answered the call.

Faolan's thin, smiling face greeted her. "Hey, pet! I see you've managed to keep that bucket of your brother's in one piece."

"Hi, yourself. How are you feeling?" She didn't like how skinny he'd become or the gray pallor his skin had taken on. "You're looking good."

"Bullshit. I look like death on two legs. No fear about my dying today though. But enough about me. How are you making out? I was surprised to get a transmission from the *Geilt* and not from the planet. Everything okay?"

She wasn't about to wear him down with the details. The less Faolan had to worry about, the better. "We're good. Alec had a run-in with an old friend and we took to the sky. We're on our way to a place where we're going to continue work on an antidote for you."

"Mace, sweetie, I told you not to bother with that foolishness. I'm dying—"

"No, you're not!" The words came out sharp, but she really didn't care. She wasn't going to roll over and accept his death when there was something she could do about it. She wouldn't let him go easily. "We're really close to getting this figured out. You just need to hold on and stay healthy long enough for me to shoot this cure into your sorry ass."

Faolan's mouth tightened into a thin line, but he nodded. "Just be careful, please. The last thing I want is for you to die on a fool's errand and your brother to be left alone after I'm gone."

"Faolan, you're not going to die."

"But I might."

"Not if I can do anything about it." She hated fighting with him about this. The constant round and round never got them anywhere but frustrated. "How's Gar? Is he there?"

Faolan smirked. "He's getting cleaned up. He'll be out in a minute."

Mace couldn't stop from snorting. "Do I even want to know why you delayed in answering my call?"

"Do *not* say a word!" Gar's voice drifted over the communication channel from the background.

Mace smiled at Faolan's grin. "Your brother is a shrewd negotiator. I wouldn't dare go against the *rules*."

Gar appeared behind Faolan, his hands coming to rest on his shoulders. "Your husband is going to kick your ass if you're not careful." Leaning down to get his face into the view screen, Gar gave her a lopsided smile. "Hi, Macie."

"Hi, yourself."

Gar kissed Faolan's cheek. "I believe we had a deal."

Faolan rolled his eyes in a very Gar-like manner. "I'm going. Slave driver."

"I'll be checking up with Doc to make sure you actually made it down to the med bay this time."

"It seems I have to cut our chat short, pet." Faolan winked at her. "Are you coming home soon?"

"Soon. I promise. Be healthy."

"Always."

Gar leaned back into the screen. "Give me a second, Macie?"

"Go, go." She waved him away.

Low murmurs buzzed off the com screen, but she wasn't able to make out the sounds. If there was something important going on, Gar was sure to tell her. They had no secrets when it came to Faolan. She knew more about his sex life than she'd ever wanted to know about anyone's. It didn't matter that the details had been vague and Gar had blushed bright red when they'd slipped out.

She hated being so far away from them, knowing that if anything happened to Faolan, chances were she'd miss her opportunity to say good-bye.

"Sorry about that." Gar took the seat in front of the communicator, scratching his face. "He's missed out on his last few appointments with Doc. I had to . . . convince him to get his ass down there for a checkup."

Mace chuckled. "Explains the grin on his face at least."

The siblings stared at each other for a moment. Gar looked tired, and not in the *Hey, I just fucked the hell out of my husband* way. He'd shaved his goatee months earlier, so the scruff covering his face was an unfamiliar sight. As were the wrinkled shirt and less-than-perfect hair.

"Are you okay?" She leaned forward. "You look like hell."

"I'm—" Gar snorted, turning his face away for a second. When he looked back, she saw nothing but utter exhaustion shining back at her. "He's given up, Mace."

"Oh no." She fell back into her seat, as the pressure of the past year suddenly doubled and began to press down on her shoulders. "What happened?"

"Nothing. Everything." Gar huffed out a breath. "He was on the bridge shouting out commands. We had a Loyalist patrol jump into a sector we were passing through and we needed to make a quick escape. We jumped to another quadrant, and when we came back into real space, he threw up before passing out." Gar spoke in a clipped fashion, like each word physically hurt him to say.

"But he is okay now?" *Gods, I should be there.*

"For the time being. But we're not going to be able to dimension jump much longer given how bad his condition seems to be now. Macie, I don't think he's going to live much longer."

"What . . . what has Doc said? Is there anything she can give him to help?"

"He won't bloody well go and see Doc. He sure as hell won't take any more of the medicine. Says what's the point in dragging things out longer than need be? The end is going to catch up with him sooner, not later, and he'd rather not prolong the pain."

"But we're so close to an antidote!" Tears blurred the image of her brother on the screen. Mace jerked the heels of her hands across her eyes, clearing them. "He can't give up on me now. Not after everything I've done to try to make this better."

"It's not that so much as . . . He's so tired, Mace. I know he hardly sleeps anymore. He spends most of his time on a computer or datapad, writing down his thoughts and telling me things he thinks I'm going to need to know once he's gone. I'm finding it so hard. Harder than anything else." Gar wiped at his own tears and let out a soft laugh. "I never cry."

"You cry all the time. Big baby."

Gar rolled his eyes. "I wouldn't have to if you and Faolan would stop torturing me. I'm a damn former bounty hunter. Nastiest one in the galaxy. Gods, the guild would have a field day if they knew what's become of me."

"Speaking of bounty hunters, I have a question for you."

Gar wiped his face. "Oh no. What's up?"

"An old friend of Alec's, ex-lover actually, showed up a day or so ago. It was one of the reasons we left the planet when we did. He's a bounty hunter with the guild. He said a bounty has been put on Alec's head and everyone in the quadrant is out to get him now."

"The guild? Who is it?"

"Byron."

Gar sat up straighter. "You're kidding. Byron? Big guy, weird silvery eyes? Shoot first, leave other people to pick up the pieces later?"

Mace smirked. "I see you know him."

"He was one of the few people I met during my tenure there that I could tolerate. One of the few I could count on to actually watch my back and not shoot me when I wasn't looking. He and I ran the occasional mission together."

"So you trust him?"

"I wouldn't go that far. But if your Alec is a former lover of Byron's and he went through all that trouble to find him, then I would say you're safe as long as he doesn't perceive you as a threat."

Given Alec's revelation in the bed, she really wasn't sure where she stood with either of them any longer. "I'll keep that in mind."

"The last I'd heard of Byron, he'd taken over running the guild after Krieg's death. If he's left Zeten and the guild to go off on his own, there must be a major power struggle happening now to determine who'll run the show. I'll have to alert some of our friends to stay extra cautious of guild ships for the next little bit. Any old agreements to look the other way may suddenly be null and void."

"Great. One more thing for us to worry about."

Gar waved her concern away. "The guild has been around for too many years for it to implode. Someone will step up and fill the void, they always do. Things will settle. Where are you now?"

"Pymiran sector. Know it?"

"It's an old guild safe zone. There are a few planet bases Krieg set up over the years in case the Loyalists got annoyed with him and he had to go on the run. If Byron brought you there, he'll be taking you to the second planet from the gas giant."

She typed in the coordinates. "I see it. I'll run a scan to make sure things are safe before we get too close. Anything else I should be aware of?"

"No. Just . . . stay in touch, Mace. In case I need you."

He didn't have to tell her why. "I will. Please try to get some rest. You're no good to him if you're sick too."

"I will. Love you."

"Love you too."

The channel went black as she ended the call. Dragging her fingers through her hair, she fought the urge to break down in tears. She'd never shied away from any challenge in her life and somehow she'd always managed to come out on top. But this? It was almost too much.

Faolan couldn't die. She'd lost too much of her family to bear to lose him too. She wouldn't let it happen.

The door chirped at her, announcing the presence of someone in the main area of the ship. Knowing it was likely Byron, she pulled herself together and tried to figure out how much she should tell him about her connection with Gar.

She stood and opened the cockpit door, stepping out into the room. Before she had a chance to say a word, a large hand grabbed her and slammed her back against the wall. It took her a second to recognize Byron through his pissed-off expression, as the oxygen rapidly depleted from her brain.

He held up a datapad for her to see. "What the hell is this?"

"A datapad?"

Byron leaned into her body a bit harder. "Don't be a smart-ass."

She managed to suck in a strangled breath. "How the hell am I supposed to know? It's not turned on."

With a single press of his thumb, the screen came to life, revealing a coded document. "This very much looks like a guild bounty warrant."

The pad was a leftover from Gar's old life. "Quite possibly it is."

Byron dropped the device to the floor, crowding in close until he filled her vision. "I didn't have time to really look at the ship when we first got here. But Alec is resting and I was able to check things out. I know this ship and its owner. And you're not *him*." Lifting a blaster to her head, Byron growled. "What have you done with Gar?"

CHAPTER
SIX

There were very few people Byron respected in the guild, even fewer he'd come to like. The one fellow hunter he'd managed to develop a friendship of sorts with was Gar Stitt. Byron had teased him, calling him "Ice Man," trying to force a crack in Stitt's armor . . . but in the way he'd have teased a little brother, with fondness behind it. When Byron tried to give the younger hunter advice, Gar would refuse to listen to him, usually following the brush-off with a punch. Byron learned early to duck. It was as close to camaraderie as either of them got.

Then Gar had been given a shit deal and taken advantage of by Jason Krieg, the former head of the guild—but he'd somehow beaten the odds and made an escape. The last time Byron had seen him, Gar had been running away from Krieg's charred remains with his arms around another man. Byron could have stopped him, but he could tell something had changed in Gar, and it didn't take a genius to know it had to do with the man he'd been holding.

The idea that Gar Stitt's ship had somehow fallen into the hands of this upstart, mercenary female pissed Byron off to no end.

"I asked you a question." He wasn't sure what angered him more, the possibility that Gar was dead or that Mace might have moved on to Alec as her next victim.

Byron knew he could be intimidating when he wanted to be. Normally, though, those he slammed against walls and threatened to kill didn't start to smirk and chuckle. Mace looked more than a little amused.

"You think I did something to Gar?" Mace somehow shook her head, despite the little space she had. "I'll have to make sure to let him know you care enough to get pissed off on his behalf."

Pulling back, he let the blaster tip slide from her head. "You know Gar?"

Mace rolled her eyes in a hauntingly familiar way. "You could say that. I'm his sister."

"What? No, he told me his sister was dead. Dead and burned. He'd seen her corpse."

Mace gave him a not so gentle push, giving herself enough space to slip away from the wall and make her way across the room. "Krieg murdered our parents. He would have killed me as well, but I managed to get away when his men came after me. Faolan and his wife grabbed me when they were fleeing the planet and kept me with them."

"Faolan? As in Faolan Wolf?" Gar sure knew how to pick them.

"That's him." Mace tucked her hair behind her ears and hooked her thumbs into the top of her pants. "Krieg got another body—I have no idea how and I don't want to know—and burned it. He convinced Gar it was me and kept him around. Gar didn't know what had happened until he was sent to bring in Faolan and Krieg attempted to have him killed."

He hadn't known the whole story behind the events that had ended in Krieg's death, even after he'd let Gar and Faolan escape the planet three years ago. Krieg's personal records had autodeleted when Byron had tried to break the encryption code. None of the guards knew anything beyond what Krieg had told them.

Now the pieces began to fall into place. The slight Zeten accent in Mace's speech. The familiar way she rolled her eyes and the way she attacked everything head-on.

"So you're a Stitt as well? The boy continues to surprise me."

"Actually it's Simms. Gar changed his name when Krieg took him in. It was why I wasn't able to find him."

Byron nodded. "So he's okay, then?"

Mace turned her face away, but not before he caught the flash of something in her eyes. "Yeah, he's alive and kicking, still being a pain in my ass."

"But?"

She bit down on her lower lip. When she looked back up, Byron's throat tightened at her expression. "It's Faolan."

"What's wrong?"

"He's sick. Krieg had him dosed with *ryana* poison. We thought he was going to be okay for at least a while after we found some medicine, but it isn't helping him anymore. He's dying."

Byron was a bastard. With the exception of Alec, very few people were able to worm their way past his defenses. But standing there, watching Gar's little sister cry for a man who was slowly being murdered, Byron's heart broke. He crossed the room and pulled her into an embrace, ignoring the way her body stiffened.

Finally she relaxed against him.

"I'm sorry," he said softly, pressing a kiss to the top of her head. "And that's why you were with Alec. You were hoping he could work out an antidote."

She sniffed, turning her face so her cheek rested against him. "All the information I could find, what little of it there was at least, pointed to this mysterious backwater scientist being the best hope for a cure. I forged the credentials I needed and went to Naveeo to find Alec and help him. But I don't think we're going to have time. Faolan's dying faster than we'd originally thought."

Fuck. Of all the concoctions Alec had developed over his years as a Loyalist, *ryana* was one of the worst. It certainly wiped out the genetically engineered "invasive fungal spore mutations" Alec had designed it to eradicate. But what it did to humans . . . was beyond cruel. Byron hadn't learned about its use as a slow, painful murder weapon until after he'd left the Loyalists and joined up with the guild. He knew Alec's motives had been innocent, but even he had briefly hated the man who'd brought that evil stuff into existence.

"Does Alec know any of this?"

Mace sniffed again and pulled back. He gave her a minute to compose herself, and ignored the redness around her eyes.

Finally she shook her head. "No. He doesn't know. I'm wanted for a few unpleasantries I've perpetrated over the years. I couldn't take the chance he would either turn me in to the authorities, or kick me out the door. And if it got out that Faolan was critically ill, there would be more than a few enemies trying for the opportunity to take his ship."

"There's a safe house in this sector. It was the reason I brought us here."

"Gar mentioned it."

"You were talking to him?"

Mace nodded. "I wanted to make sure you weren't flying me into a trap. I've already plotted a course toward the second planet."

"You're efficient, you Simms kids. There's an old base we can hide out in. This sector is pretty much off the grid for most of the guild now. Hopefully, anyone familiar with it is either dead or not in the least interested in us. It's been years, but I'm pretty sure there's a place for Alec to set up a lab. He can make himself a cure for the Brasillian syndrome, or at least whip up a palliative, and the two of you can continue your work to save Faolan."

"Is he okay?" Mace sat down on the old couch in the middle of the room. As she spoke, he could hear her unspoken questions, her hesitation to ask what she really wanted to know. "Alec, I mean. I hate knowing he punished himself like that. Gods, he could have died and then he would have been no good to anyone."

Knowing Mace felt the same way about Alec made Byron hopeful she could eventually look past his being responsible for *ryana*. Still, if Faolan actually died, there was no telling how she'd react. Despite sympathizing with her, he wouldn't let her do anything to hurt Alec.

"He does that. Years ago when I first met him, he was so excited about the science but couldn't relate to the politics. Smartest man I've ever met, but a complete idiot in some ways."

"And you looked out for him."

Of course, they hadn't started that way. Byron hadn't been able to stand being in the same room as Alec when he'd been assigned to the scientist's protection detail. Alec wasn't his type at all—too book-smart, and terrible at following simple directions. It wasn't until the political pressure started to build and Alec realized how dangerous the Loyalist infighting could be that he came to Byron asking for help. Byron started out guiding Alec on how to handle certain members of the council, telling him what to say in certain situations. The more time they spent together, the closer they'd become.

The first time Alec had kissed him, Byron thought it was nothing more than basic attraction. The first time Alec had dropped to his knees and begged Byron to tell him what to do, he'd known there was a lot more to it than that.

"I did try to look out for him and give him what he needed. For the record, I'll do whatever I can to keep him safe."

Mace cocked her head and gave him a good hard look. "Do you love him?"

"There was a time when I thought I might have been able to. I thought he had feelings for me. Now?" He shrugged.

"Because he ran away?"

"Because he didn't trust me to help him." Gods, he'd been furious for days, long after his incarceration and subsequent dismissal from Loyalist guard detail. It was as if Alec had flown into a black hole. "I still don't know exactly what happened. And I don't know how to ask him."

It didn't matter how many years had passed, he'd never given up looking for Alec. He'd used every case from the guild as an opportunity to search for him without drawing unwanted attention.

The Loyalist government had made it painfully clear he was supposed to leave Alec the hell alone. The order had only encouraged Byron to dig deeper. He'd hit a wall when he learned the government had lost track of Alec as well. His lover had been written off as dead and irrelevant. They should have had no reason to put a bounty on his head.

So who had?

Mace seemed sympathetic. "I guess it isn't the sort of topic you can easily approach."

"Not really. 'Hey, darling. Sorry we lost track over the past seven years. So, how many people have you managed to kill unwittingly?'"

"Exactly." She sighed, leaning back against the couch. "We should be within scanning range of the planet soon. If Alec can hold on long enough to tell me what he needs, I'll be able to help manufacture a treatment for the Brasillian symptoms."

"We may have to force it down his throat, but hearing Faolan's story might work as well."

Mace flinched. He moved to the water processor along the back wall, sensing she was about to ask him a question he really didn't want to answer. The reclaimed water was cool as he swallowed it down, reminding Byron how long it had been since he'd taken any time for himself.

"Did he do it?" The too-calm tone of her question made his stomach sour.

"Do what?" It was a feeble attempt to deflect, but he really didn't want to have this conversation.

Her eyes flared with annoyance and anger. "You damn well know what I'm asking. Was Alec really the creator of the *ryana* poison?"

Another swallow of water, this time to force the rising bile back down his throat. "Yes."

Her muttered curse summed up his feelings exactly.

"Are you okay?" He turned back to face her, hoping to get a line on her emotions. If she was going to snap and do something everyone would regret, he wanted as much warning as possible.

Mace looked up for a second before her gaze snapped to the door. Alec stood there, a blanket wrapped tightly around his half-clothed body. Byron fought the impulse to go to him, knowing neither Alec nor Mace would appreciate the sentiment. But gods, did he want to.

"I—" Alec gave his head a soft shake. "Where are we heading?"

Alec glanced at Mace, but she dropped her chin to her chest, breaking eye contact. Byron took a half step forward. "Pymiran sector. It'll be safe, so we can get you healthy. Once you take the medicine, then you'll be able to continue your research."

"Because you are *going* to finish it," Mace added, steel behind her words.

"The *ryana* antidote?" Alec waited for her to answer. When she didn't, he turned to Byron. "What happened?"

"Mace and I had a little heart-to-heart. Seems a good friend of mine is her brother. Thought she was dead when it turned out she'd been rescued by a pirate."

Before he had a chance to continue, Mace was on her feet and moving across the room to stand in front of Alec. Byron followed but stopped a short distance away when he realized she wasn't touching Alec.

"Faolan's been infected. I owe him *everything*. So you are *going* to take whatever medicine you need to get your head straight enough to help me find an antidote. Then we are *going* to find the *Belle Kurve* and you are *going* to make sure it works and Faolan is going to be okay.

If everything works out, I *might* consider letting you live. But if he dies, you're next."

Byron opened his mouth to say something, but Mace spun around, her finger pointing at him. "And don't tell me not to threaten him. If our positions were reversed, you would feel *exactly* the same."

She stared him down until he backed off. Nodding, he conceded her point. "Fair enough."

Mace swallowed, letting her hand fall to her side. A soft chuckle slipped past her lips. "I hate this."

Alec shuffled closer to her, reached out, and squeezed her shoulder. "I know the words are meaningless, but I am sorry. I never knew what they were really doing with the things I created. I was a cocky kid who didn't think, and trusted that the people I worked for were giving me all the information. But I'm going to make this right, Mace. I promise."

She stiffened. "I hate knowing it was you. When the creator was some faceless monster cackling with glee over his latest method of torture, it was easier."

"But knowing the monster was an idiot, someone who believed the *ryana* poison was going to be used as a way of removing a blight of mutated *ryana* fungus from a farming colony, doesn't quite make anything better." Alec's voice was strangely sympathetic.

A tear slipped down Mace's face as she reached up to cover Alec's hand. "Yeah."

Byron hated feeling useless. He wanted nothing more than to blow something up or beat the shit out of someone. Standing here watching them try to feel their way through this fucked-up situation was worse than a knife wound to the gut. He needed to get them on the planet and make this right. For both of them.

Instead he reached down and scooped up Alec's glasses from where they'd fallen earlier. Holding them out, he brushed his fingers against Alec's when he took them. Byron knew if he could keep the three of them together, they could work through this.

He did his best to ignore the softer emotions welling up in his chest. "Mace. You're exhausted. Why don't you and Alec go lie down and I'll make sure the ship lands on the safe zone."

She pushed her hair behind her ear and wiped the tear away. "If you do anything to hurt this ship—"

"I'll castrate myself. I remember your brother's rules. Go rest."

He watched as Alec tugged on her shoulder. "I'm still feeling a bit woozy. I might need your help."

Mace turned, reluctantly wrapping an arm around Alec's waist, and the two of them disappeared down the hall. Byron stood in the middle of the room alone and did his best to fight through the rising tension in his body. This wasn't what he'd expected to find when that warrant crossed his desk. He didn't have a clue how to fix this.

SEVEN

There were many things in Alec's life he regretted. Hurting Mace—even unknowingly—was very close to the top of his list. With his feet hanging off the side of the bed, he sat and watched her pace. She was clearly tired and angry, most of the latter emotion directed squarely at him.

Escaping his Loyalist keepers and letting them think he was running scared or dead had been the only way he could be free to work without restrictions and find cures for all the shit he'd cooked up; it had also meant escaping the pain and guilt of having to look the victims and their families in the eye. Living a furtive life in a squalid, obscure waypost settlement was far too easy a punishment for his crimes.

Except now there was Mace.

"You should sit down," he managed to say after her fifth circuit around the room. "Maybe have a rest."

"Yup." She kept moving.

Alec pinched the bridge of his nose and ignored the burning starting up in his blood again. Damn it, he was going to have to get himself off soon just so he would be able to think. "I can leave. I'm sure there's more than one cabin I can lock myself in if you don't want me in here. It will give you a chance to have a shower and unwind a bit."

Mace stopped short, turning her head to stare at him. "I don't think that's a good idea. You still look like hell, and Byron will murder me if something happens to you."

"I'm clearly making you uncomfortable, so it might be for the best."

He'd started to push himself up when she strode across the room, stopping him with a hand on each of his shoulders.

"Don't be an idiot. Stay there."

Not wanting to give up the contact, he covered her hands. He'd lost count of how many times they'd been in a similar position over the past few months. Encouraging one another to rest, to eat, to try again. He'd taken it for granted. "Mace, I'm—"

"Don't." Muscles jumped along her jaw as she clenched her teeth. "Just . . . you're not the only one on this ship with a past. I'm not an innocent princess who can pass judgment on you with a clear conscience, but that doesn't mean I'm not furious right now."

He'd often wondered what had brought Mace to him. Sure, he was the expert, but there were many other doctors both in and out of Loyalist influence who could have helped her almost as well.

"Bry said he knew your brother. Another bounty hunter?"

"Yeah. He thought I was dead and ended up working for Krieg, the head of the guild before Byron took over. And a complete bastard."

Taking a chance, Alec tugged on her wrist, coaxing her to sit beside him. Mace resisted briefly before letting him pull her down. Not wanting to break the fragile truce they seemed to silently have created, he laced his fingers through hers, enjoying the softness of her skin. Giving her a squeeze, he was relieved to feel her return the gesture.

"So your brother went to work for the guild. Where did you end up?"

"Pirate ship. I probably have a bigger bounty on my head than you do. I figured Byron was after me when he showed up on the planet."

A few standard days ago, he couldn't have imagined his sweet-tempered research assistant doing anything that would warrant a bounty on her head. But a *pirate*?

Still, it made a strange sort of sense. The way she held a blaster and the sharp temper he'd seen emerge proved that Mace was a force to be reckoned with. After her showdown with Byron, he could easily imagine her raiding a Loyalist cruiser and taking no prisoners. He suspected she could easily kill him barehanded if she were so inclined. "What are you wanted for?"

A small smirk tugged at her lips. "I blew up a Loyalist weapons facility a few years ago. It was part of a raid that allowed the Borjan Five colony rebels to drive out the Loyalists during their coup."

"Have you ever killed anyone?" It wasn't the sort of question he expected anyone to answer honestly, but somehow he knew with Mace it was different.

She tried to pull her hand away, but he didn't let go. She relented after a moment and squeezed tighter, her gaze locked on the floor. "Yes, I have."

"Self-defense?"

"Self-preservation. He was a pirate, one who didn't follow the code. We got wind he was coming after Faolan. When he blew up a base where several pirates were meeting, because he thought Faolan was there, the Admiral put out notice to have him killed."

"The Admiral?" Gods, there was a lot beyond the Loyalist borders he still didn't know. "Who the hell—"

"Best not to ask." A small smile twitched at her lips. "Me and one of the other crew members had to go after the bastard and put him down."

Mace was protecting others.

"You had no choice."

"Doesn't make it right or take away how it makes me feel." She finally looked up at him, her eyes full of anguish. "He was a complete bastard who got off on pain and torture. I know I did the universe a favor by killing him. But there was a brief second before I pulled the trigger when he looked right at me. *Gods*, Alec. He looked terrified. *I* had done that to him."

Byron had always brushed off the action of taking a life as an unpleasant but sometimes necessary part of the job. Mace seemed to feel the same way Alec did, know the same cold dread that seeped through his body at the knowledge he was responsible for snuffing out the spark in another being. Needing to offer comfort as much as he had to take it, Alec leaned forward and captured Mace's mouth in a kiss.

Unlike Byron, he didn't dive in with force. While a part of him still loved Byron and his domineering ways, there was another part of him that wanted softness and comfort couched in strength. He wanted Mace.

There was a chasteness about the press of their lips together. In any other circumstance, he could have laughed off the gentle contact. He might never have pursued Mace at all, given where their relationship had been even a few days ago. But now, here, sitting on the side of a bed floating through space, totally unsure of where the future was taking them, he couldn't pull away.

Mace moaned as she reached up and ran her fingers through his hair. Alec ignored the feeling that he was taking advantage of the situation. The fire burning through him pushed past his warring emotions, forcing his growing need to a crisis point.

The kiss turned angry and urgent, and he knew Mace was taking what she needed from him.

He pulled back, gasping, dizzy at the sight of her swollen lips and glazed eyes. "I've wanted to do that from the moment you walked into my lab."

"Why didn't you?" She rubbed her thumb across his temple.

"I told you before, you weren't serious." He'd spent his years after leaving the Loyalists trying not to take advantage of others, and he'd tried to resist his growing attraction to his lab employee. But Mace was the strong pirate, not the meek assistant. She might even be able to handle the darkness swirling around inside his head. They were on equal footing.

Mace lightly sucked her bottom lip into her mouth, finally nodding. "But I am now."

A wave of lust welled up inside him. Without thinking, he grabbed her by the shoulders and pressed her firmly back into the mattress. "If you're going to change your mind, I need you to do it sooner rather than later. The Brasillian symptoms get worse when I'm . . . well, right before they get better. I won't be able to think about anything but that after a certain point. I don't know if I'll be able to stop myself."

"I'll probably kill you if you try."

"You might want to do that anyway now that you know the truth."

In a move that would have impressed Byron, Mace rolled them over on the bed so she straddled his waist. Lowering her face so she was only an inch from his, Mace spoke in a low and firm voice.

"Let's get something straight. I'm still pissed as hell at you for what you've done. Don't be foolish enough to think everything is okay. I might *still* kill you. But there is *something* between us and I'm not willing to walk away. Not yet. Got it?"

"Yes, ma'am."

"Now are you going to fuck me or not?" She stripped off her vest for the second time in as many hours.

Alec's world tilted on its axis. For once, he wanted to be the one calling the shots in bed. He needed her to know he was capable of giving her something other than pain and heartache. Without any warning, he rolled them back over until they were in the middle of the mattress, then shifted down to unfasten her pants and pull them off. He was grateful she hadn't put her boots back on when she'd abandoned the room earlier.

He yanked his own pants off and crawled back up to where she lay waiting on the bed, watching him with a measured, appraising gaze.

He fit perfectly between her legs. The moisture from her pussy now trickled down her thighs to wet his legs and cock. Mace moaned, bucking her hips up to force the connection between them, sending another rush of lust through him. It was powerful but bordered on the edge of his control.

"I wanted our first time to be something special you'd remember." He kissed her shoulder. "I didn't expect it would end up being a pity fuck."

"Technically," she gasped as he bit down on the juncture of her neck, "this is the second time. And who said anything about pity? Now if you don't do something soon, I'm going to call Byron on the coms and get him to come down here and—"

He smothered her tirade with a kiss. Her lips parted instantly as her tongue probed his mouth. He jerked his hips forward, forcing the length of his shaft across her swollen clit. Mace moaned, digging her nails into the backs of his shoulders and answering with a buck of her own.

He could have come from the novelty of it all. Smooth skin and soft curves, covering a layer of strong muscle. From her near-frantic thrashing beneath, he knew Mace wanted him to do more, take her out of herself. He'd felt that near-blinding need more than once with Byron—silently begging someone else to make the hurt and confusion simply go away. But just because she wanted to lose herself didn't mean she was going to hand control over to him the way he did to Byron.

He covered her hands with his, spreading them until Mace's arms were stretched out to the side. Breaking their kiss, he couldn't stop grinning at the look of frustration on her face. She struggled against his hold and tried to maneuver her legs so she could leverage herself off the bed. Spread wide like she was, she didn't stand a chance.

"None of that, Mace." Alec tilted his hips, trapping her. Her eyes widened as a startled gasp escaped her. Rubbing his lips across hers, he grinned down at her. "I'm still on fire in here and need some relief. I want to come in your pussy again."

"Oh yeah?" There was defiance and more than a little eagerness in her voice. "Are you going to make me?"

"Is that what you want?" He tightened his grip on her wrists. "Because I have no problem playing rough. Given my current state, I think rough is the only thing I can manage."

Mace snorted. "I doubt you know what rough is."

He couldn't let a challenge like that go unanswered. Transferring both her slender wrists into one hand, he reached down with the other to pull on the back of her knee. He knew if he encouraged Mace to wrap her leg around his waist, she would, but it would totally undermine the mood they were setting. Instead he pressed her knee to the mattress, pinning her open.

Thanks to the enhanced olfactory neurons provided by his spliced-in Syrilian DNA, and the keen need forced on him by the Brasillian syndrome, the scent of Mace's arousal hit Alec hard. Without pausing to think, he gave in to his impulses and drove himself completely into her waiting cunt.

Mace cried out as her back arched off the mattress. Alec pulled back to give himself better leverage. He didn't stop. Hell, he didn't even slow down. Instead he picked up the pace until he was pounding into her steadily. His mind seemed to sharpen every time her slick passage clenched around his shaft, making him aware of details that would normally have escaped his notice.

A bead of sweat slipped from his hairline to roll down the side of his neck, teasing his ear as it passed. The air cooled the wet trail before more sweat gathered on his skin. Mace's breathing came out in small, stuttered gasps. The air caught in her throat on every thrust. The small surrender she gave him sent a thrill through him.

For the first time in a long while, Alec was the one in control. Instead of the pain and suffering he'd given Mace and her family, now it was pleasure. She deserved more, better than what he could offer, but for now it would have to do.

He squeezed her wrists, leaning a bit more pressure on them. "I want you to keep these here. No touching me or yourself. Understand?"

Mace moaned, nodding once.

It wasn't good enough. "I said, understand?" His voice was harsher than he would have liked.

And maybe it was what Mace needed. She opened her eyes to look fully at him. "I understand."

With those two simple words, he knew Mace now belonged to him . . . at least as long as he made it worth her while. Free to shift her where he wanted, he grabbed her other leg and pulled it up to mirror the position of the other. There was now no place for either of them to hide.

The openness of her body let him see his cock as he pumped into her. It was stunning to see her pussy swallow his length completely. Her lower lips were flushed red and slick from her desire. Her clit shone out from beneath the thatch of dark curls, and for a moment he wished Byron were here so Alec could watch him suck on her. *Next time.*

"I think we should shave you bald." Alec pressed down on her knee to ensure she wouldn't move, before shifting to suck his thumb. Only when it was sufficiently wet did he reach between her thighs to brush against her clit. "A treasure like this shouldn't be hidden from sight."

"No." Mace's eyes closed, and she turned her face to the side.

"Look at me!" She instantly complied, looking surprised. He rolled his thumb across the top of her clit, enjoying her reaction. "You've been hiding from me, Mace. There's not going to be any more of that. If I want to see your bare cunt, then that's what we'll do. Byron will want it too."

Mace shook her head, and he started to back off, make a joke to ease the tension—but she was biting her lip, breathing harder and arching into him. Her splayed arms and legs never moved. She had made it clear from the outset besting him physically was something she could easily do. Maybe all Mace needed was some encouragement to let go. A little push and a whole lot of trust and he knew he could make things so good for her.

Like Byron had for him.

He didn't expect Mace to tilt her head, gaze still locked on his, and whisper, "You hid too."

He faltered in his rhythm, forcing himself to catch his breath and slow his pace. Of course he'd hidden from her—why would anyone want to know the truth about the monster hiding in plain sight?

Trying to shake off the gathering fog in his head and heat in his veins, Alec broke eye contact and slid out of her. He rolled her to her side and pressed himself along her back, then bit down hard on the side of her neck as he thrust into her.

"I may have hidden some things," he muttered against her damp skin, "but you saw all the important parts. I'm still me."

"Shut up and fuck me," she managed to say, though there was little venom to her words.

Mace lifted her leg and draped it backward across his thigh. Unable to resist the opportunity before him, he reached down and rubbed two fingers along his cock, capturing some of her juices. Then, as he snapped his hips forward, Alec massaged the damp tips of his fingers over her clit.

"You can't come until I tell you to." He licked the side of her neck. "But you can tell me when you're close."

"Yes." Arching back against him, Mace reached down and covered his hand with hers. She didn't try to stop him. It was like she wanted to connect with what he was doing.

The fire heating his blood now flared to a roar, and he swore he could feel every muscle and bone rubbing together with increasing agony as he moved. But his body had only one goal, and it was starting to consume him. *Come, come, come.*

Sliding his hand down to between her legs, Alec began to flick her clit in time with his thrusts. He forced himself to exhale and slow his pace, wanting so badly for them to build toward release together. But it didn't take long before his frantic need to come outweighed his restraint. Alec sucked and bit a trail up to Mace's ear lobe, while at the same time he increased the pressure on her clit.

Mace tried to buck back in time with his thrusts, but she was pinned down, locked in place and spread open. Alec knew he wouldn't last much longer and wanted to feel Mace come first. He wanted to give her at least that much. Releasing her ear, he spoke soft and low against her, his lips brushing her skin with every word.

"I watched you every day. Moving around the lab, trying to hide how fucking hot you were under that damn lab coat. It didn't work. I noticed and I couldn't do a gods-damn thing about it. But you're mine now. Mine to fuck or kiss, anything I want. And right now I want you to *come*."

Rubbing her clit at the same time he snapped his hips forced Mace over the edge. Her body tensed beneath him as she screamed. Alec could barely register the near sob that spilled from his lips as his own orgasm overtook him. Wave after wave of pleasure shot out, taking with it his last ounces of pain and suffering.

After collapsing back onto the mattress when every muscle in his body betrayed him, Alec came to life enough to kiss the top of her shoulder.

"Thank you."

Mace nodded and moved her leg so he was now free from her grip. "I still haven't forgiven you."

"I'm not expecting you to." Gods, it still hurt him to know what he'd done to her. "But I'm hoping there's a chance we can work on this."

"The cure?"

"Yes, but I was also thinking about *us*."

Mace was quiet for a long time. He knew she hadn't fallen asleep. Her breathing was far too irregular to be mistaken for peaceful bliss. When she gave no indication she would respond, he pulled his arm away. He'd nearly escaped when she reached up to clutch at his fingers.

"I won't promise you anything," she whispered. "But I'm not going to run."

As if his body had finally been given permission to relax, he fell back down beside her on the mattress. All the tension he'd been holding in his sore muscles bled out of him, making him suddenly aware of how exhausted he was. With the pain pushed down to a low background ache, he thought he might even be able to rest for a few hours.

"Stay with me?" he asked, no longer sure of her reaction.

Thankfully Mace seemed to have lost what was left of her fight. "As long as you don't steal the blankets. I get cold."

"Deal."

For the first time since Byron had shown up, Alec closed his eyes and slept.

CHAPTER

EIGHT

Mace slipped the belt end through the clasp and finally felt like herself again. For however long she lived, she swore she would never pretend to be someone she wasn't. Her blasters hung heavy from her hips in their twin holsters, and the knife Gar had given to her two years ago on her birthday was safely ensconced in the sheath along her back. This was who she was—killer, fighter, pirate.

Alec had still been sleeping when she'd gathered her clothing to change in the bathroom. While they'd been out of it for hours, she didn't have the heart to wake him just yet. The gods only knew how affected he was by the Brasillian syndrome, and despite her smoldering anger toward him, Mace couldn't stand the thought of him being in pain.

She'd deactivated the light and was nearly out the door when she heard Alec move. Cringing, she stopped at the sound of his soft, "Hey."

"Go back to sleep. I was just going to make sure Byron hadn't crashed my brother's ship into anything."

"Bry is a good pilot. I'm sure everything is fine."

"Me too, but I need to do something."

Alec pushed himself to a half-sitting position. His hair was flat on one side, sticking up on the other. His eyes were only half-open and a light darkening of stubble now covered his chin and jawline. He looked far sexier than he had any right to. She hated how her body reacted to the sight of him.

"I'll get dressed and join the two of you soon."

Mace wanted to argue.

She'd spent the better part of the last three years fighting with Faolan about his health, forcing him to take things easy. When she'd gone undercover, pretending to be a young research assistant with no particular worries, she'd felt guilty about the measure of relief she gained from the quiet, predictable daily lab work. Her time with Alec had given her a brief reprieve from the constant anxiety and danger back home. Now, standing here looking at him, she might have well returned to the *Belle Kurve* and rejoined Gar at his post by Faolan's bedside. The target was different, but the concern was achingly familiar.

Alec was sick, but more than his current illness weighed on him. His past was eating at his soul, a darkness she'd only caught a glimpse of when they'd both been pretending everything was fine. If he didn't sort himself out, eventually there would be nothing left.

"Why did you do it?" The question was from her before she even registered the thought. At Alec's confused scowl, she clarified. "Why did you infect yourself? The real answer."

Alec stared at her. There was no expression on his face to read, nothing to give away the emotions she knew were simmering below his surface. "I thought it was only fitting for me to suffer the same way my victims did."

"They weren't your victims. You weren't the one who poisoned them."

"I'm surprised to hear that coming from you. How is your brother-in-law doing these days?" Alec jerked the sheets from his body and pounded his feet to the floor. "I'll be on deck shortly."

Mace's stomach turned as dread rolled through her body. She was as surprised as Alec over her concern for his well-being. It wasn't right, her defending him, trying to justify what he'd done while he insisted on his culpability. She had no idea what was true, what his motivations had really been, whether he had manipulated her somehow into feeling this way. And she didn't want to talk about it until she at least had a handle on her own motivations. Frustrated, tired despite having slept, she nodded and left Alec to face his demons on his own.

It wasn't until she was at the door that she reached into her pocket. There, hidden in the smooth leather, was the necklace Gar had shoved into her hands as she was leaving the *Belle Kurve*. The priceless trinket that had led to Faolan and Gar's meeting, and ultimately reunited Gar and Mace. The legendary pendant that wasn't a legend, and gave the wearer the ability to read another person's thoughts.

It was an invaluable tool for a pirate, and Faolan had used it to his advantage in more than one negotiation. She hadn't wanted the responsibility or risk of keeping the gem safe. Most passed it off as an attractive bobble when they saw it, but if anyone discovered exactly what it did, her life could be in danger. But Gar had insisted she take it.

"If for no other reason than to make sure the person you're working with doesn't suspect you of anything."

She'd only worn it one time, to ensure Alec was on the level when it came to his intentions to find a remedy for the *ryana* poison; then she'd tucked it safely away in her room, well hidden from any possible intruders.

The stone felt cool in her palm and the familiar itching in her brain urged her to put it on. Because she'd connected to Alec once before, she was more aware of him, the turmoil of his emotions and spinning thoughts, than she would have been with a stranger. But there was something else, another mental tug that reminded her they weren't alone.

Byron.

Stepping out into the main area, Mace quickly decided, slipped the necklace from her pocket, and put the chain around her neck. The stone nestled nicely in her cleavage as a rush of awareness surged through her.

The *Geilt* shuddered, and Mace could feel the change as they approached a planetary atmosphere. She must have slept longer than she'd originally realized. Marching to the cockpit, she stopped midstride as Alec came through the hallway entrance behind her. He came beside her, placing a hand on her shoulder as he had dozens of times in the past.

Except now she wore the stone. She barely repressed a gasp as her mind came into sharp contact with his. Because of the previous link, the connection was immediate. And unlike the last time, she knew to look past the veneer of surface information to the truth underneath.

Why doesn't she hate me? Alec's thoughts invaded her head with a marked difference from his calm demeanor. Self-loathing and guilt came off him in waves and it took tremendous effort not to flinch away from his touch.

Alec frowned. "What's wrong?"

"Nothing. I just have a bit of a headache. I need to eat, and I'll be fine." She made a point of waiting a second before she slid away from his touch. "It feels like we're close to the planet. I was just about to check on Byron."

"And I was coming to see how the two of you were doing."

She turned to see Byron lounging in the now open cockpit doorframe. *Fuck, he's hot like that.* She blinked when she realized the thought had come from Alec and not herself. Not that she disagreed with the sentiment. Byron had abandoned the goggles from around his neck and had taken off his jacket. Now wearing only a thin shirt and hip-hugging pants, Byron looked more like a character from one of her more erotic dreams than a bounty hunter.

Shaking herself from her musings, she gave him a little smirk. "We're good. I was sleeping until I felt you start to bump my ship into the atmosphere, and I had to make sure you weren't going to break anything."

Byron snorted. "Please. I told you I wouldn't do anything to Gar's baby. But I could use a copilot to help get us down."

Mace narrowed her eyes. "You mean *I* could use a copilot. I'm taking over. You can navigate."

"Listen, girl, I'm used to being the one running the show." Byron lowered his chin and glared at her. "Don't push your luck."

Mace's breasts pressed against Bry as he fucks her. I wonder if Bry will let me fuck him at the same time. Alec shifted his weight and cleared his throat. "Are the two of you going to bicker like this all the time? If so, I'll find a new place to conduct my research."

"You're right!" Mace said, far louder than the conversations called for. "Let's just get down to the planet and see what we have to work with."

She didn't wait to see either man's reaction before she marched into the cockpit.

Byron was still in the doorway, and he was huge. She couldn't avoid brushing against him as she passed—it wasn't her intent to establish a firmer connection with him. The last thing she wanted was a bunch of warring male thoughts rattling around in her head while she tried to fly—or navigate—a spaceship. So it was a complete shock when the buzzing she'd noticed earlier snapped into a crystal-clear thought.

Man, I'd like Alec on his knees sucking my cock right about now.

Shaking, Mace lowered herself into the pilot's seat and set about programming in the descent protocols. She pushed back the images trying to bounce into the forefront of her mind. "Where exactly are we going? I want to make sure I hit the right trajectory."

"You okay?" Byron fell into the seat beside her. "You've gone pale."

"I'm fine. Coordinates?"

"You don't look—"

She twisted in her seat to glare at him. "Just give me the coordinates, Byron."

"All right, all right. Don't get your leathers in a bunch." He typed in the command as Alec came into the cockpit behind them.

Nice move, Byron. Smooth as ever. "Everything okay in here, you two? You're not going to crash the ship as you fight over who's in control?"

Byron winked over his shoulder at Alec. "I'm always in control." *And that's just the way you like it, boy.*

Mace snorted, though at which comment, she wasn't sure. "Coordinates locked in. I'm starting the approach vector for orbital descent now. Alec, you might—"

"Want to strap myself in, I know." *She can't really care about what happens to me. I killed her friend. I should die too.* "I'll make myself comfortable out here, then."

She looked up at him, grabbed his hand as he started to leave. Byron cocked an eyebrow at her, but there was nothing she could say that wouldn't give away her secret. Instead, she shrugged and smiled at Alec. "Use the seat by the computer consol. The straps are secure and you can help us monitor the descent."

Disbelief crossed his face, but Alec's thoughts were surprisingly vacant. "Aye, Captain."

He left the cockpit, but she triggered the door so it would stay open. The last thing she wanted was to cut Alec off even more than he seemed to be doing to himself.

If she hurts him . . . Byron's voice betrayed none of the menace she heard in his thoughts. "I've popped the coordinates in. There's a minor asteroid field just above the upper atmosphere we'll need to contend with, but other than that, it should be a smooth dive. Once we get near the base, though, your piloting skills will be put to the test."

"I'm not going to do anything to hurt him." Mace was surprised by the softness of her voice. It didn't matter that she shouldn't have known what Byron was thinking, she couldn't let it pass. Keeping her gaze locked on the controls in front of her, she added just as quietly, "He's hurting himself enough as it is."

"Don't make promises you can't keep."

"I don't—"

Byron slapped his hand against his thigh, causing her to jump. "This is not the time for this. Get the ship on the ground and we'll see what's left at the safe house. We'll worry about cures and praise or blame once we know what we're facing. Now fly."

Mace stiffened in the seat until she thought her spine would snap in two from the tension. Nodding, she set about guiding the *Geilt* down through the asteroids toward the surface.

"Alec, are you secure?" Byron called out, not bothering with the coms. "It's gonna get bumpy here in a second."

"I'm good," Alec shouted back. There was a soft hiss of static, followed by his voice echoing through the com. "Bry, is there some sort of perimeter security we need to be aware of?"

"Not up here. Why?"

Mace's heart began to pound as she glanced at the monitor. "Shit, I see them too."

"What?" Byron leaned in close to the scanner, tapping his finger against the screen. "I don't see . . . damn it!"

"Hold on." Not waiting to hear his suggestions, Mace threw the *Geilt* into a far steeper dive through the upper atmospheric shell than was healthy, then veered in a hairpin turn back away from the planet's surface. The sudden change in their trajectory jerked the two small security probes out of their orbit. The objects followed, trailing behind the ship in an intercept path. "Left over from your guild friends?"

"Krieg was a paranoid bastard, but this level of technology wasn't his style. He hated spending credits if he didn't think there would be a payoff. More likely to send someone to blow you out of the sky than lay a trap like this." *Shit.*

Images and thoughts of Krieg flashed through Byron's mind, none of them complimentary. Mace wanted to rip the bloody necklace from her throat, not needing the distraction as she bounced the *Geilt* off the atmosphere and back into the asteroid field.

"I'm going to get rid of these pests before we make any approaches. With luck, they won't have transmitted our coordinates to whoever put them out here."

Don't count on it. The simultaneous thought of both men echoed in her head. She couldn't stop laughing as she throttled up the ship, taking them directly into the path of the largest of the rocks. "Watch and learn, boys."

The hull rattled as she increased speed, nearing the minimal gravitational field of the space boulder. Mace aimed for dead center, knowing her timing would have to be perfect to force the probes to crash while ensuring her ship didn't. The computer sensors started to scream at her as the probes fell into weapons range.

"We could blow them out of the sky." Byron tensed beside her. "No reason for this."

"If they haven't sent the transmission, then whoever comes to check on them later will think they simply malfunctioned and crashed."

"And if they've already alerted the owner, you're putting our lives at risk for nothing."

Mace grinned. "But it's fun."

Foolish, cocky kid. "I'd rather settle for getting us down safely." Byron's fingers flew across the console. "Less than a thousand meters from the asteroid."

"Hold on, Alec." Mace waited until the last possible second before jerking the nose of the *Geilt* straight up.

The force from the shift in their forward momentum made her stomach pitch and roll with the ship as the artificial gravity tried to compensate but was half a second too slow. Alec's low moan crackled out from the coms, while Byron chuckled as the closer of the two probes smashed against the asteroid.

"One down," she muttered, steering the ship in a corkscrew arc back down toward the planet. "That's what I want."

Twin rocks at least double the size of the *Geilt* were locked together in a swinging dance of repulsion and attraction. The gap between them as they pulled apart would be just wide enough for her to slip the ship between, leaving the probe no room when the asteroids contracted together again.

No, no, no, don't do it. "Mace . . ." Byron's low growl would have terrified anyone. "Don't be a fool. Let me blow it up with the lasers."

A small part of her felt bad for what she was about to do, but the rest of her had total confidence in her ability to pull the maneuver off. Next to her brother and possibly Faolan, she was the best pilot on the *Belle Kurve* and had been since she was seventeen. Without another comment, she engaged the throttle, pushing the engines to capacity as she entered the gap.

"Shit." Byron spun in his chair to face the side computer. "We're not going to make it." *I'm going to kill her.*

Mace sucked in a breath as she watched the asteroids start their inward swing. She'd brought the *Geilt* over halfway through their path, the probe only a hundred meters behind them, as the gap rapidly began to close. The timing had to be perfect; a silent count ticked off in her head as she watched the sensors closely. She felt Byron stiffen beside her as, at the last possible moment, she side-rolled the ship, giving them just enough room to clear the colliding rocks.

The probe didn't make it.

"Woooooo!" Air rushed from her screaming lungs, and she let her body relax back into the seat as she took a deep sigh of relief. "See? Not a problem at—"

Pure, incoherent red rage filled her brain. Byron jerked her chair around and grabbed her by the neck. His fingers dug into her flesh as he leaned in close, his face only inches away.

"If you *ever* do anything stupid like that again, I will happily put a blaster to your head and pull the trigger. If you want to kill yourself, that's fine. But I'm not going to sit idly by while you take others with you. Understand?"

She jerked away, driving her palm into his solar plexus to drive him back. He puffed out all his air in a sharp blast, surprise clear on his face as he struggled to regain his breath. Not wanting to give him a chance to recover, Mace yanked a blaster from its holster and pressed it to his temple.

"Let's get something straight. In the bedroom you may be the one who takes control, but on this ship, I'm in charge. *My* ship. Not yours. If I want to fly us straight into the bowels of hell, then that's exactly what I'm going to do."

Byron licked his lips, his eyes glinting with internal fire. He panted a few times as his lungs finally refilled, then answered as if it hurt him more than the punch had. "Yes, ma'am."

She didn't retreat, her anger fueling her attack. "And for the record, I may have fucked you once, but don't count on a repeat performance. It takes more than a bossy attitude to get me hot."

That brought a smirk to Byron's lips. "I think it's exactly what gets you hot."

Mace pressed the blaster harder against him and did her best to ignore the *She looks fucking gorgeous when she's pissed off* that flashed through her head.

"Are you going to let me fly my ship now? I'd like to get to this base of yours sometime soon. Alec might need to rest before he gets to work."

I want to work on you, I want you begging and pleading for me to fuck you until you scream. No, not good, Byron, shut that down, not the time. Relax. Breathe. "Then we better get moving."

He reached up and gently pushed the blaster away, slowly enough that Mace could have stopped him if she were so inclined. She wasn't. She could hear him talking himself down, more calmly and reasonably than she ever could have.

Straightening, she reholstered the blaster. "I've never wanted to shoot someone so much in my life." She snorted and dropped back into her seat. "Except maybe Faolan."

"Lucky he's in your good books at the moment or else you might not be so keen to find him a cure." Byron went back to work on the computer, pausing only briefly to cast quick glances at her. "All programmed in. We'll be able to set down close to the base. It's in a bit of a valley, so the *Geilt* will be hidden from visual scans, and the metal and mineral content in the surrounding mountains should mask it from computer scans. They'll only see it if they trip over it."

Deciding she couldn't handle any more conversation with him, Mace simply nodded and concentrated on getting them through the atmosphere with as little trouble as possible. Gods, she hoped they'd be able to get an antidote or treatment for Faolan figured out soon, so everybody could go their separate ways. If she had to keep butting heads with Byron, one of them would end up dead. And it wouldn't be her.

Unlike their first attempt at a landing, the second went smoothly. Almost too smoothly for Mace's comfort. Things weren't supposed to be easy—not for her. So she was almost relieved when the valley Byron had described wasn't readily visible as they approached. She hated being forced to rely on the *Geilt's* computer sensors to guide her down to safety. Still, flying blind wasn't new to her. With hardly a shudder, she lowered the landing gear and touched them down gently.

Smug satisfaction made her grin. "I've done my part. Now let's see what your base looks like."

Strip her naked and wipe that grin— "Let's get the boy, then, and find out how bad things are in there."

Byron strode out into the main area ahead of her, to come face-to-face with a pale and shaking Alec leaning against the back of the chair.

"I'm not a boy."

"Shit." Mace tried to move to Alec's side, but Byron beat her to him. "Are you okay?"

Alec waved her away, even going so far as to lightly shove at Byron. "Fine. Just need to lie down soon. Let's see what's here so we can get started."

Gods, I hate to see him like this. I need to help. My boy, my responsibility. "Alec, I think you should rest first."

Mace shuddered at the emotion Byron packaged with his thoughts. Not able to take any more, she freed herself from the necklace and shoved it in her pocket. Byron noticed, cocking an eyebrow in question.

"The chain was irritating me." Jerking her chin toward the door, she stepped past the men. "We better move before he can't. I'll take the lead. Byron, bring up the rear. Alec, if you see anything weird, yell."

"Gods, I didn't realize you were quite so bossy, Mace." But despite his protests, Alec fell into step behind her as they left the ship.

The air on the planet held the putrid scent of sulfur. Mace had to suppress a gag as she caught the first whiff. They would need to get inside to avoid getting sick. Blaster in hand, she swept the area as they moved across the cracked and split landscape on their way to the camouflaged bunker door barely visible in the sheer side of the mountain. Clearly, the safe house was designed to go unnoticed by anyone who wasn't aware of its presence to begin with.

The hair on the back of her neck stood on end as a large shadow silently passed over their heads. Twisting around to look above them, she caught sight of an airborne creature as it disappeared past the cliff overhang.

"I thought you said there was nothing on this planet, Byron?" She kept the blaster pointed at the sky, even as she resumed their trek to the bunker. "That was a very large *something* up there."

To his credit, Byron was also pointing his blaster upward, using his other hand to nudge Alec along faster. "We'll talk once we're inside. I swear to gods we killed all those bastards last time we were here. Your brother helped."

A bloodcurdling screech reverberated in the stone valley, sending a chill through Mace. "Then I'm betting they won't be pleased to see us here. Let's hurry."

Knowing better than to tempt fate, she took off at a jog toward the bunker. The stone-clad door was pitted and the bottom was covered in a layer of muck, blown up over the years of disuse. Byron thrust the blaster into Alec's waiting hands and dropped to his knees in front of the small access panel.

"It should only take me a minute to get into this. The codes cycle through a series of twelve permeations. I'll know which one based on the prompt."

Two more large shadows crossed the ground, followed by another screech. Alec and Mace exchanged glances.

Alec shifted his stance, trying to peer around the ledge above them. "Want to move a bit faster, Bry? They sound hungry."

"Just . . . one . . . second . . . There!" The door hissed loudly but only opened partway, apparently glued in place by the built up layer of silt. Byron squeezed his body between the door and the frame, wedging himself in tight. "Give me a second to . . . get this bitch . . . open." Grunting, he forced the door the last few inches they needed.

Mace waited for Alec to get safely inside before following suit. It took all three of them to push it back closed, blocking the outside safely away. The musty stench of stale air filled the tiny vestibule. Byron grabbed a light from his belt, and shined it on the corridor ahead.

"Looks like people really did forget about this place. Should help us keep off the radar for now." Stepping forward, he led the way through halls that at one time must have been the epitome of guild prosperity. Now they were littered with debris, covered in inches of dust, and appeared to have housed any number of creatures over the years.

Mace was surprised the place was still standing and hadn't simply caved in under the mountain's weight, given its current condition. "Might want to fire your cleaning staff, Mr. Head of the Guild. They clearly haven't been living up to their end of the contract."

Alec snorted, only to stumble over a crack in the floor. "How much farther?"

"Getting horny again? Because I'm good for another round if you are." Byron winked at them from over his shoulder.

"And he wonders why I ran away from him," Alec muttered.

Mace would have laughed if it weren't for the flash of hurt she saw on Byron's face. As quickly as it was there, it was replaced with the now familiar cocky grin. "Couldn't keep up with my libido. That's why Mace here is going to be your helper, Alec. I'm more man than you can handle and she's your backup."

Bastard. Mace didn't need to have the necklace on to know Byron was more hurt than he'd let on and Alec was emotionally damaged. If she were smart, she'd abandon the two of them here and go off to find someone else to help develop a *ryana* antidote. There wasn't time to indulge their relationship issues, let alone possibly add to them by acting on the fantasies that plagued her.

"If you two are done with the pissing match, we need to find some usable living space and the lab. I want to get started on the research again as quickly as possible."

They spent a few minutes clearing a path to what ended up being a common room. From there, they had access to the living quarters, as well as to several powerful computers that were tucked into a side room and appeared intact.

Byron blew dust from a keyboard, sending a cloud of particles up through the flashlight's beam. "I'm pretty sure Krieg had some science whacks working on a special project for him a few years ago. There might be more equipment in one of the other labs if this isn't enough. We'll know more when we get the power on, I guess." It took him a few minutes to backtrack down the corridor. They knew he'd succeeded in finding the generator when the lights flickered on, dazzling Mace for a few seconds until her eyes re-adjusted.

She watched Alec inspect the equipment, flicking switches and waiting for the nearest computer to power up. His color was slowly coming back to normal, but he held his body rigid as he moved. When Byron walked back into the room, Alec ignored him. When the screen finally brightened into an image of the guild logo, he gave a nod but didn't direct his words to anyone in particular. "It will do."

Then, without so much as a thank-you, he pulled up a chair, slipped the backup data crystal he always carried with him from his pocket, and started to work.

Byron stared at Alec for a moment, a look of longing on his face, before turning to Mace. He licked his lips and shrugged. "I'll check out the place. See what I can find." He left before she could say anything.

Standing alone, she felt her heart begin to ache. This wasn't how things were supposed to have gone. She was going to get a remedy for Faolan, then get the hell home. She wasn't supposed to get caught between two ex-lovers. She wasn't supposed to lust after either of them. And she *certainly* wasn't supposed to have any feelings whatsoever for both of them.

So why the hell did she want nothing more than to lock the two men in a room until they sorted their shit out? More importantly, why did she want to lock herself in the room with them until she knew they were all going to be fine?

"Mace, think you can help me fill in the details of your last experiment?" Alec kept his eyes glued to the screen as he spoke; his fingers never paused on the still-grimy keyboard. "I didn't have time to save them to the backup before we ran."

Swallowing past the tightness in her throat, she did her best to push the emotions deep down before they could break through. "Yup, no problem."

Gods, she was in so much trouble.

CHAPTER

NINE

Byron hated feeling useless. For the past five days he'd been relegated to the sidelines, watching as Alec and Mace went about their tests. It had taken both him and Mace to convince Alec to manufacture and take the antidote for the Brasillian syndrome. Byron still wasn't completely convinced it had worked, but seeing as Alec wasn't climbing the walls trying to fuck everything in sight, he assumed things were better.

In a way, he wished Alec was still symptomatic.

Since their arrival on the base, Byron hadn't been able to engage Alec in anything deeper than a conversation about the weather—which was shitty. If Mace wasn't close by, Alec would practically fold inward, trying to segregate himself from Byron. Even with Mace around, Alec had little interest in spending much time with them. Byron was feeling worse than he had during those first few weeks at the Loyalist science compound, when he'd been nothing more than Alec's bodyguard and Alec barely gave him the time of day.

Even though he'd finally managed to locate Alec and make sure he was safe from the threat of bounty hunters, Byron couldn't do what he really wanted. He needed to find a way to make his former lover sit down and pay attention to him. But nothing seemed to work.

He wanted to punch something.

"What's with the scowl?" Mace slipped past him to the food replicator he'd somehow jerry-rigged into working with parts from around the base. "I'm surprised you're not out exploring what's left of your safe house."

Mace and Alec had come to an uneasy truce since their arrival. She didn't bring up Faolan's suffering and Alec kept his guilt speeches to a minimum. As a result, Mace had started smiling a bit more and her guard had dropped.

Byron couldn't stop his gaze from traveling down her body. She'd gotten some clean clothing from the *Geilt* and was now wearing a simple, form-fitting shirt and a new set of leather pants. The dark-green knit of the shirt suited her, highlighting her hair and eyes in a way that made Byron's mouth water.

The three of them had avoided anything remotely close to sexual conversations, touches, or even innuendos since they'd set up the lab. It was damn near driving Byron up the wall.

"I was saving that for my afternoon activity. Brooding and bugging you was on the agenda for the morning."

Mace rolled her eyes and let out a soft snort. "Well, I might suggest you change your schedule a bit. Alec has been doing enough bitching for the two of you."

The mug she'd pressed into the food replicator was suddenly filled with a spurt of dark liquid that smelled more foul than fair. Byron chuckled at her as she took a sniff, crinkling her nose at the aroma.

"Gods, I thought you said you fixed this."

Trapping her hand around the mug with his fingers, Byron moved it to his mouth and took a sip. The liquid burned as it passed down his throat, only to curl hot in his belly. Mace's gaze was locked on his mouth. He licked his lips and ran his tongue along the rim of the mug to capture a drip before it could travel down the side.

"It's better than the first day." He kept his voice low as he spoke. Mace met his eyes, and he smiled when she shivered. "I programmed the replicator to add a nice dollop of Grandalian brandy to the mix. Smells like shit but tastes amazing."

"Good to know." She swallowed and tried to tug her hand away. "Mind if I get this back?"

Without answering, Byron took another sip, and gently squeezed the mug, soaking in the feel of her skin and the heat of the drink. When she frowned at the wall and he saw her jaw clench, he reluctantly released her. It had been a very long time since a woman had caught his attention the way Mace had. He was finding it just as difficult keeping his distance from her as he was giving Alec the space he apparently needed.

For all her bravado, Byron had quickly come to realize Mace was unsure of herself. Not in her skills as a pilot or even in a fight, but in her allure as a woman. He was certain she hadn't been abused in any way—there wasn't the defensiveness in her actions he normally associated with that kind of harm. No, he thought her uncertainty was entirely consistent with the history he knew about her: She'd spent her teen years and adulthood almost entirely among men. And not just any men, but pirates. Rough, tough, muscled bundles of testosterone who probably banged the first willing targets planetside . . . but who all knew Faolan Wolf would kill any crew member who laid a finger on Mace.

She might have picked up a few lovers in port over the years. But she had no idea how appealing she really was, because she'd spent her formative years flirting and bantering with a ship full of tough guys, and never getting anywhere with any of them through no fault of her own. She'd never had the chance at a relationship. So she had zero confidence in her own appeal once things progressed past a quick fuck during a supply run.

As far as Byron was concerned, that was akin to a crime against nature.

So in addition to Alec and his mountain of issues to resolve, he now had Mace's problems to consider.

It was a good thing he was more than up to the task.

Turning so they stood side by side, he randomly pressed some buttons on the replicator and hoped the end result would be edible. "So what's gotten into our boy this morning? Is he still upset we shoved that cure down his throat?"

A serving of something that resembled meat was manufactured from the machine onto Byron's waiting plate. Mace didn't answer, so he started to move away, but she stopped him with a hand on his arm. She didn't look at him, but he could feel the tension bleeding off her.

"He's getting . . . frustrated. I think now that he knows about Faolan and how sick he is, he's pushing himself even harder to find an antidote. Too hard, I think."

He remembered what Alec was like when his frustration kicked in. "It's making things worse. He was always his own worst enemy when he tried to solve problems."

Mace nodded. "I spent the last hour trying to convince him to take a break. He snapped at me to get out if I wasn't going to be helpful."

"Typical stubborn ass. Some things never change."

"I was hoping you'd talk to him." She shrugged. "Maybe convince him to come out of the lab for a bit and recharge. He's no good to anyone if he gets himself into a mental block."

Unfortunately Byron was also familiar with Alec's stubborn streak. In the past, he would have locked the overworked genius in a room and fucked him so hard and so long, Alec wouldn't be able to think at all. Alec would always come out of their marathon sessions better for it—clearheaded and physically relaxed, able to focus properly on the task at hand.

Byron doubted the suggestion would be appreciated in their current situation.

"Byron?"

He shook his head. "Sorry. Anything I would have done in the past to help him involved sex. I doubt he'd be a willing participant right now."

Mace sucked in a breath but didn't retreat. Instead she turned to press her back against the wall. A blush colored her fair skin, but she didn't break his gaze. "I wanted to ask you something."

Cocking an eyebrow, he waited for her to continue. He had a notion what the question might be, but even if his guess was right, it was up to Mace to verbalize it.

"Back on the *Geilt*, when we first went through the dimension gate and had to . . . take care of Alec, you were very . . . forceful."

His cock twitched as his body responded to the memory. "Is that a question?"

"No, no. But I was wondering if that's something . . . I mean, when you have sex . . . are you always . . . ?"

"Do I always dominate Alec when I'm fucking him?"

The blush deepened as Mace nodded. "I got the impression it was more than just you making sure he was going to be okay."

Shoving the plate back on the replicator, Byron grabbed the mug from Mace and set it down on the counter. Then, in a long-practiced move, he snatched her wrists in one hand and held them against the wall above her head. She didn't struggle, not even when he slid his thigh between her legs, forcing them open.

"I think it's fairly obvious," he said quietly, "that I'm an overbearing bastard. But Alec needed someone to help him. There was so much stress on him all the time. To be perfect, be smart. To help the Loyalist government. It was too much for one man to handle."

Mace squirmed against him, her pussy grinding down on his thigh. "So you helped him."

He lifted his leg to increase the tension where he knew she wanted it most. "In my own way. Alec didn't need to be anyone for me. He could let everything fall away and be himself, knowing I would take care of him. When I fucked him, he didn't have to make any decisions."

"No pressure." The words left Mace's lips on a sigh. She wasn't referring to Alec.

"No, little one. No trying to deal with problems bigger than yourself. I see it in you too." He leaned forward until his mouth hovered inches above hers. "You were so good for me on the *Geilt*. Did everything I asked when I asked it. And that wasn't even me taking over. Would you like that, Mace? Want me to lock you in a room and look after you like that? I think I'd like it."

Closing her eyes, Mace turned her head to the side, her breath coming out in barely controlled pants. Holding herself back, even though she seemed to want to give in. She wouldn't be the first to walk away from his offer. Normally by this point, Byron would have walked away himself. He didn't have the patience to deal with lovers who couldn't allow themselves to admit what they wanted.

But he knew why Mace hesitated just when she should have felt most confident. And he'd already seen how she responded to him. If she let herself have this—if she let him take control—the result would be so worth the wait, for both of them.

"Leave her alone, Bry. She doesn't need your bullshit."

Mace stiffened, but Byron didn't react to the threat in Alec's voice. It was a challenge to keep from spinning around and pressing Alec against the opposite wall, but Byron managed. Instead he lowered his mouth to Mace's neck and pressed a soft kiss to the sensitive skin.

"He always had poor timing. It was one of the things I constantly worked on with him." He dipped his mouth lower to drag his teeth across her collarbone. "I wonder if you would be better at it than him? I think you would. Pilot instincts."

"Byron, leave her."

It might have been jealousy coloring Alec's impatient tone, or simple frustration. Either way, he wasn't about to listen to his ex-lover. Since Byron had left Alec alone in the bed back on the *Geilt*, something had changed in Alec. It had nothing to do with Mace. No, this was an old fight—back and forth like a planetary ocean tide—Alec's desire to give up his control warring with his guilt and conscience, driving him to resent Byron for giving him exactly what he'd asked for.

With his free hand, Byron burrowed under the smooth material of Mace's shirt until his fingers grazed the soft flesh of her stomach. The muscles beneath his touch fluttered and flexed as she tried to hold still. The effort made Byron smile against her skin, encouraging him to place another kiss to her throat.

"I think now that his brain is clear, our boy has forgotten what it's like to have a good time. Did he try to fuck you down on the planet?"

He felt her breath hitch and a low moan catch in her chest. "No."

"Didn't think so."

The growl from Alec wasn't unexpected. "I wasn't going to take advantage of her like that. You know I wouldn't. You shouldn't be either."

"I would never take advantage of her. She's a grown woman. And she raised the subject in the first place. I'm just answering her question."

Byron noticed a sound over the steady background hum of the generator and the higher whine of the replicator—a gentle, rhythmic tapping, like rain on a faraway metal roof, soft and soothing. He wondered about it for a moment, but quickly found he didn't care. Not when he had Mace's flawless skin beneath his touch and her scent filling his head. The heat poured off her body as she writhed against him.

"What are you doing, Byron?" Alec's voice again, but this time there wasn't any anger or resentment. It was calm, and for once Byron couldn't help but answer honestly.

"I'm trying to seduce her." The words slipped from him before he gave them much thought. Still, it was the truth, and he wasn't exactly hiding his intentions. He had Mace pinned against a wall with his hand up her shirt.

"Did you give her a choice? Are you just taking what you want, like always?"

Byron bit down on the juncture of her shoulder and neck, but not quite hard enough to break the skin. Mace gasped, her back arching away from the wall and her hands pulling against his restraining grasp.

"I want her." He licked the abused area, enjoying the salt from her skin. "She's mine."

Somewhere in his brain, Byron knew he shouldn't be answering Alec. It wasn't his style. But right then he really couldn't give a fuck. Mace was wet and willing in his arms, something he would never say no to. If Alec wanted to watch the show, then he was more than welcome.

Sliding his hand up to cup her breast, Byron flicked her nipple with the pad of his thumb. He trapped her gasp, covering her mouth with his in a deep kiss. His tongue matched the teasing flicks of his thumb until he knew Mace would be beyond thought. It was only his need for oxygen that forced him to pull back.

Byron forced himself to look at Mace. Her eyes were screwed shut as her breath came out in heated puffs against his skin. The flush now covered her throat, spreading down to beneath her shirt. If he pulled it off, he had no doubt the red glow would cover her breasts.

The rhythmic tapping increased in tempo, in time with Mace's breathing.

"Mace? Do you like what Byron is doing? Do you *want* him to do that?" The uncertainty in Alec's question almost made Byron turn to face him. Almost.

Mace opened her eyes, licking her bottom lip once she locked her gaze on Byron's. "Yes. So much."

As quickly as the tapping began, it stopped. Byron's mind cleared from a fog he hadn't noticed. It was like someone had pulled a blanket from his head, and the air around him felt clearer and cooler.

Mace stopped her struggles and gave her head a shake. Though she looked confused, she wasn't Byron's immediate problem. He heard the shuffling of Alec trying to slip away.

"Don't move." The command came out as tersely as Byron could manage. "Don't you dare move, Alec."

Finally turning to look over his shoulder at Alec, he resumed his sensual attack on Mace's nipple with his thumb. "You came in here telling me I was taking advantage of her. Clearly I'm not."

Alec swallowed, looking more than a little guilty. "Byron—"

"No, it's my turn to ask questions. Does it bother you to see us like this?"

"Bry—"

Byron lifted his leg until Mace was nearly off the ground. She moaned, straining on tiptoe, grinding against him until he thought she was going to come.

"Answer me, Alec. Does it bother you?"

Alec stepped back until his shoulders were pressed firmly against the wall and his palms were flush with the surface. Byron recognized his wide-eyed stare, and knew Alec was aroused by what he was witnessing.

"You see, Mace, our boy loves to watch almost as much as he likes to participate. I can't tell you how many times I'd tell him to sit still and watch me fuck someone else. He'd come really hard those nights when I eventually let him. Didn't you, Alec?"

He didn't think Alec would respond at first, but after a few heartbeats, he nodded.

"Yes."

A quick glance at Alec's groin proved he was responding exactly the way Byron had hoped he would. "Good. I want you to take your cock out and start stroking. You're not allowed to come until I say, and you can't look away. Just like old times."

Alec groaned as his head bounced against the wall, but he didn't break eye contact. Byron was pleased to see that it only took him a few moments to comply, pulling his already hard cock out. He gave it a few tentative strokes before falling into a slow, steady rhythm.

Mace sucked in a breath, and Byron turned to see her attention fixed on Alec. This was going to be easier than he'd first thought. And a much better few hours than the other two would have spent if he hadn't stepped up. A threesome trumped research in his books every time.

"That's right, Mace. You just keep looking at him. You're not going to come until I tell you to either. We want to make sure we give Alec the best show we can."

"We shouldn't be doing this," she whispered.

Byron yanked her shirt up, looping it over her head so her bare breasts were on display. "You said yourself we were all working too hard. That we needed a break. Consider me the break enforcer."

Bending down, he caught her nipple in his mouth and sucked hard, causing Mace to cry out and twist beneath him. Byron held her body still and continued to suck and tease her. "Gods, yes, *Bry*."

Hearing Mace moan out Alec's nickname for him sent a jolt to his cock. Momentarily increasing the suction, he waited for her to moan again before finally releasing his grip on her wrists and sliding down to his knees.

"What do you think, Alec?" He pressed his nose to the hollow of her ribs below her breast. "Should I lick her pussy until she begs me to let her come?"

Dual moans assaulted his ears, drawing a smirk from him. With very little effort, he popped the button holding Mace's leathers up. Thank gods she hadn't bothered to put on her blaster holster. He wasn't sure he was coordinated enough to work the buckle just then.

Mace took the opportunity to take off her shirt, throwing it toward Alec. Then she helped Byron maneuver the leathers down over her hips and thighs. They got stuck as he tried to maneuver them down over her boots, but he managed to jerk them free. Finally finished, he looked up to admire the woman before him.

Mace was the image of sex itself, standing there in nothing but her knee-high boots, her gaze flicking down to him every so often, but mostly fixated on Alec. Byron's cock throbbed in complaint—he should be buried balls-deep in one of them by now.

Unfortunately for his cock, his mind had better restraint than that. "Mace, I want you to put your leg over my shoulder. Shift your weight so you're leaning against the wall."

The heat from her thigh on his shoulder contrasted with the cool, hard boot leather against his back. Mixed with the sight of Mace spread open, cunt staring him in the face, begging him to lean in and suck her clit—yeah, he wasn't a fucking saint. He was going to need to get naked himself soon or he'd suffer irreparable injury.

The second his tongue connected with Mace's wet clit, she gasped. The heel of her boot dug into his shoulder blade, forcing him closer. Who was Byron to argue with a lady? His head spun with perverse pleasure from the sounds she made as he ran his tongue up the entire length of her pussy. He'd always gotten off on the power of seduction—reducing Mace to a quivering mass would be nearly as heavenly as when he finally gave in and fucked her.

Alternating long licks with short bursts, Byron brought her to the edge of orgasm before pulling sharply away. Her body shuddered with the strain of her denied release, and she thumped her head on the wall behind her.

"Bastard."

"No coming until I say. That was the rule."

"Stupid rule."

"Necessary rule. If I'd let you come already, you wouldn't be in the right frame of mind to enjoy it when I did this."

His fingers met no resistance as he pushed two of them into her pussy. Moist muscles clenched around him as he screwed his digits into her. He pressed against the front wall of her cunt, rubbing her from the inside. He knew he was hitting the right spot when Mace began to moan and buck down onto him.

Byron set a slow but even pace, and glanced over at Alec. Their eager voyeur matched his own strokes to Byron's. Even from across the room, Byron could see the tip of Alec's cock leaking pre-cum at a generous pace.

"Look at you." Byron's whisper was harsh in the space between them. "All hard and ready to fucking blow. I'd bet you'd come all over your hand right now if I told you to. Wouldn't you, Alec?"

He didn't have to do any other prodding to get Alec to nod.

"Yes."

"Good boy. She's so wet. I bet you can hear my hand pumping into her." Byron smacked Mace's ass hard. "Don't move, Mace."

"Bry, please." Mace bucked her hips, practically forcing her mound into his nose. "Let me come."

"No." Another smack. "I'm not done with my fun. The two of you will come and run back off to your lab and leave me alone. So no, you're not allowed to come. Yet."

Not one to punish himself, Byron leaned in and sucked her clit into his mouth again. When she tightened around his fingers, he pressed harder against the front wall. Cream flowed down his hand and along his wrist. Gods, she was ready.

Without giving her any warning, Byron rose to his feet, letting her leg fall to the ground with a *thump*, and held her against the wall. Capturing her mouth in a searing kiss, he yanked open his pants and shoved them down just enough to get his cock out.

"I'm going to fuck you, baby. I'm going to pound into your sweet cunt until you're screaming. And once you've come, I'm going to pull out and come all over you. Then if Alec boy is very lucky, I'll let him come too."

"Stop fucking talking and get on with it," Alec bit out.

Byron knew when not to push his luck. Instead, he lifted Mace up, cupping her ass with his hands, and impaled her on his shaft. Grinding his teeth to keep from crying out at the perfection of her tightness, he slammed into her at an unrelenting pace.

Mace dug her nails into the back of his neck and shoulder, trying to match his rhythm. With her every downward thrust, he was taken deeper into her body. If she kept that up, he wouldn't last long at all.

He knew it wouldn't take much to push Mace over the edge, not after all his teasing. Shifting so his body pinned her still, he reached down and pressed her clit with his thumb, circling her tip after every thrust.

"You're gorgeous and you don't even realize it. Do you?" He buried his face against her neck, letting her hair caress his skin. "Every man who's ever met you has wanted to fuck you, and I doubt you even noticed."

She shook her head, rolling it back and forth against the wall.

"It's true. Even Alec wanted to fuck you." Byron pulled back and was rewarded by the sight of Alec down on his knees, panting hard, his hand flying over his cock. Byron increased the pace of his thrusts once more, not bothering to hold himself in check any longer. "If I gave him the word, he'd walk over here and take you right now. But I won't. I want you to come now. Right now."

Mace tensed, her face contorted, and a scream escaped her as she came. Byron felt every flutter of her muscles around his cock, drawing his orgasm to the point of inevitability. Letting her legs go, he pulled out, stroked his cock twice, and shot cum across her stomach. The pleasure was so intense, his body froze for a moment, then relaxed all at once. He collapsed against Mace with a muted groan, pinning her to the wall as they both panted.

"Wow," she whispered.

"Yeah." Byron turned his attention back to Alec, whose hand was practically a blur as it moved over his shaft. How Alec had kept himself from coming, Byron hadn't a clue. He was clearly desperate.

"Come for me, Alec."

Almost before the sound of Byron's voice died on the air, Alec threw back his head and screamed. Moments later he slumped to the ground, an exhausted, sticky mess. The look on his face was one of utter contentment.

When his knees began to quiver from the strain of keeping upright, Byron shifted Mace around until he was able to slide down to the floor, arranging her so she sat cradled on his lap, facing Alec.

It was odd how peaceful, almost normal, this felt to him. Sure, he and Alec had shared lovers in the past, but with Mace it was different. She was practically a buffer for the tension that had risen since their arrival. As much as he would be able to start things up with Alec once they'd solved whatever issues he had, Byron wasn't an idiot. It was going to take a lot more than a few quick fucks to fix what had gone wrong.

Alec finally opened his eyes again, a half smirk on his lips. "Well, that was a bit unexpected."

Mace chuckled as she adjusted her head on Byron's shoulder. "We more than needed the break."

"That's what I'm here for, kids. Useless with the science crap, but more than able to screw the tension out of you."

"Don't." Alec shook his head, stretching his legs out to their full length but not bothering to tuck his cock back in his pants.

"You're more than a bounty hunter, bodyguard, or a convenience fuck. I hate it when you do that." The last was little more than a mutter.

Byron knew he shouldn't antagonize Alec, especially since he was trying to win the other man over—but this was another old argument. Tipping Mace's head back so she could see him, he rolled his eyes for effect. "Alec's of the impression I've got more in my head than I do."

"Who's saying you don't?" She scrunched her face in what Byron was sure she meant as a scowl; it came across as more of a pout. "I very much doubt anyone can be the head of the guild without having a certain degree of intelligence."

"You're as bad as Alec." Pushing her gently aside, he stood and fixed his clothing. "What I do is completely different from what the two of you can do. No comparison."

Alec snorted. "Byron, you know that—"

"How's that antidote coming along?" He knew he was close to yelling, but he wasn't in the mood to have his life put under a microscope at the moment. "Any closer to saving Mace's friend?"

Mace stiffened as Alec's gaze darted between the two of them. She got up and quickly gathered her clothing. "We were getting closer, but there are still some issues with cellular degradation."

"That's what I came to tell you." Alec followed suit and tucked his now soft cock away. "I think I might have discovered a way to boost the potency of the compound without damaging either the cell structure or causing genetic decay."

Byron let them chatter as they exited from the room. It was funny how quickly he felt the emptiness return, even after some of the best sex he'd had in years. Still, despite what Alec thought, he'd never really had much of a place in that world beyond, except being the brawn.

He was so wrapped up in his own head, he nearly missed the sensor alert blinking on the computer in the side alcove.

Frowning, he strode over to the machine and checked the readings. "Did either of you go out the side exit to the collapsed section of the compound?"

Mace was by his side, leaning over to scrutinize the monitor. "I sure as hell didn't. I thought you said the base was empty."

"It is. Was." A surge of protectiveness flooded him, mixing dangerously with his lingering anger. "You two stay here. I'll go take care of our unexpected guest."

"Bry, don't be a fool." Alec was already reaching for the blaster Mace had found for him on the *Geilt*. "We're all here, we can all look."

Sure, take that away from me too. "You two just keep working on that cure. I want to get us out of here as quickly as possible." Mace opened her mouth to join the argument, but he silenced her with a kiss. "Keep on your toes."

He bolted out the door, trying not to look behind him. He pulled his blaster as he turned the corner to the long service corridor, looking down when it snagged on the holster. There was a noise followed by shouting. He didn't realize he'd been shot until the scent of burned flesh hit him. His vision blurred as he stumbled backward, falling to the floor.

CHAPTER

TEN

Mace had her blaster in hand and pushed past Alec before he had a chance to register the sound of weapon fire. Every instinct he had was screaming at him to follow her. Byron was out there—alone. Gods only knew what they were facing, and if Byron was pinned down, Mace might need his help.

But one look at the computer reminded Alec that the data took precedent. They were under attack, and he had no idea if they would have to leave the base—or ever be able to return if so. Jumping to the computer station, he started downloading the details of his latest experiment onto his data crystal. He'd be damned if he'd lose everything they'd worked so hard for because of a bunch of trigger-happy bounty hunters.

How the hell had the hunters found them anyway?

Another volley of blaster fire echoed in the hall, sounding dangerously close. "Come on, come on, come on," he muttered.

"Alec!"

His body froze at the panicked note in Mace's voice. *Oh gods, please let them be okay.* The computer beeped its completion, and he snatched the crystal away and shoved it deep into his pocket. Grabbing his own blaster, he raced through the door.

"Mace?" A light cover of smoke filled the hall; the sound of blaster fire was louder out here. "Where are you?"

"Go left!"

It took him only a matter of seconds before he knew he'd reached the center of the fight. Mace was across the open hallway, crouched low and firing down the hall at the attackers. She acknowledged him with a quick glance before letting loose another torrent of fire.

Lifting his blaster, Alec ran through the steps Byron had taught him years ago. Deep breath, focus on movement beyond the blaster beams. Don't hesitate to shoot first.

Byron.

"Where's Bry?" He called out before sliding past the safety of the corner to unleash a series of blasts.

He nearly froze when Mace moved to the side enough to reveal Byron's body, slumped against the wall. His heart must have stopped for a few beats, because when it started up again, the rapid rhythm almost made him pass out.

"Bry?" There was no way he could have heard Alec over the shouts of their attackers or the noise from their weapons.

"Get over here." Mace only gave him half a second to acknowledge her before she stood up and laid down cover fire.

He bolted across the opening, the heat from the lasers so close the hairs on his skin curled. He returned fire as he passed, not bothering to check if he was actually hitting anything. Nearly running Mace over, he fell to the floor on the other side of Byron, checking out his wounds.

"Not dead," Byron slurred, wincing as Alec tore open his shirt at the shoulder where the blaster had hit.

A cursory look told Alec his stubborn-assed lover would live to annoy him another day. "We need to get out of here and back to the *Geilt*. Can you move?"

Mace pulled on Byron's good arm, looping it around her neck. "Can or not, we have to go *now*."

Alec supported Byron's other side, and they raced as fast as they could down the hall toward a security blast door—the even better-hidden back door to the complex, that led out into the recesses of a natural cavern in the mountainside. Alec let Byron and Mace go first before securing the door behind them. The computer beeped, but the ubiquitous silt and mud hadn't been cleared from this entrance, and the locks didn't fully engage.

"Shit." He tried again with no better result. "This won't hold them for long."

"We won't need it," Mace said over her shoulder as she continued to haul Byron down the rough, narrow passage between two rock faces. The rock was damp and reflective, and there was just enough daylight filtering in from the cavern's distant opening that they could make their way without a flashlight. "The *Geilt* is just down here."

Alec took up Byron's other arm, and they increased their pace. "Pray they don't have someone guarding it."

"Who the hell are they? They don't look like guild hunters." Mace kept looking back, her blaster still in hand. "And how did they find us here?"

"Not guild," Byron ground out. His teeth were clenched, and his body shook in their hold. "Freelancers."

Oh, that is very bad. Freelancers were less interested in negotiations and credits and more concerned with kills. They were all in serious danger if Mace wasn't able to get them out of here on the ship. "Did you recognize any of them, Bry?"

"More important," Mace demanded in a harsh whisper, "why the hell are they after us? You said this base wasn't known by anyone."

Byron stumbled and groaned. "Shoot now. Talk *later*."

Alec wasn't sure if the chuckle that popped out of him was one of panic or because the entire situation was beyond ludicrous. Either way, Byron glared at him while Mace rolled her eyes and shushed them both.

They slowed their approach as they rounded a set of stalactites into the widest part of the cavern, then crept as quietly as they could along one wall toward the opening where the *Geilt* lay beyond. Three men and a four-legged beast that looked like a pumped-up *ragnate* dog were pounding on the hull. Mace chuckled when they tried to attach what looked like a bomb and the ship let out a low level EMP blast. The device landed on the ground with a loud *thunk*, followed by a series of curses from the men.

"They won't be able to do anything to the ship," she murmured with a smile. "Gar made sure she had the best defenses credits can buy."

Alec peered around the edge of the opening as best he could, not wanting to risk being spotted. "We still have to get past them."

"I'll take the two on the right, you aim for the mutt." Mace slipped free from Byron, taking an extra moment to press her second blaster into his hand. "Alec, you'll have to get him to the ship. Bry, think you'll be able to help?"

"Just point me in the right direction and I'll take them down."

Alec knew better than to argue with Byron. "Point and shoot. Got it."

"Give me a three-second head start, then come out firing. Ready, boys?"

Gods help me. "All set."

Byron reached out and caught her shoulder in a squeeze. "Don't get yourself killed. Your brother will never forgive me if you do."

"Are you kidding? He'd find a way to bring me back just to bitch me out. I plan on getting back to him in one piece to avoid that." Before either of them could react, Mace leaned in and placed a quick kiss to each of their mouths. "Here we go." She sucked in a deep breath, winked at them, and with a final rakish grin, ran out into the clearing.

One. Alec adjusted his hold on Byron, watching as the wind whipped up around Mace, tossing her short hair madly around her face as she opened fire on the unsuspecting men.

Two. Byron lifted his blaster and adjusted his stance. Alec saw Byron's wound was now bleeding, despite the cauterizing nature of the blast. It was going to take him quite a few treatments to get fixed up again. Mace better know a good doctor.

Byron shifted closer, squeezing Alec's side with his hand.

Three.

They moved as one, Alec barely needing to haul Byron along. The smell of burning ozone trailed in Mace's wake as she cleared the way for them. If he'd had time, Alec would have appreciated the picture she made, face contorted in a scream as she sliced through the increasing number of guards.

Three more attackers had come from the front of the ship, forcing Alec to redirect his aim. Mace had reached the *Geilt* and was quickly releasing the security lock. The hatch slid open and she jumped inside, covering them while they ran as fast as Byron could manage.

Alec landed on the ship's floor in a heap, Byron under his body, and was forced to duck his head down as Mace jumped over him on the way to the cockpit. "Why am I always running for my life with you two?" The hatch slid up behind her, blocking out the furious faces and shouts of their pursuers.

Byron chuckled, shaking Alec. "Go help."

"You need me more."

"Won't matter if they blow us up. Go."

Growling, he rolled away, ran for the cockpit, and threw himself into the copilot's seat when he got there. "What do you need me to do?"

"It's just like an atmospheric shuttle. You've driven those planetside. Except we're going to pop into deep space. Put the commands into the computer when I read them out. Okay?"

He knew little about ships, but a computer was a computer. His hands seemed to know what to do on instinct. He set the computer to warm up while the *Geilt* blasted off and began a rough, fast climb against gravity's pull. He heard Byron groan from the other room when the ship pushed up through the atmosphere with a hard shudder.

He knew he shouldn't react. Hell, he was still pissed off at Byron, but he'd let himself get distracted by the wild escape from Naveeo, then by the damn Brasillian syndrome. Then by sex and a bunch of useless emotions, plain and simple, no way to blame it on anything but his own weakness. The same weakness he'd always had where Byron was concerned. If he'd been thinking even a little bit, he would have turned around back on the planet and run screaming to the nearest Loyalist enforcer building. It would have been less harmful to his psyche if he had.

"Alec!" Mace slapped the top of his thigh. "Here and now. You can brood once we're safely away from these assholes."

"I wasn't brooding."

"You're always brooding. At least now I know why."

He bit down hard on his tongue and hoped it was enough to keep himself in check. A little pain always went a long way toward helping him focus. "Coordinates?"

"Theta, gamma, one. Zero, zero, delta. Go!"

The ship kicked forward, breaking the last of the upper atmosphere and settling into the silence of space. Surprisingly, there weren't any ships waiting for them, only the ghostly asteroids dancing together. It would have been beautiful under any other circumstances.

"How the hell do you think they found us?" He turned to face Mace and could see she was wondering the same thing. "If any of the original bounty hunters were tracking us, they would have been there much sooner. No one could have spotted the *Geilt* from orbit, so once we'd landed there was no indication we were there. And that base had been abandoned for ages. It's not like somebody just happened by."

"Byron."

Words to defend his ex-lover were in his mouth before he had time to think. "Absolutely n—"

Mace cut him off with a wave of her hand. "I don't think he did anything intentionally. But it's a guild safe house and he put in several codes to get things turned on. Maybe . . . maybe someone is tracking *him*."

"That doesn't make sense. Why the hell would anyone be after Byron? He said the bounty was on my head."

"Alec, he's the head of the guild. If even half the stories my brother told me about them are true, then he's at more risk for assassination than either of us."

It made sense. Of course it did. No one knew where Alec had been hiding, and it had taken Byron no small feat of detective work to locate him. And if Byron hadn't done that—to warn Alec about the new bounty on his head—he would still be safe and sound in the middle of some guild-protected area with bodyguards and more weapons than a small army could use.

Alec had been the bait to lure Byron into the open.

"Shit." He turned away from Mace to focus on the computer.

"It's not your fault."

Gods, he hated the sound of sympathy in her voice. "Yes, it is. Bry would never have allowed himself to be vulnerable if he hadn't thought someone was trying to kill me."

"You can't know—"

"Mace. Please let it go."

He knew he wasn't being fair to her, but he had never been one to deal well with his emotions. They weren't some nice, neat little scientific problem he could figure out with experiments and computers. They were messy and confusing, most of the time causing him more pain than he'd been able to handle.

Only during the short time he'd spent with Byron had he seemed to settle down into any kind of normalcy. Then he'd put Byron at risk, so he'd gone on the run. Now here he was, putting Byron in danger all over again.

Clearing his throat, Alec checked the computer again as Mace flew them straight for the dimension gate. The treatment they'd rigged up for the Brasillian syndrome better work. He wasn't sure he'd be able to face either one of them again if the insane sex cravings came back.

As if reading his thoughts, Mace snorted. "Promise me you won't try to fuck me until after we get through this thing. I'm not sure how good my multitasking skills are these days."

He chuckled. It felt good to let some of the tension bleed away. "I promise."

The gate drew closer as they picked up speed. Apprehension burned in his stomach like a ball of acid, worsening as they drew near.

"If this formula doesn't work . . ." He licked his lips, considering how best to put it. "If it doesn't work, I want you to lock me in one of the rooms. Byron is hurt and you need to fly the ship. I'll be fine for several hours before you'd have to knock me out."

"I don't like the idea of doing that to you."

"Mace, we don't have a lot of choice. Do what you have to do to get us someplace safe. I brought this shit on myself. I'll handle it." He cleared his throat and made a crude jacking motion near his crotch, as if Mace needed any clarification.

She shook her head. "You're being stubborn."

"I'm not sure where Byron would suggest we go, but there are a couple of planets a few jumps from here we could land and get lost on. I'm sure there's medical care we could buy. But we won't be able to stay long. They'll be on our trail soon."

He could feel her looking at him, the heat from her stare enough to make his cock twitch in interest. *Time and place, Alec.*

"Damn it, Alec." She let out a huff. "Screw this. I'm going to take us someplace where I can get the two of you fixed up. One I know for a fact is safe."

"Where?"

She didn't answer, and he was forced to watch as the dimension gate activated in front of them. He had a few seconds of panic as they got close. Byron wasn't strapped in. The Brasillian syndrome could come back stronger. Heart racing, he closed his eyes as they flew through.

The sensation of the universe collapsing around him wasn't one he'd ever grown used to. He'd done so little space travel in his youth, relegated to the confines of a Loyalist colony, he'd never developed the space balance many experienced travelers had.

His brain felt like it was being taken apart molecule by molecule and thrust back together out of order. His lungs compressed and his cock stiffened as the rush of the universe flowed around them.

Then they were free, and he sucked in a deep breath.

His head buzzed and his lungs itched as his body righted itself. He waited for the burning lust to hit him, the pulsing uncontrollable desire low in his body to spread like lightning through the rest of him.

It didn't come. His face felt warm, his bones ached slightly, his head still spun a bit . . . but that was all.

"Alec?"

He opened his eyes to see Mace's hand hovering a few inches above his arm. Heat from her body prickled at his skin, and he knew the cure hadn't been completely successful. He fought back a sudden sharp impulse to rip her clothing off and fuck her right there over the back of the chair.

Closing his eyes again, he took several deep breaths to try to regain his control. He eventually opened them again and smiled at her concerned expression.

"You're safe."

She frowned. "It didn't work, did it?"

"It was enough to let me stay in my right mind. We'll be fine until I can get somewhere and work on it properly."

He wanted to laugh when Mace's gaze slipped down to his prominent erection.

"Are you going to be able to handle two more jumps?"

"Just swing by the nearest pleasure planet on the way and I'll be good."

Mace rolled her eyes and keyed something into the com unit. She waited, flying the ship in a lazy pitch and roll through the sector they'd arrived in. From what Alec could see, there was nothing here—wherever here was.

The computer chirped at them in a tone he'd never heard before. Mace frowned as she checked the readings.

"It's going to take us an hour before the jump drive is ready to go again. I'm getting our new coordinates now. Why don't you check on Byron?"

Shit. He was on his feet and out into the main room before she could say anything else.

Byron had pulled himself over to the couch but hadn't managed to get on top. He sat with his back propped against the base, panting. Alec's erection softened at the glassy look of pain in the other man's eyes. He'd forgotten him—even if it was only for a second. He'd forgotten that Byron was injured and in pain not five meters from him.

Carefully he knelt beside Byron, grimacing at the smoldering, bleeding hole in his shoulder.

"We get away?" Byron's words were a low slur.

"Yeah. Mace is taking us someplace safe. We have about an hour before the next jump."

"Don't know . . . how they found us."

This wasn't the time to be presenting him with any theories. "We'll figure it out."

"Mace . . ."

"I trust her to get us somewhere we won't get killed. Right now I need to get this wound cleaned up. Let me get a med kit."

Byron reached up and ran his thumb along the back of Alec's wrist. "'M okay."

"You're not, you stubborn ass."

It took a bit of searching, but Alec found the med kit tucked away in a storage compartment under one of the couch cushions. He was back at Byron's side ripping the remains of his shirt away within minutes.

The skin was black and peeled where the laser blast had connected. The muscle beneath was clearly damaged. Gods, Byron was going to lose some range of motion. As gently as he could, Alec began to spray the damaged area with antiseptic. At least the numbing agent would make things less painful.

He also pressed an injector filled with painkiller to Byron's neck. The effect was obviously immediate, as Byron finally relaxed, letting out a soft sigh.

"Could have used that first."

"You're lucky I gave it to you at all." Alec knew his lingering anger was unreasonable. But he didn't want to believe Byron's life was in danger because of him again. That someone had used him as a means to draw Byron from safety. "You're more trouble than you're worth some days."

Byron stilled Alec's hands with a simple touch. Alec finally made eye contact with him, and despite his words, he knew he'd missed Byron more than he'd ever be able to admit.

"What's wrong?" Byron frowned. "While it hurts like hell, this isn't going to kill me. So why are you so upset?"

Alec's heart pounded. He looked away and bit his bottom lip, hoping the pain would help clear his head. "Mace and I think the attackers are after you, not me."

Byron's mouth snapped shut.

"We think they were looking for your codes. When you activated the safe house, they were alerted to our location. We think they put the bounty on me because it was the one thing that might bring you out from under guild protection."

When Byron said nothing, Alec went back to work on his shoulder. He was able to clean up most of the mess and secure a bandage over the wound before his hands started to shake.

Sitting back on his heels, he let his gaze take in Byron's body. He'd been purposely avoiding anything akin to emotional intimacy with Byron, scared of where it would take them. Now that he knew he was the instrument others had chosen for Byron's downfall, he hated himself a little bit more. Felt even less worth somebody's time or attention.

"Boys, we're going to be ready to make another jump soon. You might want to finish what you're doing and strap in."

Mace and Byron. He shivered at the memories of the three of them in bed, and back at the safe house. He'd gone from not wanting anyone to being obsessed with two people. Despite the gore he'd been cleaning up, his cock was semihard again. Another jump wouldn't be impossible, but it wouldn't make things any easier.

"You okay?" Byron made no move to touch him. "Did the stuff work?"

Alec shrugged, no longer able to lie. "Mostly. It will be harder for me to control it with every jump we take."

"Then we need to get where we're going fast so I can take care of you."

He grimaced and shook his head. "Bry, you don't have to—"

Byron slapped the floor with his hand. "Let's get something straight right now. You're *mine*. You've always belonged to me. I will take care of you whether you want me to or not. So get your ass into the cockpit and go do something useful for Mace, because once we're safe, you and I are going to have a nice long talk."

Swallowing past the lump in his throat, Alec nodded. "Yes, sir."

Without looking back, he made his way to Mace, knowing without a doubt he was screwed.

CHAPTER

ELEVEN

Mace was not one for prayer. There had only been a few significant times in her life when she'd indulged the need, using the words her mother had taught her as a child. As they sat there floating in space, waiting for the *Belle Kurve* to show up, she started reciting those words in her head.

Alec sat beside her, still strapped into the chair. He hadn't moved since the completion of their second jump. Sweat covered his face and neck. He wasn't as bad as he had been during the jumps away from Naveeo, but clearly they'd done something wrong when they'd created the treatment for the Brasillian syndrome.

Doc would be able to help. At the very least they'd have a proper facility to work with. Then they could continue to develop the antidote for Faolan. Gods, she needed to see him again. Gar too.

"How much longer?" Alec's voice made her jump. It felt like forever since he'd spoken.

She checked the computer. "Not long. We should be getting a signal from them soon. Are you okay?"

He nodded. "I will be. It's not as bad as before, but I'll need another dose of the stuff once we get to your ship's med bay."

"We weren't thinking. We should have made extra just in case something like this happened." She knew she hadn't been thinking straight when she'd helped him develop the supposed cure. Normal procedure was to make backup doses of whatever compound they were developing. Even in the lab, it was always better to have extra than not enough. This time she'd been so angry, so focused on getting Alec healed, that she hadn't paid attention to procedure. She'd made obvious, avoidable mistakes. No excusing that.

"There wasn't time." He reached out and squeezed her hand. "It's not your fault in any way. You're in charge on the *Geilt*, but I'm supposed to be in charge in the lab. It was my responsibility to do things right, but I wanted to get better so we could start again on the *ryana* antidote. I cut corners. It's a bad habit of mine."

The computer let out a three-tone pulse, letting Mace know the *Belle Kurve* had entered the sector. The tightness in her chest, neck, and shoulders lessened, letting her breathe easily again.

Alec wiped his hand down his face. "Is that them?"

She could tell he was nervous about going on board. Not that she blamed him in the least. Coming face-to-face with a man he was indirectly responsible for poisoning must be a terrifying prospect. Especially when the man was a notorious pirate captain.

Serves Alec right . . . but please don't let Faolan and Gar kill him. Part of her was still furious at him for what he'd done. For not seeing the dangerous potential of his deadly creations. But more and more she was coming to accept that he wasn't the monster she'd always imagined the poison's maker to be.

Alec moved to pull his hand away, but she stopped him. She gave his fingers a gentle squeeze, then reached up with her free hand and cupped his cheek.

"They'll blame you at first. To be honest, my brother will probably try to kill you. But everyone on that ship trusts me. If I tell them you're a good man who will help us find a way to make Faolan better, then they'll listen."

"I don't think I would be so generous. I'm a mass murderer."

She couldn't handle knowing Alec thought of himself that way. Leaning awkwardly over the chairs, she kissed him. He didn't respond, forcing her to increase the pressure on his lips. Finally he gave way, letting her slip her tongue in to tease and taste him.

Lust flared between them, and she felt her pussy grow wet with anticipation. Alec's response was explosive. Reaching down, he cupped her ass with both his hands and tried to pull her over to him. Their positions and the lack of space between the chairs didn't allow her to straddle him, so instead she reached between his legs to cup his cock. Gods, he was hard as stone and pulsing in her hand.

Alec groaned, thrusting up against her as the computer let out another signal. She broke the kiss but didn't move away from him. "Shit, the *Belle Kurve* is looking for a response."

"Don't care." He surged forward and bit down on her neck.

She gasped, squeezed his cock, and let her eyes roll back in her head. "No . . . time."

Alec licked the hypersensitive spot on her skin and moaned. "Don't think I can stop. Not now."

Gods, she'd gone and done it. She knew he was close to the edge of his control. Byron was injured in the other room, unable to do anything to help. With the *Belle Kurve* nearly on top of them, the last thing they needed was for Alec to lose it in front of Gar and Faolan.

"Mace . . ." Alec fumbled with her vest, fingers seeking skin. She could feel the heat rolling off him as his temperature rose. "Help."

Fuck it. Standing as best she could, she got behind his chair and spun it around. Dropping to her knees, she yanked his belt open and tore at the buttons holding his pants closed.

"I'm going to give you the best blowjob you've ever had." Her fingers shook as she grabbed the top of his open pants and began to tug. "Up."

He lifted his hips and did his best to help her. He was gulping large lungfuls of air and his cock was leaking pre-cum. Mace pulled his pants down just far enough to give her access to his balls and ass.

The scent of his arousal was nearly overwhelming. The warmth from his cock inches from her face made her mouth water and her cunt tingle with longing. No time for that, but later she'd take advantage of her bed back on the *Belle Kurve* and fuck him until she couldn't see straight. If Byron was up for it, she'd probably fuck him too.

Another beep from the computer was the prod she needed to move. Without any preamble, she took Alec into her mouth, sliding halfway down the length of his shaft. He groaned and placed a hand on the back of her head, encouraging her.

Not about to let him control her, she slid up, her teeth grazing the underside of his cock until only the tip was in her mouth. She circled his head, lapping at the bitter fluid before increasing the suction and sliding down even lower.

The hand on the back of her head held her still, and for a second she thought Alec wanted her to stop. It wasn't until she heard Byron's chuckle that she realized why Alec was reacting.

"I thought I smelled sex."

Abandoning Alec's cock, she turned to face him. Byron's wound was now bandaged, and he'd used what was left of his shirt as a makeshift sling. Even wounded and exhausted, he was an impressive sight. She leaned forward enough to allow her nipples to graze the seat edge as she moved. Using her teeth once again, she kept her gaze locked on Byron as she started a steady rhythm on Alec.

"Is she as good as she looks, Alec?"

Alec bucked his hips in response.

"Easy now. You don't want to hurt the poor girl." Byron shifted so he was leaning back against the wall. "Mace, I want you to reach up and tug his balls. Not too hard. That's it. Hear him? Our boy likes a bit of pain with his pleasure."

He swelled in her mouth, and she sucked harder. Byron's gaze shifted from hers, drifted lower. Her heartbeat increased as she tugged on Alec's balls. Byron smiled.

"Good girl. You want this to go fast, right? Want me to show you something else?" He licked his lips. "Slide one of your fingers in your mouth. Get it nice and wet for him."

She didn't hesitate to comply, ignoring Alec's moan of protest when she abandoned his sac. Saliva coated her lips and dripped down her finger and onto his shaft as she sucked and tongued both. The sounds coming from Alec had her cunt clenching with want. Gods, it was going to be harder than she thought not giving in to her own desire.

She closed her eyes and let images fill her head—Alec fucking her while Byron watched, her watching the two of them together, both of them fucking her at the same time. Before she knew what she was doing, she squeezed her thighs together, trying to gain some friction.

"Stop, Mace!"

Her whole body froze. Opening her eyes slowly, she was surprised to see a scowl on Byron's face. "This isn't about you, girl. Alec needs to have his head straight before we get on that ship of yours. So you're going to make him come hard now, and later we'll look after you. Understand?"

She moaned but nodded as best she could.

"Good girl. Now take that wet finger of yours and tease his asshole. Don't press in yet."

Alec's body tensed, and he spread his legs wider.

Byron chuckled. "See, he likes that."

The tips of her fingers rubbed gently against the sensitive skin. The shift in her hand position made it easier for her to brush her thumb against the divot between his testicles, where it was slicked by her saliva rolling down his cock. She resumed her sucking, this time adding in a push of her finger on every down stroke.

They quickly fell into a rhythm—Alec wordlessly encouraging her on with every touch she offered. Byron directed her, telling her how much pressure, when to change, where to touch, until he finally said the words she'd been waiting for.

"Now press inside him."

Careful not to cut him with her nail, Mace increased the pressure on Alec's anus until the tip of her finger was swallowed up by his body. He arched up and clenched around her hard as his hips bucked off the chair.

"Relax, Alec. She can't get to where you want her like that. Relax and we'll look after you."

Slowly he complied, and Mace was able to work her finger in deeper with even strokes. She knew in theory about the prostate. Faolan loved to tease her with facts she really didn't want to know about how good her brother was in bed. But when she found a hard bundle of tissue and pressed against it, she was thankful for the information.

Alec cried out. His legs began to tremble beneath her as she continued to swallow him down. Again she rubbed her finger against the firm knot, knowing she'd hit the mark.

"That's a good girl. He won't last much longer like that."

Throwing everything she had at him, she sucked the entire length of Alec's cock into her mouth. Only when her nose touched his pubic hair did she pull back and press hard against the nerves.

Alec's cock pulsed, the only warning she had before he screamed. Cum filled her mouth. She swallowed as much as she could, but some escaped her to spill down her chin.

Byron hummed his approval. "Gods."

Finally pulling back, Mace returned her attention to Alec, who sat limp and panting. Slowly he opened his eyes and leveled a steady gaze at her.

"You weren't kidding." His sex-tinted voice sent a shiver down her spine.

She licked her lips and cocked her head. "About what?"

"That was one of the best blowjobs I've ever had."

"I think you just like an audience."

"Of course he does." Byron shifted against the wall. "It's my payback for making him watch last time."

The computer interrupted their banter. Slowly getting to her feet, Mace ignored the ache of her jaw and fell into her chair.

"Shit, the *Belle Kurve* is in full coms range."

Alec frowned, tucking his cock back in his pants. "Why's that a bad thing?"

"Because Faolan will want visual contact before he gives me rendezvous coordinates, and I'm pretty sure I look like I've just been sucking cock."

In her periphery, she saw Byron frown and push away from the wall to come stand beside her. "Turn this way."

Mace spun her chair a quarter turn so she faced him. He bent over her, and she held her breath as he licked from the corner of her mouth, down along her chin. When he was through, he wiped away the remains of his saliva and grinned.

"There. At least you won't have to talk to your brother with cum on your face."

She felt herself flush but couldn't stop a chuckle. "Because that would be awkward."

"It would be for Alec when Gar tried to flay him alive with those blades of his."

Alec coughed. "*Blades?*"

"Not to mention Faolan's sword." She turned to smile at Alec. "Did I forget to mention that?"

"We don't really need to go on board, right?" Alec straightened in his seat. "I'm not in the mood to be gutted today."

Byron patted him on the shoulder. "I'll protect you."

Alec glared as the com beeped again. "You better answer that, Mace."

After taking another few seconds to compose herself, she finally signaled the acknowledgment. Instantly the face of Faolan's pilot popped into sight.

"Ricco!" Mace gave him a genuine smile. Ricco was the closest thing she had to a favorite uncle; he'd also been the man Faolan trusted to teach her hand-to-hand combat during her first months on the *Belle Kurve*. "Faolan still letting you drive his baby?"

"He has little choice these days. Ready for coordinates?"

Shit, she didn't like the sound of that. "Let me have them."

"Get back over here soon, girl." Ricco's normally dour face was more so than normal. "Need you to help out again."

The communicator winked off. Mace nearly didn't register the sound of the coordinates being fed through to the navigation system, her mind still playing Ricco's words over and over in her head.

Alec's hand on her shoulder pulled her back in.

She shook off the gloom. "Sorry. Entering in the rendezvous now. The auto-engage will take us where we need to go. There'll be one more dimension jump, Alec."

"I'll be fine. What about you?"

I'll be better once I see Faolan again. "I'll get back to you on that. Byron, you'll need to get secured. This last jump will be a bit rough."

"I don't even want to know how we're going to do a jump without a gate, do I?" Byron pushed away from the wall and sauntered out to the main cabin.

The *Geilt* slid silently through the empty sector of space. Knowing Ricco and Faolan's preferences, the coordinates would land them in some little-known quadrant where the *Belle Kurve* would be able to monitor if there was anyone around who shouldn't be there. Mace had been on the other end, directing things, enough times to know how it worked.

She was surprised when the rendezvous data led them to an ion cloud near the center of the sector. Purple and green gases spiraled out in crisscross patterns across the black of space. The *Belle Kurve* wasn't going to pop in and scoop them up for another jump like she'd assumed.

Mace had been here once before, shortly after her arrival on the *Belle Kurve*. It was where Faolan had held the memorial service for his late wife and her crew.

Oh no.

"Mace?" Alec spun her chair around, his worried gaze directed squarely at her. "What's wrong? You look like you're going to pass out."

She swallowed down the bile creeping up her throat. "Faolan thinks he's about to die." Surprised she sounded as calm as she did, Mace gave her head a shake. "We won't be jumping again. This is where he said he wanted to be buried if anything ever happened to him."

The muscle in Alec's jaw shifted as he ground his teeth. Looking away from her, he took a moment to compose himself before standing. "Then let's get over there and make sure his funeral is put on indefinite delay."

The rational part of her mind knew the chance of their finding a remedy in time to save Faolan was growing slimmer and slimmer with every moment they waited. They'd lost so much time in the past few days, the odds of pulling off a last-minute miracle seemed impossible.

The take-no-prisoners pirate part wasn't willing to back down and give death even an inch.

"Tell Byron about the change in plans. I'll get us into docking position and come back when it's time to open the hatch. Grab whatever you need from here and I'll take us right to the med bay."

As Mace moved the ship into place, waiting for the telltale clunk of the docking clamps connecting to the *Geilt*, she tried to get her heart, head, and stomach all under control. She couldn't handle this. Faolan was too important to her, too important to Gar to lose now.

No. He wasn't going to die. She wouldn't let him. She didn't want to be alone again.

Once the *Geilt* was in final position, she bolted from the cockpit and into the main room. She ignored Byron and Alec and the odd looks they were giving each other. Triggering the ladder, she started climbing before it had fully extended.

"You boys stay there for a minute. We have a shoot-strangers-on-sight policy, and I'd hate for Byron to wind up with two bad arms."

"Don't worry about me," he drawled. "I'm more than capable of looking after myself."

Alec snorted. "I think that attitude concerns her more than anything."

"Just stay here. I'll call down when things are safe."

"Very welcoming ship." Alec scratched the back of his head. "We'll be here."

She scrambled up the rest of the way to the hatch. She banged three times, paused, then twice more before spinning the valve and opening the small round portal. Even so, the sound of blasters being engaged filled the room as she popped her head through.

"Ricco, if you shoot me, I'm going to fucking kick your ass." She pulled herself up and stood straight, grinning. "Hey, blue boy. You're looking good."

Ricco didn't crack a smile but cocked his head and holstered his blaster. "You've lost weight." It was the closest thing he got to an insult with her. "Faolan will give you hell."

The few crew members who'd come to greet her quickly waved and returned to their duties. Neither Faolan nor Gar were anywhere in sight.

"How is he doing?"

Ricco stepped closer, his gaze dropping to the floor. "He asked me to come here a standard week ago. I don't like this."

"What did Gar say?" She hated hearing the quiver as she spoke, but knew if anyone understood what she was going through, it was Ricco.

"He's mad as hell but trying not to show it. I've heard him trying to convince Faolan to fight, but the stubborn bastard won't listen. Now that you're back, I hope he'll change."

"Well, I'm not alone." Mace turned and leaned over the opening. "Come on up, boys."

"I'll inform your brother." Ricco didn't wait, and marched over to the com unit. Mace ignored the fact he'd drawn his blaster again, holding it along his leg.

Byron came up first. Anyone looking at him would know he was still a major threat, even half-naked and clearly wounded. She watched him scan the room, looking for dangers, his gaze pausing on Ricco before moving on. Only when he seemed satisfied did he move away so Alec could come up.

"Move your slow ass," Alec muttered.

"My slow ass has saved yours more than once."

Mace rolled her eyes. "And if you both don't learn to shut up, I'm going to kick both your asses."

Ricco chuckled. It was a sound Mace hadn't heard often in her life. Turning, she cocked an eyebrow at him. "What?"

He shook his head, the smile slipping from his face nearly as fast as it had appeared. "Your brother is on his way. I need to get back up front. Be safe, girl."

Ricco gave both Alec and Byron a good glare on his way past. Mace would have chuckled under normal circumstances, but she couldn't get Faolan out of her mind.

"Did they tell you anything?" Alec was at her side, hand hovering close but not touching.

"I'm sure Gar will fill us in as soon as he gets here." Byron ran a hand down across his face. "Let's just hope he doesn't try to kill you, Alec."

It was amazing how close they'd all gotten since leaving Naveeo. It had only been a matter of days, but Mace knew she would do anything possible to make sure both men were safe as could be in her home. "Don't worry about Gar. Once he knows Alec is Faolan's best chance at survival, he'll give him anything he needs to make the antidote. Just let me do all the talking."

The seconds ticked off in Mace's head, louder and louder as each one passed. Gar was punctual to the point of being disturbing. If he wasn't here now, it meant there was a problem—most likely with Faolan. She was about to leave the men to go in search of her brother when the door opened with a hiss.

Gar stood at the opening, an arm looped around a very tired looking Faolan. Mace didn't hesitate, and ran over, throwing herself in their arms. "Oh my Gods, I missed you."

"I told you not to bother going out there, sweetie." Faolan kissed the top of her head. "I missed you too."

Shifting over, she gave Gar a hug but pulled back when she felt how rigid his body was. "What's wrong?"

"You brought company." Looking down at her, he raised an eyebrow in that infuriatingly superior way he always managed. "Here to help, Byron?"

Mace stepped away, walking backward until she stood close to Alec. Byron had also moved closer—the two of them stood like a wall between the pirates and the scientist, ignoring Alec's protests.

Gar and Faolan were far from stupid, and Mace saw the moment they both realized something was wrong. Faolan pulled away from Gar's hold and stepped toward them.

"Mace, I've met Byron here before. Thanks for letting us go back then." He winked. "Saved our asses."

Byron gave Faolan a lopsided smirk. "Happy to help."

"But I don't think I'm familiar with the other gentleman." Taking another step forward, Faolan held out his hand, peering around Byron's bulk. "Captain Faolan Wolf. Welcome aboard the *Belle Kurve*."

Byron stiffened, and Mace was about to say something when Alec nudged the two of them aside, moving to stand directly in front of Faolan. Mace wanted nothing more than to jump in and rescue him, but she held her peace. Faolan had surprised her on more than one occasion. She owed both him and Alec the respect to wait and see what would happen.

Alec cleared his throat and reached out to take Faolan's hand. "Alec Roiten, Captain. I wish we were meeting under better circumstances."

Faolan chuckled. "Son, I'm a pirate. There's no such thing as better circumstances where I'm from. Given that we're not under attack and the universe hasn't decided to open up a hole to swallow us down, I think we're doing okay."

Alec turned his head toward her. Grim determination clouded his face, and she knew what his next words would be, even without the aid of the psychic stone.

"I'm the man responsible for killing you."

Mace had forgotten how unbelievably fast her brother could move. Before either she or Byron had a chance to react, Gar had come forward, activated the black-bladed knives he wore hidden beneath his shirt sleeves, and pressed them to Alec's throat. It didn't take Byron long to respond. Yanking his bad arm from the sling, he pulled his blaster from its holster and pressed it to Gar's head.

For the first time in her life, Mace didn't know how to respond. Her loyalties would always lie with Gar and Faolan. They were family. But given how close she now felt to Alec—hell, even Byron at this point—she couldn't decide on the spot.

"Put the fucking blades away, Gar." Byron's gritty voice sounded even rougher than normal. "I'll blow your head off if you so much as nick his skin."

"He said he's the one killing Faolan." Gar's gaze never left Alec, even as his body shook from what could only be rage. "And you brought him here."

Finally finding her voice, Mace punched both Gar and Byron on the arms. "The two of you back the hell off! No one is dying here. If either of you do something stupid, I'm going to rip you both apart piece by piece. They'll be lucky to find your skin cells when they do a bio scan of the ship!"

The echo of her shouts was still bouncing around the room when it was joined by Faolan's chuckle. All four of them turned to look at him, and Mace couldn't believe what she was seeing.

He almost looked like his old self again.

"This is the most fun I've had in months." He paused his laughter long enough to wipe away a tear that had escaped his eye. "Gods, I missed having you on board, Macie. You always knew how to liven the place up."

Faolan put one hand on Gar's shoulder and another on Byron's. "Okay, boys, the only person who has any right to kill someone on my ship is me. Given the circumstances, I'd much rather talk for the time being. If he annoys me, I'll blast him out an airlock."

Gar and Byron exchanged looks, both pulling their weapons away at the same time. Mace released her breath and did her best to slow her pounding heart down. "Well, this is going better than I thought it would."

"You back up too, Mace." Faolan waved her away. "I want to talk to our Mr. Roiten."

She and Byron each took a step back, but Gar stubbornly didn't move. Faolan reached up and cupped Gar's cheek, forcing Gar to look him in the eye. "You too. I'm fine."

"You're not—"

"Please."

Mace never knew if it was because Faolan and Gar had used the stone to connect to each other more than any other person, or if they'd simply gotten to that stage in their relationship where they knew each other so well they didn't always need words. Either way, after a few moments of silent communication, Gar nodded and stepped away.

Faolan let out a soft huff before turning to face Alec once more. "Let's start this again. You say you're the man responsible for my death here, but I *know* who it was that poisoned me. Mind explaining *exactly* what you meant?"

Alec began to explain. And it was at that moment Mace realized she'd fallen in love with him.

Without deflecting any blame from himself, he described his work as a Loyalist scientist, how he thought he'd been helping others by creating the *ryana* poison. By developing other chemical agents, some of which had also ended up as weapons. By designing the poison that had killed so many Syrilians . . . and the virus that had saved them, but at a terrible cost. A small part of her heart broke when he told them about the moment he'd learned of the tragedy on Syrili Prime and realized the truth. When he got to the part about his decision to flee—after a Loyalist security director had threatened to tear his life apart if he stopped developing products to the specifications he was given—Mace had to bite her tongue to keep from comforting him. Alec didn't come right out and say Byron's life had been threatened, but she was able to read between the lines.

Based on how Byron tensed, he could as well.

"I did my best to cover my tracks, moving from one backwater planet to another. At first I wouldn't stay longer than a few standard months in any one spot. I'd been over a year on Naveeo, though. I figured once they realized I wasn't going to reveal any unpleasant truths about them, they'd leave me alone. I thought I'd been doing well until Byron tracked me down."

Gar snorted and rolled his eyes. "Don't feel bad. Byron has an uncanny ability to find shit."

Faolan crossed his arms and studied Alec. "So you're telling me Mace didn't just find some loony scientist who happened to specialize in *ryana*—she managed to find the one person in the entire universe who is the most likely to save my sorry ass, even after he'd done his best to hide from everyone?"

Looking back at her, Alec smiled. "It seems like there are two uncanny trackers on board."

She knew she was blushing, but for once she really didn't mind. There was something about the way Alec was staring at her that melted her insides. Gods, she wanted him.

The sound of Byron clapping his hands together made her jump, breaking the moment. "Now that we're past the whole 'trying to kill each other' phase, I suggest we get these two set up in a lab or med bay so they can continue to work on a cure."

Despite his words, Byron clearly wasn't comfortable on board. The sooner they were able to get into some sort of routine, the better things would be for everyone. Mace was about to say as much when Faolan let out a low groan.

"What's wrong?" Gar was beside him in a flash, one arm around Faolan's waist even as his body started to sag.

"I'm not—" Faolan's face went white and his eyes rolled back into his head a second before he passed out.

TWELVE

Byron hadn't moved in far too long. Back against the wall, he switched feet, taking his weight on the right one and pressed the left flat against the surface behind him. He was bone-tired and thirsty, and he kind of needed to use the head. But his gnawing desire to get out of the corridor where he'd taken up residency was squashed every time he glanced across the med bay door. Gar stood there, motionless, mirroring his position. Byron wouldn't abandon his compatriot.

Doc had kicked them both out of med bay after Gar's hovering nearly caused her to drop a bio scanner. She'd kicked Byron out just for the hell of it. *At least she patched my arm up first.*

Gar refused to move farther than half a meter from the door, even after both Doc and Mace tried to convince him to go rest. Byron didn't bother wasting his breath on futile pleading. One look at Gar had told him that nobody would convince the man to leave his husband. Gar was staying put.

It was what Byron would have done if it was Alec lying in there.

"He thought he was dying."

Byron's head snapped up. "What?"

"He didn't actually say the words," Gar admitted. "But I suspect it's why we're here in the ion cloud."

Byron nodded. "Mace mentioned as much."

When Gar shifted his gaze from the spot on the floor he'd been examining, Byron was surprised to see his eyes were red-rimmed, bright with unshed tears. "The stupid bastard has given up."

"You know, Alec and Mace are amazing with that science crap." Byron pushed away from the wall to move closer to Gar. "Ice Man, if anyone is going to be able to find a cure in time to save your guy, it's those two. Alec is a fucking genius and Mace, well, she's pretty damn smart too."

Gar snorted. "Most people are terrified of Mace when they meet her."

"I can imagine. She's almost as fast as you are with a blaster. Hell of a good pilot too. She was pulling some maneuvers in that bucket of yours you would have been proud of."

Hell, the more he thought about her, the more Byron wanted to be with her. She'd slotted so neatly into his way of thinking, he hadn't realized she'd done it. She was right there in his mind beside Alec. The two of them were a pair, not only balancing each other out, but filling the gaps in Byron's life.

Alec fed his need to see the wonder in the universe. Byron's father had done what he could to educate him, but he'd been a mechanic on a middle-grade outpost world. The world of books and higher learning had been so far out of Byron's reach, they weren't in the realm of possibility. With Alec, he had a chance to touch a wisdom and way of seeing things he'd never considered before.

Mace . . . Gods, he hadn't ever expected to feel so close to a woman. His mother had died when he was a baby. After her death, his father never sought a female companion for anything more than a quick fuck, and he'd never brought one home. Byron had done the same thing for years, never realizing how much his father's narrow outlook had affected his own. By the time he'd gotten some enlightenment, he'd already been in the guild, aiming for more power but half expecting to die each time he left for a mission. And still so angry at Alec's disappearing act that he hadn't considered a new long-term partner of whatever gender. Quick fucks were all he could manage.

Mace had been a surprise in every possible way. She was strong and capable and skilled . . . and soft and comforting and small enough to fit perfectly under the curve of his arm. Where Alec reasoned and considered, she dove headfirst into most aspects of life despite the risks. Even in her one area of vulnerability, she'd taken a risk. She'd told Byron what she wanted, and trusted him to follow through. Only one other person had ever trusted him that way.

And gods help him—having the two of them in bed was the best fucking sex he'd ever had in his life.

"Do I want to know what you're thinking about to put that look on your face?"

Byron snapped his attention back to a now amused Gar. "Since it involves me doing dirty things to your sister, probably not."

Gar rolled his eyes. "I guess it goes without saying, if you do anything to hurt her, I'll put a laser through your brain so fast you won't have time to blink."

"And yet you still felt the need to say it."

"I know you, Byron. I've seen the revolving door to your bedroom. Men, women, it's all the same. Never more than a night. Mace deserves more than that."

So does Alec. He knew Gar was right and only had his sister's best interests in mind. It still pissed him off to know Gar thought so little of him.

"You're saying I'm not good enough for her, Ice Man?" Byron crossed his arms and stood directly in front of Gar. "You'd rather she end up with someone like you? Someone safe, who'll protect her but never let her wild side out to play? I was good for Alec, and I'm just as good for her. Both of them."

Gar blinked, and for a moment Byron thought he was going to get a punch to the jaw. Instead the other man chuckled. "Now I understand."

"What the fuck are you talking about?"

"Back on Zeten when you caught me and Faolan escaping. You looked at me and saw the one thing I hadn't even admitted to myself. I wasn't sure how you'd been able to do that. I get it now."

Byron was about to drill him about what the hell he meant when the med bay door opened and Mace stepped out.

"How is he?" Gar grabbed her shoulders with his hands. "Can I see him yet?"

Mace appeared more than a little wrung out, black smudges shading her eyes and her skin paler than Byron had ever seen it. Her gaze flicked to him for a split second before she concentrated on her brother.

"Doc has him sedated for now. He's stable, but his immune system is starting to break down. Alec thinks he'll be able to manufacture a booster that will buy us some time." Mace reached up and covered

Gar's hands with hers. "We are so close to a solution. You just need to get him to hold on a little longer."

The expression on Gar's face turned Byron's stomach. He knew that expression, knew the feelings that went along with it and how they ate at a person from the inside. Reaching out, he gripped Gar's shoulder and gave him a squeeze.

"Alec is the best researcher I've ever come across. He makes these jumps in logic and understanding . . . I don't even pretend to understand what he's talking about. He'll find a remedy. An antidote or something to help counteract the effects of the poison. *Something*."

Mace was nodding before he'd even finished speaking. "He wants to see you, actually. He has some questions about Faolan's condition and how it might have changed over the past few months. Some things that Doc and I didn't have the answers to."

Gar glanced between the two of them, and Byron knew him well enough to practically see the wheels spinning in his head.

"You both trust him? Completely, without reservation?"

Byron straightened. "Ice Man, other than yourself and your sister, Alec is the only other person I *do* trust."

It seemed to be enough for Gar. Without another word, he stepped past them and strode into the med bay. Once the door had closed, Byron couldn't help but pull Mace into a hug.

"You look like shit," he muttered, placing a kiss to the top of her head. "You should try to get some rest."

Warm breath heated his chest, and he thought he felt her return his kiss. "So you trust me?"

Of course she would pick up on that. "You think I'd fall into bed with just anyone?"

"Yes."

He snorted. "While that might be true, there aren't many people who I've let myself get . . . close to. Alec was the only person before now."

Mace hesitantly brushed her fingertips along his jaw. "And you're starting to feel close to me? You haven't known me that long."

Byron had seen too much of the shitty part of the universe to be convinced a softer emotion like *love* had that much power over him. He didn't know if that word, that idea, was strong enough to match what he felt when he looked at Alec. And lately, the same stirrings built low in his gut, took over his breathing and heartbeat, governed his every nerve ending when he let his gaze sweep over Mace. Reaching up to tuck a piece of her hair behind her ear, he smiled. *Close*, she'd said. Yeah, that too.

"I think I might be. The length of time doesn't seem to matter."

"I think . . ." Mace swallowed and smiled back softly. "Thanks."

"How is our boy doing? While I can stand here and say how confident I am in his ability to work miracles, I don't have a clue when it comes to that science shit. I know he gets frustrated when things don't go the way he wants."

She pulled away and shrugged. "He's as tired as I am, but I don't think he'll rest. We'll need to keep an eye on him or else he'll burn out and be useless to Faolan. At least with Doc here we have another set of eyes to help work on the problem. Honestly I'm just as worried about Gar at this point."

Byron frowned. "Why?"

"Doc said he's been running himself ragged. Not sleeping. Taking over all of Faolan's duties on top of his and mine. It's been too much for him."

Thank the gods. At least this was a problem Byron could do something about. "I can help with that. Once he gets out from checking on his man, I'll get him to put me to work."

Mace broke out into a blinding grin that both loosened the tension in his chest and sent a surge to his cock. "Thank you so much, Bry. It would mean a lot to me."

His body seemed to move on instinct, walking Mace forward until her back was flush against the wall. "How much would it mean?"

Her full-body shiver and the gentle buck of her hips against his groin had him growling. "I'd be very grateful. I would even owe you a thank-you."

Closing his eyes, Byron pressed his forehead against the wall by her head. "You're going to kill me talking like that when I can't do anything about it. You and Alec . . . fucking killing me."

Pushing away from her, he ground the heel of his palm against his straining cock. "Go and rest, Mace. I'll get your brother and we'll get things straightened out on this ship. I'll make sure everything is fine."

"Bossy."

He snorted. "You like it, so don't even bother with that. Now go, so we can cure your captain and get back to a normal life for once."

Mace nodded and slipped back into the med bay, leaving him alone.

Byron raked his fingers down his face. *A normal life?* Gods, he didn't even know what that was.

The muscles in the back of Alec's neck were screaming at him. He'd been at this for three days now, nearly every moment he had since finishing his reevaluation of the antidote based on the new information he'd obtained. He did his best to ignore the discomfort in his body as he waited for the latest test results to come through. It was better to think about the positives—like the advantages of coming to the *Belle Kurve* to work on the antidote. Not only might he be able to help Faolan—a man he owed this to, and would never have met if he hadn't made his dash for freedom seven years ago—but he had all the live samples he could ever desire to test his formulas on. He was also able to see how the poison had mutated over time as it interacted with Faolan's immune system, something he hadn't been sufficiently accounting for in his previous antidote attempts.

"Your spine is going to snap in two if you don't relax." Faolan's amused voice filled the med bay. "My gods, you've got a stick up your ass to rival Gar's."

The first few days of Alec's renewed testing, Faolan had been unconscious. Three days ago, Alec had found an odd cellular mutation floating in Faolan's latest blood tests that had led him to making an improvement in the immune booster. In a matter of hours, the captain was awake and getting back to his old ways, if Doc was to be believed. How the fiery redheaded doctor hadn't killed Faolan from sheer annoyance before now, Alec wasn't sure.

"I think this one might be close, Captain. I need to make sure there aren't any glitches."

"Alec, you won't miss anything."

He couldn't help but turn at Faolan's exasperated tone. "What the hell does that mean?"

"I've been awake for four days now, and I've yet to see you miss a detail, forget a note, or be unable to recollect any aspect of any of the tests either you, Mace, or Doc have run. Relax."

Alec stared at him, not quite believing what he was hearing. "If I miss something, you will most likely die. We're barely slowing the progress of this thing as it is."

Faolan's bright-blue and very amused gaze locked onto his. "Me dying isn't the end of the universe."

Alec stomped across the med bay to stand at the foot of Faolan's bed. "Are you fucking kidding me?" Anger swelled through him, exploding out. "Gar and Mace would be devastated if anything happened to you! Do you think I'd ever be able to live with myself if you died and I had to look at them every day knowing it was my fault your body was floating out in the middle of an ion cloud? So pardon me if I'm going to do everything possible to save your sorry ass."

Faolan's smirk never left his lips. "Really, I know I'm harping on a theme here, but I never thought I'd meet anyone who was more of a tight-ass than Gar. It's really something to see. You've got so much emotion bottled up inside you, I wouldn't be surprised if you actually exploded from the pressure."

Alec bit down on his tongue, not wanting to take any more of Faolan's bait. Of course he had emotions, but rarely did they do him any good in situations like this. He kept very tight control over himself, like a good little Loyalist scientist. The only time he ever let go was when Byron pushed him, forced him to relax and give up his control. Or even better, when Byron and Mace were both with him. Then he felt like everything else around him could melt away. He could simply be a man with normal concerns and not carry the weight of his sins on his shoulder.

Gods, he missed them. He'd segregated himself from them as much as possible, not willing to risk the distraction. Mace was a constant presence in the med bay, either visiting Faolan or helping with the antidote, but the work took all their attention. Fortunately at least Byron was busy elsewhere on the ship, only stopping by to visit when Gar did. Those times were tenser than anything Alec could ever remember between them. He knew there was so much they needed to discuss, but he couldn't do it—not now.

"That is some serious thinking if I ever saw it." Faolan shifted in his bed, crossing his arms over his still-sizable chest. "When was the last time you took a break?"

"I don't see what that has to do—"

"You are the man who is trying to find a cure for the thing killing me. I want to know if you are in a suitable mental state to be working on this. Now answer the question."

It took Alec longer than he would have liked to think back so he could provide the response. "Twelve hours."

Faolan rolled his eyes. "Go. Find Mace and that other fella and get laid. Eat, drink, I really don't care. I don't want to see you back in here until tomorrow morning."

"You're not in any position—"

"I am still the captain of this ship!" He dropped his congenial face and sat up as high as he could in the bed, suddenly exuding the powerful menace of a lethal predator . . . like his ancient Firstworld namesake, an animal most dangerous when wounded or defending its family. The glare Faolan leveled at Alec made him shiver. "Until I can't draw another breath, I *can* boss around each and every body on this bucket. That includes you. Doc will be here in a few minutes. *She* can check the test results. *You* are to leave and not come back until you've eaten, slept, and fucked. I don't care in what order. Do I make myself clear?"

"Yes, sir."

"Dismissed."

Alec left the med bay, ignoring the sounds of the computer signaling the end of the test scan, and Faolan's chuckle.

While he'd been on the ship for a week, he still didn't know more than the most basic routes. He'd started down the corridor before he realized he wasn't quite sure which way to turn for the mess hall. And even though the appealing idea of food was now in his head, the thought of falling into his bed was even more so, and he took the path he knew the best: the one leading to the quarters he was sharing with Mace and Byron. Alec wasn't even sure what the ship-standard time was, or where the two of them would be. He really couldn't face them, not like this. If the universe were being kind, one or both of them would be on duty somewhere.

The moment the door to their quarters slid open, Alec knew the universe was still angry with him. Byron was just emerging from the bathroom, shirtless, water still clinging to his face and head from what looked like a recent shave. Mace was stripped down to a black tank top and a pair of skin-hugging shorts. Alec stopped barely a meter inside the door and simply stared at them as it *whooshed* closed behind him.

Byron clucked his tongue and raked his gaze down Alec's body. "You look like shit."

"Byron." Mace shot Byron a deadpan glance. "We talked about this. That is not an endearment. But he's not wrong," she admitted, turning back to Alec with an apologetic shrug. "You *do* look like shit."

"Faolan kicked me out. Said he wouldn't accept any treatment from me if I wasn't rested." Alec sighed. "The bastard made it an order."

Mace made the same clucking noise Byron had. "Did he pull the, 'I'm still Captain so you better listen to me' bit?"

"Yeah."

"I forgot to tell you to ignore him. Now he'll be insufferable about someone actually following his commands." She cocked her head. "Though in this case I'm glad you did. Maybe I should give him more credit for having good leadership skills."

Alec turned to leave, but before he got half a step toward the door, both Mace and Byron pulled him back. He would never have admitted it out loud, but it felt so good to have their hands on his body. Their touches felt like caring, something he wasn't used to.

He wanted more.

"Where do you think you're going?" Byron's breath was hot against his ear. "I don't think wandering the corridors is considered a restful activity."

"Like I'll get any peace with the two of you here. Don't you have places to be?"

"Doc won't let me near med bay for at least eight hours." Mace leaned close to Alec's arm, her lips only a few inches away from his skin.

"Gar said as much to me. Apparently he'd been running the bridge just fine before my arrival." Byron rolled his eyes similar to Gar and Mace. Apparently it was contagious. "I told him the only way I'd go was if he promised to rest later while I covered for him."

Alec nodded and did his best to ignore the tight way his pants pulled across his hardening cock. "So, we've all been sent to our rooms."

"Seems that way." Byron reached up to turn Alec's face so he had no choice but to look at him. "All to the same room. Whatever shall we do?"

Alec shuddered, warring emotions clashing inside him. "We should sleep."

Faolan's orders had included fucking, but Alec wasn't sure he deserved the solace being with Byron and Mace would offer him. Gods, did he want it, though.

"I don't think so. I haven't seen either of you for more than a few minutes in the past week. I can't even remember the last time all three of us were alone." Byron released him and strode over to the chair propped in the corner of the room. Sitting down in one smooth move, he laced his fingers behind his head and nodded in the direction of the bed with a smirk. "I'm in the mood for a show. Now both of you strip."

CHAPTER
THIRTEEN

Mace was wetter than she'd ever been in her life. Byron's words would have been enough to send her over the edge if she'd been a little further gone. Alec wasn't unaffected either, if his soft gasp and clenched fists were anything to go by.

She knew Byron was doing this more for Alec's benefit than his own. It was something she'd learned over the past few days of watching him. Between seeing him interact with the rest of the crew, and learning a few more things about him from Gar, she felt like she was finally getting a handle on the bounty hunter.

When she looked over at Byron, her heartbeat quickened. There was something about the way he held his body, the raw power he controlled that made her itch with want. Byron was a blaster charge, building energy waiting to explode.

Mace knew Alec would try to resist what Byron was doing. She'd seen enough of his self-loathing to know he would continue to berate himself until he found a remedy for Faolan—or Faolan was dead.

Fuck, no, she couldn't think that way.

Stepping away from Alec, she moved to the spot Byron had indicated and stood still. She kept her gaze fixed on Byron and did her best to hold still until either Alec relented or Byron issued another command.

"Mace?" Alec's voice was softer than she ever remembered hearing it.

"He wants a show." She reached up and hooked her thumb under the strap of her tank top. "I'm game."

The air in the room seemed to heat in an instant. She waited until Alec stood beside her—close but not touching.

Air tickled the side of her neck as he took a deep breath and let it out with a stutter. "Gods forbid if Byron doesn't get what he wants."

The man in question smirked. "Good boy. You're always amazing when you do what I tell you."

Mace fought the urge to explode forward, jump onto Byron, and take what she wanted. But that wasn't the game . . . and she liked the game. It almost killed her to hold herself back, but she knew it would be worth it. He'd shown her that back on the *Geilt* and at the safe house. She wanted more, wanted to go as far as Byron was willing to take her. Take the three of them.

"Alec, I think you're wearing too much. Mace, I want you to take his shirt off. And his boots. Leave the pants for now."

Turning to face Alec, she bit back a curse when her hands shook as she reached for the hem of his shirt. "I'll need you to help," she murmured.

The heated look in his gaze told her he was more than happy to oblige. Unwilling to give him the upper hand, she made sure to drag her nails along his sides as she moved the cloth up his body. The neck caught momentarily on his head before she tugged and pulled it free. She wasn't tall enough to yank it all the way off Alec's arms, so she had to wait for him to toss it aside.

She paused, making sure Alec was watching her before she dropped slowly to her knees in front of him. His breathing grew more ragged the closer she got to his cock, and he swallowed hard when she passed by without so much as an accidental brush. Finally, she turned her gaze down and concentrated on the task of removing his boots and socks. His feet were warm and appeared sore from the hours he'd been standing on them. Without thinking, she bent her head down and placed a kiss on the top of each one, not minding the ripe, pungent mix of leather and sweat on his skin.

"Now that's fucking hot."

Byron hadn't moved, but she could tell by the strain in his voice he wanted to.

"Mace, I bet you didn't know Alec has very sensitive skin. The spots above his hips, on his sides. Kiss him there."

She shuffled near, careful not to accidentally touch Alec's erection through his pants. The faint scent of sweat and arousal strengthened as she pressed her face to his side and opened her mouth to kiss where Byron directed. A thrill passed through her when Alec moaned and swayed to increase the contact.

"Don't you dare move, Alec," Byron bit out. "You've been hiding away from us for days now. It's our turn for some attention. If I want to torture you for the next eight hours, then I will happily do that for you."

"You'll like it," Mace added, keeping her lips in contact with Alec's skin. "You know you will. Want more?"

He closed his eyes and balled his fists at his sides. "Yes."

Mace moved and mirrored the kiss on his opposite flank.

"Does he taste good, Mace?" There was a tremor in Byron's voice. "Gods, I can smell the two of you from here."

She was so damp now, she could imagine how wet her fingers would be if she were to reach between her legs and run her fingers across her lips. "His skin is salty. But sweet too."

The sound of Byron shifting in his chair rang loud in her ears. "I know. I remember. Kiss his stomach now, but don't touch his cock."

It was a bit tricky to reach, given her shorter height and the very large bulge forcing Alec's pants away from his body, but she managed. The dusting of hair covering his skin tickled her nose and chin as she placed wide, openmouthed kisses along the ridges of his muscles. He lifted his hands up for a second before letting them fall back down to his sides with a frustrated growl.

"I know you want to touch her," Byron said, clearly amused. "I think I might allow it. Mace, stand up."

Her legs shook far more than she expected as she slowly got to her feet. It made her body tremble and sway, bringing her dangerously close to Alec, so she was nearly pressing against him without Byron's permission.

And when had his permission to do anything to Alec become so important to her?

"Your turn, Mace. Alec, take her shirt off, nice and slow."

She didn't miss Alec's wicked smirk, and anticipated what was coming even as he started to move. She sucked in a sharp breath as his nails lightly grazed her sides in a slow upward line. He pulled the tight-fitting top from her body; all she could do was lift her arms in compliance and wait for him to tug it free from her arms.

Her nipples stood out hard, tightened from her excitement and the slight chill in the room. She couldn't keep herself from pulling in several deep gulps of air in an attempt to slow her pounding heart. Alec reached up and cupped her cheek, frowning slightly.

"You okay?"

Nodding, she forced herself to relax. "Just been a while."

Byron gave a disapproving growl. "Too busy looking after everyone else."

The quick glance and snort Alec shot him told her Alec was aware of all Byron had been doing to help out. None of them had focused on anything other than helping Faolan and Gar since coming on board, especially not sex. That really needed to change.

Biting down on her lip, she turned to look at Byron. "Please."

The bounty hunter was on his feet and next to them in seconds. Wrapping an arm around each of them, he led them over to the large bed and gently shoved them both down before joining them.

"I want to fuck you both." He caught her mouth in a bruising kiss, then gasped as he pulled away to do the same with Alec. "I want to watch you fuck each other. I want to mark you both so no one comes anywhere near either of you. You're *mine*."

Alec rolled to his side and pressed his cock hard against her hip. The shift of their weight on the bed pulled her underwear tight over her clit; the pressure dragged a low moan from her.

"You could come right now, couldn't you, Mace?" Byron pushed Alec away from her and bent over her body to lick a swipe from the top of her breast to her shoulder. "You're so tense, and you've been working so hard. I bet you haven't even taken the time to play with yourself. Have you?"

"No." She bucked her hips up. "Byron . . ."

"Soon, little one. But first we need to take care of Alec. He's been punishing himself again, and I don't like that."

She recognized the glazed look in Alec's eyes. Even without the Brasillian syndrome at work, something about play with Byron quickly put him beyond rational thought. It was the same look he'd gotten back at the safe house. This time she didn't want him to find his release on his own. She knew Byron could give him what he needed, but she wanted to be a part of it as well. Alec needed to know that she forgave him for his unintentional part in making Faolan sick.

Rolling to face Alec, she let her gaze slip down his half-naked body. "Bry, tell me what to do."

His kiss to her temple made warmth explode in her chest. "Good girl. See, she wants to take care of you too, Alec. You don't need to worry about a thing."

Mace relaxed her body and let Byron shift her around so her face was near Alec's clothed erection and her cunt was by his face. Byron stayed positioned behind her, a large hand resting on her hip. Reaching across her body, Byron undid Alec's pants and pulled his engorged cock free.

"Suck him in, Mace. Show him how well you can use that tongue of yours."

She didn't wait for a response from Alec. Instead she leaned in to suck the head of his cock. His hips jerked forward, forcing his shaft farther into her mouth. Her head spun from the sheer pleasure of the heat and weight of him along her tongue.

When Byron wove his fingers through her hair, she pushed her head into the touch as she pulled back on Alec. Alec shivered beside her, a puff of his breath blowing across her swollen clit.

Her world dissolved into pure sensation—heat from Alec's groin warmed her face, and the scent of his arousal filled her lungs. Byron's steady presence at her back gave her an added burst of reassurance that whatever she was doing was right, was sexy, was good for all of them. Under Byron's firm direction she felt confident, competent, more daring than ever. Reaching down, she threaded her fingers through Alec's hair and tugged him forward.

Byron leaned over her, and pressed his lips to Alec's ear. "I think she wants you to lick her. You want to taste her the way she's tasting you? Gods, I can see how wet she is from here. Do it, Alec."

The first touch of his tongue to her clit had Mace moaning, her hips bucking forward, chasing the feeling. Four hands simultaneously held her still and opened her up. Byron lifted her leg so it rested on his shoulder, making room for Alec to move closer to her core.

"Yes, that's it." Byron's voice shook as he rubbed a pattern on her thigh. "You two have no idea how beautiful you look together."

She let her eyes close and resumed her sucking. Alec's cock pulsed in her mouth, and the tangy taste of pre-cum filled her mouth. Alec's steady laps against her clit lulled her into a mindless space where her brain refused to think.

Byron rubbed his erect cock against the back of her thigh. She wanted to thrust back against him but couldn't. Moaning again, she bucked as best she could.

"I think she wants something else, Alec. Use your fingers and open her up."

There was no teasing this time. Two thick fingers came into her cunt in perfect unison with his tongue. It was too much. Pulling off Alec's shaft, she cried out and pressed her face to the mattress.

"That's it, girl, just give in to it."

Opening her eyes, she watched Alec's head bob and his hand increase its frantic pace. Byron had a hand in Alec's hair, gently guiding his motions. She waited, staring at Alec, doing her best to hold off her impending orgasm.

Finally Byron looked her way. His pupils were blown wide and his lips were wet from where he'd licked them. She could only imagine how he saw her—naked, panting, and moaning with a man between her legs.

"Mace," he whispered.

She groaned in response. Alec was thrusting three fingers into her pussy now, and she could feel her juices covering the insides of her thighs. It was too much, all of it. Her body hummed and her mind grabbed hold of the only two things in the universe that mattered to her in that moment.

"Mace." Byron's voice dragged her back to him. "Let go."

As if her body were no longer hers to command, the orgasm she'd been resisting snapped out from her cunt and spread like a fire through the rest of her body until it erupted from her chest in a scream. The only thing keeping her from smothering Alec's face with her legs was Byron, holding her open for the universe to see.

Alec's moan vibrated against her pussy, prolonging the waves of pleasure. It seemed an eternity before Byron finally ordered, "Alec, stop."

With a care she wouldn't have associated with the bounty hunter, Byron lowered her leg and helped her move onto her back. Her lungs burned from lack of oxygen and the deep breaths she sucked in did little to help. It was only when Byron leaned over her and pressed gentle kisses to her forehead, nose, and lips that she finally relaxed.

"So beautiful." His words were spoken with awe. "Alec, she's . . ." Byron shook his head.

"Bry?" Alec's voice shook.

The look on Byron's face wasn't right. Reaching up, Mace cupped his cheek and ran her thumb across his bottom lip. "What's wrong?"

He stared for a moment before chuckling and shaking his head. "Nothing. Not now. What we need to do is take care of our boy."

Alec moaned and flopped onto his back, a reverse mirror of Mace's position. "Gods, please."

She couldn't stop the wicked grin she knew was on her face. "I think he's horny."

Byron cocked an eyebrow. "Can't imagine why."

"Should we help him with that?"

"Perhaps. If you feel he's earned it."

Alec bucked his hips up. "I *am* right here."

His cock bobbed tantalizingly close to her mouth. Turning to look at Byron again, she licked her lips. "What do you want us to do?"

Byron ran a hand down the back of his head and shivered. "Alec, I want you to fuck Mace while I fuck you."

Mace's cunt pulsed at the thought. "Gods, yes, Alec."

This time she didn't wait for Byron to say anything else. She shifted so her head was on the pillows at the top of the bed, and spread her legs wide. For a second neither man moved, their gazes locked on her body. She couldn't remember a time when anyone had ever looked at her that way. No man or woman had bothered to see past the image she projected of the tough pirate. Those who did know the "real" Mace were all members of the crew; they saw her as a sister or daughter, not a potential lover . . . or partner.

But the way Byron and Alec devoured her with their eyes, the unrepentant lust and something a little bit more shining out to her, was enough to make her want to combust.

Spreading her legs as far as she could, she looked directly at Alec. "Now."

He crawled up her body, dragging his cock along the length of her leg until finally settling between her legs. He didn't thrust into her immediately, instead pressing kisses between her breasts, slowly approaching one nipple.

"Byron forgot . . . how much . . . I love breasts." He licked a circle around her now swollen tip. "You have the best pair I've ever seen."

Mace giggled and lifted her thigh up so she pressed against his balls. "You lie."

"Never about this. I take breasts very seriously."

"He does." Byron was behind him now. She couldn't see what he was doing, but it was clearly something Alec liked, judging by his sudden gasp. "He's as serious about boobs as I am about ass. And Alec's ass is one of my favorites."

"Are you going to fuck him?" Mace reached up and directed Alec's mouth so he latched on to her nipple. "He's been so good and worked so hard. So have you. I want to feel you fuck him, Bry. I want you both."

Their eyes met across Alec's body. In that instant she saw more than sex in his eyes. She knew she meant more to Byron than what was happening now, in this bed, between the three of them. It was an odd realization to have as Byron grabbed a packet of lubricant, tore it open, and smeared it over his fingers, all without breaking eye contact with her.

The truth of it was comforting and arousing.

Alec gasped against her wet nipple when Byron pressed a heavily lubed finger into his ass. Mace shivered at the burst of cool air on her skin as he sucked in a breath.

Byron grinned. "Gods, you're always so tight at first, Alec. Your ass is clamped around my fingers so hard. I know it's going to feel good when I get my cock in there."

Byron glanced at Mace, then nodded toward Alec, and she knew the time for them to look after Alec had come. For the next little while, their pleasure was secondary to his—and Mace loved knowing she would be part of bringing Alec to the place of pure bliss he'd taken her minutes earlier.

Fighting the urge to buck against him, she waited until Byron moved Alec so he was now firmly between her legs. The head of Alec's cock pressed against her pussy but didn't penetrate. He was doing what she was—waiting for the command, for Byron to lead them where they wanted to go.

This was the dynamic of their relationship. Without daring to put words to it before her admission to Byron, Mace had wanted something like this all her adult life, and now it was hers to be a part of. Byron continued to thrust his fingers in and out of Alec's body. With their position adjusted, every time Byron pressed into Alec, the head of his cock nudged her clit. It only took a few seconds for renewed arousal to spike again.

"Please, Bry," Alec begged from between gritted teeth. "Can't wait."

"Yes, you can." Byron slapped Alec's ass, forcing him hard against Mace. "You'll do exactly what I tell you to do, when I tell you to do it."

Another sharp slap, followed by a third, had Alec panting. Mace saw and felt that far from trying to escape the abuse, Alec was bucking his ass up into Byron's hand. The look of concentration on the bounty hunter's face was all the warning Mace had that the game they were playing was about to change.

Byron braced Alec's hips with one hand, pulled back with the other, and began to spank him in earnest. Not sure exactly what to do, Mace wrapped her arms around Alec's upper body and held him to her chest. He'd turned his face, so his cheek now lay flat against her breast. She could feel his tears against her skin but somehow knew this was something he needed. He was in the same state she'd experienced back in the safe house; he certainly could have escaped if he'd really wanted to—but he didn't try.

"You want to be punished?" Byron slapped him three times in rapid succession. "That's my job. I determine when you deserve this. I'm the one who looks after you and gives you what you need."

Another volley of spanks left Alec openly sobbing. "You weren't there."

"I am now!" A sharper slap echoed in the room. Byron bent over Alec's body and pressed a kiss to the other man's temple. "I'm here now. So is Mace."

"So many people died."

Mace's heart twisted. She knew he wouldn't listen to reason, not when it came to this. Instead she leaned up and kissed him the same way Byron had. "We forgive you."

As she spoke the words, she realized they were true. The anger and betrayal she'd felt toward him had melted away over the days he'd frantically searched for an antidote. He'd done so much to make amends. Even if it didn't make what he'd done all right, Mace couldn't fault him for turning his back and running away on his responsibilities.

She didn't miss the look of thanks on Byron's face. "That's right, Mace and I forgive you. That's all that should matter."

Byron lined his cock up with Alec's ass and thrust in. Alec groaned, pressing his face hard to Mace's body. She swiveled her hips, working them until Alec's cock was lined up perfectly. Byron's next thrust forced Alec into her pussy. She sighed and pulled her knees up to brace them against Alec's sides.

"Oh yes." Byron shifted one of his hands from Alec to cup her knee. "Her cunt is so hot and wet, isn't it? It's like I'm fucking you both at the same time."

Then the words stopped, and Mace could do nothing but absorb the incredible sensations of Byron's powerful body thrusting into Alec and the hard planes of Alec's muscles driving against her. Both these men wanted her as much as each other—she completed them as much as they completed her.

Her hips took on a life of their own, bucking up to meet Alec's thrusts as best they could. With every movement her clit ground hard against Alec, pulling her far faster than she wanted to a second orgasm. This time Byron's command wasn't necessary. Mace screwed her eyes shut, her mouth opening in a silent scream, her body tensing below the two men. Alec's pace stuttered, throwing off the rhythm for all three of them as the pleasure swept through her and she gasped and tightened around him. When she finally opened her eyes again, she could see how close he was to following her over. But he didn't give in to the pleasure she knew he was feeling. Tipping her head up, she nipped the side of his neck, her gaze locked on Byron.

"I don't know how you walked away from him," she whispered in Alec's ear. "He's gorgeous and strong and cares for you. And he's also way too stubborn to come before you, so you better put him out of his misery."

Alec gasped and pressed his face to her shoulder, slamming into her as hard as he could. Mace rode him out, all the while focusing her attention on Byron. His skin was flushed from exertion, his breathing coming out in pants. She could tell Byron was holding on for Alec, but he wouldn't last much longer.

He didn't need to. Within another three strokes Alec came, his strangled cry muffled by Mace's body. Byron's look of relief would have been funny if he weren't screaming out his own climax seconds later.

Finally they fell to the mattress, a tangle of limbs and sweat-soaked skin. Alec pulled Mace into an embrace, only to roll her onto her side so she was lying between the two men. Byron reached across her, encouraging Alec closer, and held their bodies together as if they were a single unit.

"Wow," she said softly before kissing Alec's chest. "That was . . . something else."

Alec nipped at her shoulder. "What's with you and biting?"

"She's marking you." Byron snorted. "Keeping the stupid people away."

Mace rolled her eyes. "Not something I thought about before. I just did it. Does that bother you?"

"Nope."

Byron bumped her hip with his own. "Are you two done chatting? Because I think we should all get some sleep before the universe falls apart on us."

"Oh, I don't believe you just said that." Groaning, Mace thumped her head against Byron's chest. "Do you have any idea how badly you just jinxed us?"

"Mace, that's just an old space tale." Alec kissed her shoulder where he'd bitten it. "There is no scientific proof—"

The com unit across the room beeped.

Mace would have laughed at the twin looks of shock on their faces if she knew it wouldn't have made things worse. Instead she pushed her way up from them, snagged her shirt from the floor, and walked over to the computer. She yanked it on as she rounded the desk and sat down, settling the fabric in place before acknowledging the message.

Gar's frowning face on the screen told her all she needed to know. "Are all three of you there?"

Shit. "Why?"

"Macie, answer the question."

"We're here, Ice Man." Byron joined her and leaned into the camera's line of view. He had pulled on his pants but hadn't bothered with his shirt. "What's going on?"

Alec joined them, resting a hand on Mace's shoulder. "Is Faolan okay?"

Gar nodded. "He's fine. We have a bigger problem than his illness at the moment."

"What the hell could be bigger than Faolan dying?" Mace knew she sounded close to panic, but she didn't care. Very few things could take priority over Faolan's health in Gar's mind; none of them were good things.

Gar seemed to collect himself, and she recognized that he was trying to find the best way of wording what he was about to say. It didn't help prepare her for what finally came out.

"The Admiral of the Black has contacted us. He has a client on board who's apparently offered him a huge sum of money. And he's demanding we turn Byron over to him immediately . . . for execution."

CHAPTER
FOURTEEN

B yron pinched the bridge of his nose and did his best to keep his temper in check. He'd been unable to sit at the war room table another minute longer, instead choosing to stand at the window, looking out into the depths of space. "Run this by me one more time, please." *Because apparently I'm an idiot.*

Gar rose from his seat next to Faolan at the table, joining Byron by the window. "The three of you had already deduced that the bounty on Alec was a ploy to get you off Zeten and out into the open. Whoever set the bounty on you must have gotten tired of waiting on the guild, so they decided to hire somebody from the other side of the law to bring you down. A death mark—no middleman, just a straight payment in exchange for a killing. And they went right to the top of the food chain."

Faolan stayed in his seat next to Doc—who'd insisted on being present at the meeting if Faolan was determined not to hold it in the med bay—but he turned to look at Byron. "And the payment must be huge to pull the Admiral out. Not that he's got any love for the head of the guild. I'm sure that's an added enticement. But he rarely exposes himself like this."

"I understand about the death mark." Byron rolled his eyes. He wasn't that big an idiot. "But are you serious? The Admiral of the Black?"

Sure, he'd heard of the "Admiral"—the mysterious, self-proclaimed alpha pirate whose stronghold fleet ruled over some fabled thieves' quadrant of space. He'd pulled in countless bounties on pirates who claimed the *Admiral* had set them up . . . or that they'd rather be caught by him than the *Admiral*. But he hadn't believed a word of it until now. Everybody knew the Admiral of the Black was a bogeyman, a myth.

But Gar was clearly not joking. "I know. I had trouble believing it too. But I've met the man and trust me, he is as real as he is terrifying."

"It's because you're here on the *Belle Kurve*." Mace's voice sounded raw, like the words were being ripped from her throat. "And we're out here in the far reaches, so he knows he can get in and out without any risk of being spotted or challenged by Loyalist security. I'm sure he thinks we'll simply hand Bry over like good little minions and be thankful he didn't blow us out of space."

"Then it's simple." Byron turned from the window to face her. She met his gaze, clearly miserable, but Alec kept staring at the table in what appeared to be stunned silence as everyone else spoke. Byron knew how he felt. "I'll leave in a pod and get as far away from your ship as possible. It won't be the first time I've blasted out of a port. I can get through the nearest dimension gate to one of the big stations, hitch a ride back to Zeten, and hole up there until I can figure out what's going on."

"*No.*"

Byron wasn't sure if everyone in the room had spoken at once, or if there was simply one hell of an echo. "Why the hell not?"

Gar sighed. "He already knows you're here. That means he has us under surveillance. Our scanning range is good, but his is better. Somewhere out there is a scout ship. The Admiral will know if we so much as empty the waste system. And trust me when I say things won't go well if he thinks we're trying to pull a fast one on him. I've seen the aftermath when we've come across a wreck that's suffered one of his . . . visits. We need to deal with him straight-up, or we're all done for."

"You can't run, Bry. But it might help if we had any idea who else we were dealing with." Mace turned toward Alec and squeezed his arm. "Do you have *any* idea who might want to kill Byron and use you as the bait?"

Alec frowned. "You mean since the last two times I've been asked? How the hell would I know? I've been in hiding myself for seven years. Ask Byron."

"It wouldn't be somebody from those seven years, though," Mace pointed out. "It has to be someone who knew you both from before, from your Loyalist days. Well enough to realize you were still the one thing that could pull Byron out of the safety of the guild. So somebody who knew you both back then, and has had it out for Byron ever since."

Byron hadn't considered that, and from the look on Alec's face, he hadn't either. Waiting until Alec caught his gaze, Byron cocked an eyebrow and let his mind drift back to all his old enemies.

"Well, there was Jonas, the head of security at the facility. He never much appreciated the influence I had over Alec."

Alec shook his head. "He was killed a few years back. I heard about it over the link." He shrugged. "Something about a weapons malfunction that caused the cruiser he was on to explode."

"Well, it can't be Seltan. He was caught in a bar brawl over on Damasmus Four last year."

"What about Hayden?" Alec stood, moving to stand between Gar and Byron.

"Dead. Pissed the wrong person off and apparently got spaced."

Alec's frown deepened. "Huh. That's most of the security and administration of the facility who would have known us both. Really, that only leaves the people from my particular lab. Ryan and Kam, my techs. I wouldn't have said either one had a grudge against you, though."

Byron had forgotten about Alec's two lab *strats*. "We'll need to run a check to see if there's a bounty out on either of them as well. I'm sure Ryan would be fine, but Kam wouldn't survive long enough to beg for her life. No life smarts, that one. That's Ryan Xi and Kam—"

Mace was already at the computer typing. "I know their names. Researched Alec, remember?" She made an odd noise, one Byron didn't like at all.

"What?"

She sat back and pressed the heels of her hands to her eyes. "They're both dead as well. And a lot of other people. Alec, it looks like someone has been targeting everyone even remotely associated with the Loyalist facility where you did your work."

"So they *are* after me." Alec cursed. "And I've put you all in danger as well."

"It sounds more like they were trying to get you both with one swoop." Gar rubbed the back of his neck. "The point is, this seems much bigger than the two of you. Maybe even fallout from some sort of Loyalist infighting. I wonder if the Admiral's aware of this twist. Either he's not, or he doesn't know Alec is on board. He only asked for the head of the guild."

Faolan nodded. "It's not his style to get involved with the Loyalists, period, let alone mix up in their politics. He's more likely to sabotage things than help."

"Disdain for politics wouldn't stop him from killing Byron to collect a small fortune," Gar countered. "We need a plan."

"Fast," Faolan added.

Byron glanced up from the computer monitor, trying to get his brain around the new information and what it might mean. Whether it changed anything. "We have six hours until he arrives, right?"

Gar turned to him. "No. He said we had six hours to agree to turn you over. But he'll show up before then. He never tells anyone the exact time he'll be in a specific place. It's why he's survived this long. But don't worry, we don't intend to give you up. The bounty placed at the guild was anonymous. A death mark's not. It's two bad guys making a deal. If we know who's behind all this, we may be able to convince the Admiral that the price for your corpse isn't worth the risk of his getting involved with this particular client. We just need to figure out who would want to kill off the entire staff of the facility where you were stationed."

"But that could be anyone." Alec spoke softly, but didn't flinch from scrutiny. "Anyone who would have been affected by any of my creations. I have a lot of blood on my hands."

Mace snorted. "That explains why someone would want to kill you, not all the others."

"And the Admiral didn't ask for you, Alec." Byron squeezed Alec's shoulder. "Which means if it comes down to it, I'll go willingly with this asshole so you and the ship can get to safety."

He would have laughed at the twin looks of horror on Alec's and Mace's faces if Gar hadn't interjected.

"Not happening, Byron."

"Ice Man, look—"

"Don't 'Ice Man' me. We are going to figure this out and solve the problem once and for all. I'm not losing anyone else in my life." Gar swung around and pointed at Faolan. "That includes you, pirate."

Faolan grinned and mock saluted his husband. "Yes, sir."

Gar growled. "Now, I have a plan. It's stupid and dangerous, which means it's most likely to work."

Faolan leaned in close to Doc. "I love it when he gets all diabolical."

"Say that once you've heard my idea." Gar let out a huff. "What's the one thing we have that the Admiral would want more than Byron?"

The answering silence made Byron feel a little less obtuse. "I'm assuming it's something other than money?"

Gar didn't bother to look at him then. His gaze locked on his husband's.

Faolan's smirk fell from his face and he sat up a bit straighter. "No."

"Faolan, you know it's the only thing that would stop the Admiral from pursuing this. We can buy him off."

"No."

"Mace, where's the necklace?"

"No!" Faolan was on his feet and around the table to stand in front of Gar before Byron could blink. "We are not giving that madman that kind of power. Do you know what he'd be able to accomplish with it? How many lives he'd be able to influence? It was why I didn't end up trying to sell it to him three years ago."

"What the hell are the two of you talking about?" Byron crossed his arms. "Gar?"

Gar kept staring his husband down, waiting for Byron's sigh before finally letting his gaze shift over to Mace. "Where is it, Macie?"

Byron recognized guilt when he saw it, and the look on Mace's face when she reached into her pocket was pure guilt. She pulled out the necklace he'd seen her wear on a few occasions.

"I don't go anywhere without it." Mace fingered the green stone, rubbing her thumb over the surface. "Not since you gave it to me."

Alec reached out to touch it, but Mace pulled it back. She quickly pressed it into Gar's hand and bit down on her bottom lip. "Sorry."

Byron couldn't tell whom she was apologizing to, or what for. More mystery, more complications he didn't know how to manage. Annoyance bubbled up, and he had to fight back the urge to yell or hit something. "Someone better start telling me what the *hell* is going on before I completely lose my patience."

Gar held up the necklace in front of Byron and Alec. "This little baby is the reason Faolan and I beat Jason Krieg. It gives the wearer the ability to read another person's thoughts."

Alec looked from the stone to Mace and back again. "Fuck."

Byron glared at her. "You wore that back on the ship."

"I had to make sure you were . . . okay. I trusted Alec, but you were still an unknown. I couldn't risk Faolan or the *Belle Kurve*."

Faolan tapped a finger on the stone, setting the dangling pendant in motion. "The Admiral doesn't know about it or else he would have chased me down years ago." He groaned, pinching the bridge of his nose. "The bastard is going to kill me when he learns I've been holding out on him."

Gar snapped the necklace back into his hand and shoved it into his inside suit pocket. "He'll kill Byron if he doesn't get it. Which would you prefer?"

"Neither." Faolan started to say more but swayed dangerously on his feet. "Shit, I need to sit down." Doc was beside the captain in an instant; Gar took his other side to help him back to his chair.

Byron couldn't give them the attention he normally would, not with his mind spinning about Mace and her invasion into his thoughts. "How much did you hear?"

She looked away. "It wasn't like that. I only had it on for a short time."

"I don't care if you had it on for five minutes. What did you hear?" He knew his tone was sharper than it should have been, but subtlety was never his strong point.

"Enough." Her words were almost swallowed up by the noise in the room as Doc fussed over a protesting Faolan. "Enough to know how much you care about him."

Byron looked over at Alec, who reached out and took Mace's hand. "In the grand scheme of sins, listening in on our thoughts is pretty minor."

"Still, I should have said something sooner. I'm sorry about that."

Privacy was one of the few things Byron had always been adamant about in any relationship he'd ever had. Even Alec knew that Byron had a part of himself he never shared, a line of intimacy he wouldn't be pushed beyond. Byron had always struggled with the darkness in his thoughts, his urges for retribution, and the ferocity of the protectiveness he felt toward the few people he cared about. He didn't want anyone catching a glimpse of that man inside him. He didn't want to scare people away, like his father had done with the loved ones in his life.

Before Byron could formulate a response to Mace, Alec spoke up with a tentativeness Byron hadn't heard from him in a long time.

"I guess . . . Well, I think there's something I should probably tell you both as well." He coughed into one fist. "I don't think either of you will appreciate it."

"Shit." Byron tightened his hands into fists. "Get it over with."

Alec stiffened and took a half step away. "I know you suspected, Bry, but I've done some modifications to my genetic makeup. And not just to test the Syrilian cure virus."

Byron felt his stomach bottom out. Alec had always wanted to push the limits, test things on himself before putting another person through any pain. Byron had stopped him more times than he could count. But nobody had limited him that way for the past seven years. Byron could hardly begin to imagine what he might have done to himself in all that time.

Mace clearly didn't see things the way Byron did. Her look of bewilderment would have been cute if the situation had been different.

"What the hell do you mean? You can't change your genetic makeup. It would make you not human."

"You can, actually." Alec looked downright sheepish, also not cute in the current circumstances. "A little tweak here, a minor change there, and suddenly I'm one percent Draconian and have the ability to, um, influence people. After I left the Loyalist facility and didn't have Byron watching my back anymore, I wanted to be sure I could trust people. It was the only thing that would keep me alive. So I can project a low-level psychic field on others and force them to tell me the truth."

Mace gasped and stepped farther away from Alec. "The tapping. That's what you're doing. You're mimicking the ticking noise Draconians make when they're . . . doing their thing." It wasn't considered polite to mention that the intelligent, pacifist, dominant species of Draco had first evolved their psychic ability—at some point in their dark prehistory—to mesmerize prey.

Alec nodded. "I don't use it all the time. I learned a few things about some people and quickly realized ignorance is bliss in most cases. Now I'll only do it for little things. Or very, very big things."

"Bastard." Byron wanted to punch him for his stupidity. "You promised me you'd never do something like this to yourself."

"You weren't there, Bry." Alec stiffened and met his gaze directly. "I did what I had to do. You taught me that."

"Well, this is another interesting twist."

Byron jumped, and the three of them turned to face Gar. Faolan and Doc had slipped out as they'd carried on their conversation. Gar's cool gaze washed over each of them, ending finally on his sister.

"Did you know what Alec was doing when he used this ability on you?"

"Didn't have a clue. I noticed his hands more than realized he'd done something to me. And that was only because I knew him as well as I did. He isn't one of those people who taps or drums on things all the time."

Gar nodded. "Think the Admiral would pick up on it?'

"Stop right there. Absolutely not!" Byron didn't bother to clamp down on his annoyance or fear. "You've just spent the better part of an hour telling me what a cutthroat killer this man is. That all the scary stories about him are true. You expect us to let Alec try to pull a scam on him? Think again, Ice Man."

Alec scowled. "Bry—"

Byron waved him off. "Find another way." This time he marched out of the room and didn't bother to listen to anyone's protests.

The last place he wanted to go was back to the room he shared with Alec and Mace. He needed to clear his head and calm the fuck down before he did something really stupid, like punch a bulkhead. Or kick a pirate. Or cry. Or tell Alec how much he loved him.

He headed away from the quarters and wound up in the weapons training room on the lowest deck of the *Bell Kurve*, near the engine room. It was one of the first places Mace had shown him when she gave him the grand tour. Byron suspected that had more to do with Gar telling her about his need for alone time than Mace thinking he'd want to keep his skills sharp while they floated in space. But there was no reason he couldn't accomplish both.

Picking up one of the dummy blasters on the table, he aimed at the farthest practice sensor and fired.

"Damn, you really are a crack shot."

He looked over his shoulder at a very pale Faolan standing by the door. "I thought Doc had taken you back to med bay."

"She tried. I'm hard to keep pinned down."

"You're hiding, aren't you?"

"Fuck yes."

"Good for you."

Turning back, he fired off several more shots, each landing dead center of the target.

"You know Alec is going to do this no matter what you say."

His next shot went wide. "How the hell do you know anything about it?"

"I kept a com channel open so I wouldn't miss out. Nosey that way."

Byron's arm suddenly felt too heavy to hold up, and he let it fall hard against his body. "Alec always did his own thing. Only came to me when he needed help picking up the pieces. It gets tiring after a while."

"But you have Mace now."

Somewhere in his confused head, Byron knew this. It didn't make it any easier to admit his failure though. "I know."

"So why are you down here instead of upstairs making sure they don't get my ship blown up?"

"They don't need me. You said it yourself. Alec will do this no matter what, and Mace is there to help him."

Faolan snorted. "That sounded dangerously like self-pity."

"Fuck off."

"Not until Alec fixes me. The will is strong, but the body is broken."

Byron turned to face him. "What the hell do you want from me? I'm not like you and your merry band of pirates. I don't play well with others, and I certainly don't stick my nose in where it's clearly not wanted."

"Funny, I knew another bounty hunter who sounded a lot like you, once upon a time."

Byron rolled his eyes. "I'm not Gar."

"No, you're not. But that doesn't mean you're any less capable of changing than he was. You clearly care for Alec and Mace, and no, I don't need a bloody mindreading necklace to tell me that. You don't want to walk away from them only to have something happen while you're gone. Trust me when I say the guilt is more likely to kill you than a blaster."

Byron's heart raced and his stomach turned at the idea of Alec or Mace getting hurt or dying. But they would only risk that if they insisted on making this insane attempt to save him from the Admiral. He shook his head, not wanting to even consider the notion of supporting such a plan.

"It's worth the fear to be there with them. You need to know you did everything you could to keep them safe, Byron." A look of pain and understanding transformed Faolan's normally good-humored face.

"You sound like you're speaking from experience."

"My wife . . . died, and I wasn't there to help her. Maybe I would have died alongside her. I don't know. What I do know is that until I met Gar, I had given up on letting anyone else close to me. I danced on the edge so many times, I'm surprised I survived."

Fuck, he hated this. "So you think I should go back up there and help them with this crazy idea to save my life?"

"Yes."

Byron paused and let everything penetrate through the bleakness of his thoughts. Could he do it? Sit back and not get involved now that he had Alec with him again? Could he ignore the new but just as powerful feelings he had for Mace, and let the two of them walk knowingly into danger while he refused to watch their backs?

On the other hand, if he could convince them to let him give himself up to the Admiral . . .

He'd be asking for the same sacrifice from them. Leaving them with the same anguish he was facing.

"I'm a fucking idiot."

Faolan shrugged. "No more than the rest of us. Love does that to a man. We just need to accept it."

The deck shuddered. Faolan stood straight and looked over his shoulder. "We should get back to the bridge. Gods only know what they'll do to my ship in an attempt to save your sorry ass."

It was then Byron caught a glimpse of the man Faolan Wolf must have been before the *ryana* stole his will to survive. The in-charge, swaggering captain who did what he thought was right, even if it went against what others wanted. The pirate with a heart of gold.

He fell into step beside Faolan. "Alec is going to cure you, Wolf. Don't think this little distraction of the Admiral's is going to change that. He'll be even more determined now."

"One thing at a time. I'll be fine for a few hours. You won't be. We'll get the Admiral off our backs, figure out who wants you dead, and then worry about saving *my* sorry ass."

They walked the rest of the way back to the bridge in silence. Faolan took a deep breath, hesitating before triggering the door.

"Cover me if they start to get violent." He winked at Byron. "Doc will be less than thrilled that I've managed to elude her again."

"I've got your back, Captain."

Walking onto the bridge, he couldn't believe the level of chaos that had erupted. Both Mace and Gar were completely focused on the coms and navigation controls. Alec was standing off to the side, frowning as people rushed by.

"Status report," Faolan shouted, causing at least half the crew to jump.

"We have a problem." Gar's calm response was disturbing amid all the noise.

"When *don't* we have a problem?" Faolan marched over to stand beside his husband. "What in particular this time?"

Mace turned and looked at Byron. "As I suspected, the Admiral is keeping to his own timetable."

Cocking an eyebrow, he returned her gaze. "What do you mean?"

"He's here now."

FIFTEEN

When Mace was younger, Faolan would tell her stories of the Admiral. It was more to keep her in line than for entertainment purposes.

"If you're bad, the Admiral of the Black will steal you away and throw you in his prison ship, where you'll be doomed to live out your sorry days eating synthmeat gruel and hoping the guards don't decide to use you for target practice."

"If you make a mistake at the helm and navigate into the wrong part of the quadrant, the Admiral's demon crew will blast your ship to smithereens and leave no survivors."

"Try to double-cross the Admiral and he'll claim all your loot, break all your bones, and leave you bound to a post on a desert planet for the strats and kralls to feast on."

Not being a very young child, Mace had always laughed at him, teasing that he really needed to get better at being scary if anyone was going to take him seriously. She never did admit how much it bothered her to hear his descriptions of what the Admiral did to people who betrayed him. But she was too old to lose sleep over the pirates' version of the monster under the bed.

It wasn't until a few years later that they'd come across several burned-out wrecks floating in the black of space, and she'd learned that the Admiral wasn't a myth or a ghost story or some character Faolan had dreamed up for his series of cautionary tales. He was real and very dangerous. Faolan's stories all came back to haunt her dreams, and she finally took them seriously. She knew if she were ever about to cross paths with the Admiral, she'd be wisest to run the other way as fast as she could.

Which was why she couldn't believe they were about to willingly open up their docking clamps to let the living embodiment of her nightmares come on board.

Byron and Alec hovered behind her, both ignoring her earlier tirade about going back to their quarters and staying there until she, Gar, and Faolan made sure the matter was under control.

Byron turned out to be snarky when he was nervous. "Well, this is going to be fun."

"Shut up." Alec sounded as tense as Mace felt. "Otherwise I might change my mind and convince Mace to hand you over to this guy so I can be done with you for good."

The *Belle Kurve* vibrated as the Admiral's ship, the *Wyvern*, connected. Mace's heart was in her throat. Gods, why the hell was she so scared? She knew if things went wrong, Faolan wouldn't just turn Byron over. They would fight for him, even though he was little more than a stranger to most of the crew. The men and women on the ship knew Byron and Alec were important to Mace, which was all the reason they needed to defend them.

A man's voice crackled through the coms. "*Belle Kurve*, this is the *Wyvern*. We've secured docking clamps and are ready to board."

"*Wyvern*, this is Captain Wolf. We are ready to welcome the Admiral on board." Faolan clicked off the system and rolled his eyes. "Like the bastard gave us any choice."

The group moved back a few steps and waited for the hiss of the air pressurization to finalize. When the hatch opened, two men pushed through the opening. They had swords on their hips and their palms rested on the butts of their blasters; each scrutinized the group and the surroundings before taking up position on either side of the hatch.

After a moment, a man came through, ducking his head to avoid hitting it on the top of the frame. He was dressed head to toe in black—leather pants, boots, and a knee-length jacket. Even his hair was the same shade. Mace wondered if he'd had the clothing made to match the hue.

The only things that stood out were his bright-green eyes.

The Admiral.

His gaze swept around the room, and Mace knew he was making note of every person there. His gaze paused on her, then Gar before finally stopping on Faolan.

"Wolf, I'm surprised to see you still standing." His voice was deeper in tone than Gar's, and it sent a shiver through Mace. "Last I heard you'd been poisoned. I thought you'd be space rot by now."

"I'm not that easy to get rid of. You should know that, Korbin."

Mace watched, awed, as Faolan chuckled and Korbin raised an eyebrow.

"I see your inappropriate sense of humor is still healthy."

Faolan smirked. "If you can't laugh in the face of danger, then when can you laugh? Let me introduce you around. This is my husband, Gar. He's a former guild bounty hunter and one of the best. Though I'm sure you know that already."

"Admiral." Gar nodded but made no offer of his hand.

Korbin gave Gar an appraising once-over. "Yes, I had been keeping an eye on you until I'd heard of your attachment to Wolf. You were on your way to becoming someone I'd have needed to deal with."

Gar waited a beat. "I would have liked to see you try."

The Admiral's lips twitched into a small smirk. "I like you. This one will be good for you, Wolf."

"This is his sister Mace. She's my second-in-command."

Mace felt the air get sucked out of her lungs as Korbin's gaze landed on her. The weight of his stare made her heart pound, and in that moment she knew every single story Faolan had told her as a kid was true.

"Admiral." Pleased her voice was steady, she rallied her cocky bravado and held out her hand. "I've heard so much about you."

"All true, I'm afraid." Korbin took her hand, but instead of shaking it, he bowed over it, gently turned it around, and pressed a kiss to the inside of her wrist. "A pleasure."

"Let her go." Alec's ragged voice cut through the haze of swelling lust in her head. Turning, she saw both he and Byron had moved closer. The plan had been for Alec to hang back, not draw attention to himself, lull the Admiral into suggestibility from as far away as possible. Instead, Alec reached out and took her hand from Korbin's grasp. "She's not yours."

Oh, Alec, you idiot. This wasn't the time to turn gallant and brave.

For half a second, Mace thought the Admiral would kill Alec where he stood. Instead he inclined his head to the side and straightened.

"Clearly not. And who are you?"

"Alec Roiten." Alec tugged Mace closer to his body. "Pleasure."

"Ah, the scientist." The Admiral paused, and the slightest hint of a smile curved his lips. "So you're here too. Bit of a bounty on your head. Wolf, you should have told me you had another distinguished visitor." Korbin turned to look at Byron. "That would make you the man of the hour."

The next events happened so quickly, Mace had a hard time putting everything together. Korbin stepped back and punched Gar in the face, pushing him into Faolan and knocking them both to the ground. The guards yanked their blasters from their holsters, pointing them directly at Gar and Faolan. Korbin then spun around, pulling his blaster out to point it directly at Byron.

Thankfully her instincts roared to life in time for her to save Byron. Mace jumped up close enough to the Admiral to land a snap kick to his chin, sending him staggering backward. The blaster discharged, but Byron dodged, throwing his body against Alec, pushing them both out of the way. By that time Gar and Faolan had recovered enough for Faolan to pull his blaster on the guards and Gar to jump on Korbin.

Armed with his ever-present blades, Gar triggered them from their hiding places, sending them out into his waiting grasp, and he pressed them to Korbin's throat. All movement in the room stopped as suddenly as it had begun.

"Admiral," Gar managed to say between pants. "It seems like you wanted to start negotiations before we were ready."

"Well, I never claimed to be the patient type." Korbin tried to get up, but Gar pressed the blades harder to his skin. "Faolan, your crew is as good as their reputation states."

"Better, actually. Now are you ready to listen to our counteroffer or are we going to roll around the floor a bit more? I don't know about you, but if we're going that route, I think there needs to be more nudity. Maybe even some oil."

Mace couldn't help but snort, and Gar rolled his eyes. "See what we have to put up with?"

Korbin nodded. "I call a truce for now. Plead your case and I agree to listen. I cannot guarantee I will agree to your barter. Especially now that we know there's nearly double the money at stake."

"I wouldn't expect you to guarantee anything, Admiral. Gar, let him up."

Gar pulled back and got to his feet with no offer of help to the Admiral. Mace helped both Alec and Byron up, letting her hands linger on each of them, confirming they weren't hurt.

"We're fine, girl." Byron pressed a quick kiss to her forehead. "You have some kick."

"Don't you forget it. If you ever piss me off, you'll find yourself on the receiving end."

With everyone back on their feet, Korbin ran a hand across his throat. "I would love a chance to see how those blades of yours work."

"Piss me off again and I'll give you another close-up view." Gar pushed the blades back into their homes.

Faolan grinned, running a hand through his hair. "I would suggest we go somewhere more comfortable, but I don't trust you not to try to take over my ship, Korbin."

"I've clearly shown I trust you. Why not repay the favor?" When no one responded, Korbin crossed his arms. "I only brought two guards. Normally there would be more."

"Thank you for the courtesy." Gar rolled his eyes.

Faolan sighed, and for a moment Mace wasn't sure if he would go back on their plan. With a quick glance at her, Faolan winked. *Stupid damn stone, he's reading my mind.*

Faolan chuckled. "Instead of comfort, I offer you a barter. Something priceless in exchange for not only Byron's and Alec's lives, but information on the source of the bounties."

Korbin narrowed his green gaze. "It would have to be something very rare for me to give you that. Can you imagine what people would say if they learned I betrayed the confidence of my client?"

"That they had it coming," Mace said without thinking.

Instead of snapping at her, Korbin grinned. "I really do like you, girl." Turning back to Faolan, Korbin held out his hand. "I assume you have the merchandise here to show me? It better be good."

Everyone in the room seemed to hold their breath as Faolan pulled the necklace out from beneath his shirt, slipped it off, and set it gently in the middle of Korbin's hand. The Admiral didn't react at first, simply stood there staring at the stone and gold chain. Mace knew the man was smart, and she hoped he realized Faolan wouldn't try to con him.

"What happens when I put it on?" Korbin frowned and lifted the stone to his eye to gaze through it.

Mace stepped forward, pointedly ignoring the hisses from the men in her life. She wasn't about to risk things falling apart now, not when they were so close to their answers. "It allows the wearer to read the mind of another person. It takes you a bit to get tuned in to your target and it can be confusing, but it works."

"For anyone?"

"So far? Yes."

Korbin glared at Faolan, his eyes narrowed to slits. "You've had this a long time and you've never told me about it?"

Faolan snorted. "I'm not a fool."

Mace stood before Korbin, knowing the next few moments would mean the difference between life and death for Byron—hell, for all of them. When the man in black finally nodded and slipped the necklace into his pocket, she finally relaxed.

"Mr. Roiten, Byron. Do you remember a woman named Celia Kev?"

Mace turned to see both men frowning.

Alec nodded, puzzled. "She was a research assistant of mine for a year or so near the end of my time with the Loyalists. Not the best lab worker. Brilliant flashes of insight, but very unreliable with procedures and documentation. They eventually transferred her to a lab on . . . one of the big mining planets, I can't remember. It was sad: I heard she took her own life some time later." After a moment, he blushed and added, "She was . . . attracted to me, I think? It could be awkward at times. I made it very clear I wasn't interested, but she never quite seemed to let it go."

Byron groaned, rubbing the back of his neck with his hand. "She was more than attracted, Alec. He's being modest. That bitch was a nightmare. She threatened me with a letter opener once, then tried to pretend it was a joke when Ryan walked into the lab. I'm also pretty sure she was stealing classified substances and selling them on the black market. Not to mention using some of them herself. I was the one who insisted she be transferred out of there. She was completely unstable."

Korbin nodded in the direction of the open hatch. "Apparently it's a family trait. Her brother is on my ship, waiting down in the hold. He wanted your corpse, Byron, but for you, Mr. Roiten—the man who broke his sister's heart—he was willing to pay a substantial bonus for the privilege of killing you himself. He was very eloquent about how much blood he wanted to see during the process and how he planned to accomplish all that."

When both Alec and Byron moved forward, Mace whipped around, pressing one hand to each of their chests. "Where do you two idiots think you are going?"

"To settle this." They spoke as one.

For not the first time, she was struck by how perfect they were for each other—much like Faolan and Gar.

And that makes me the odd person out.

Pushing that thought away, she shook her head. "Idiots."

Byron narrowed his gaze at her. "What?"

"Admiral," she said a bit louder than necessary. "Would you mind terribly if we boarded your ship to deal with this man? As part of our original barter, of course."

"His name is Zran. And my dear, you may board my ship at will." Byron's body tensed. "Zran? Tall, dark skin, blue hair, bitchy?"

Korbin nodded. "He said he infiltrated the guild trying to get to you, but you were far too protected and cautious. Traits I admire."

"Son of a bitch."

"What?" Mace let her hand drop.

"He was the first hunter I recruited after Gar left. He was his replacement. That guy got lucky on one huge bounty, then left in the dead of night in a guild-owned ship. Which he flew straight to Zaxon and sold for cash. Fucking ship-flippers."

"You should work on your recruitment policies," Gar suggested.

"Screw you." Byron pulled out his blaster. "Let me deal with this."

"Not alone." Alec squeezed Byron's arm. "Mace and I are going with you."

Mace braced herself for a fight but was relieved when Byron relaxed in her hold. "Fine. But I want the two of you staying back until I deal with Zran."

"Sure. Backup. You got it." Only then did she let Byron pass her. One look from Alec and she knew he was thinking the same thing she was. Neither of them would stand back and let anything happen to Byron.

With a smirk of her own, she swept her arm forward. "After you."

Korbin tapped on a wrist unit as they passed. "I'll have Strand auto-unlock the correct doors for you, leading down to the hold. Zran is next to the cells, in interrogation room seven."

The air in the *Wyvern* was almost sweet to the taste. The corridor was dimly lit, and the walls seemed to recede into shadow as though some sort of visual dampening net obscured them. Mace fell into step behind Byron but was poised, ready to defend if they were attacked.

A door a few meters ahead of them opened as they approached. Mace stepped out around Byron, sweeping the entrance and side hall as she moved.

"Clear." She looked back over her shoulder at him. "Ready?"

"You're not going to let me take the lead on this, are you?"

"Nope."

Alec pushed past them both, aiming his blaster down the new corridor. "If you two are going to stand here and bitch at each other all day, then I'm going to take care of Zran on my own."

Byron chuckled, and Mace couldn't help but roll her eyes. "Gods, the three of us make a great team. We can't even decide who gets to do the attacking."

"How about we do this?" Byron stepped ahead of Alec. "Mace, you cover our backs. Alec, in the middle and make sure your weapon is hidden from sight. You shoot at anything I tell you to."

"Just move," Alec said, shoving Byron in the small of his back with the butt of the blaster.

They fell into a comfortable silence as they proceeded deeper into the ship. Door after door silently opened for them, clearly indicating that someone was tracking their progress. After a long trip down several floors in a cargo hoist, the door slid aside to reveal a short corridor with several numbered doors lining either side.

The fourth door on the left popped open with a soft click, and the muscles in her back and neck tightened. "Number seven. Looks like the place," she whispered.

"Mace, I want you to hang back a bit. Zran's not expecting you, which might give us an advantage." Byron held up his hand to silence her protests. "Please. I need to count on you to save our asses if it comes to that."

It burned her to know Byron was playing things smarter than she was. "At the least little sign of trouble, I'm in there."

"Deal." Byron winked at her. "Wish us luck."

Mace waited for them to move down the hall several meters before following. Byron didn't hesitate to enter the room, Alec a half step behind him.

"Zran, you asshole. Didn't have the balls to do your own dirty work?"

Mace moved close enough to hear a chuckle. "Oh, I did a fair amount of it myself. But look at you. Byron and Alec. The happy couple is finally reunited. How sweet."

Dropping into a squat, Mace poked her head around the doorjamb to catch a quick look at Zran. Standing in the middle of the room, pointing a large blaster rifle at her lovers, was a man nearly as tall as Alec, with dark skin and bright-blue hair. From the quick look, she could tell he was a solid wall of muscle and wouldn't be easy to take down at all.

Alec shifted closer to Byron. "Why are you doing this? Celia took her own life. Neither of us had anything to do with it. Neither did any of the other people you killed. We weren't even on the same planet."

"No one in that gods-awful facility deserved to live," Zran sneered, his finger flexing against the trigger. "I wanted you all dead. I know what you did in that lab, Roiten. You were the Loyalists' genocide specialist. Mass murder, custom designed. The military developed the plans, you gave them the weapons they asked for, and Byron kept you safe so you could continue to kill. Celia could have stopped you years ago, kept you in line, if it hadn't been for Byron. After Syrili, she blamed herself for not realizing what you were sooner. Not seeing how much you'd truly needed her."

Alec started tapping out a steady beat on his blaster. The sound was soft but quickly filled the silent spaces in their conversation.

"She was my assistant. She helped the Loyalists as much as I did. She knew as much as I did, or any other of the researchers. They lied to all of us about what the poisons would be used for. I would never have knowingly harmed a person. And it certainly isn't my fault Celia killed herself."

At the mention of his sister's name, Zran's arm shook slightly. "Not your fault?"

"Zran, you're being an idiot." Byron stepped closer, his blaster held steady. "What is this really about? Because it's sure as hell not about Alec killing people. You're a ruthless enough bastard not to care."

For a moment Mace thought Zran was going to fire on both of them. Because of how Alec had moved, she no longer had a clear shot. *Shit, this is going to get messy.* She was about to creep closer when Alec increased the tempo of his tapping.

"Tell us why you really want us dead."

"She was completely in love with you, Roiten! Do you know how many com messages she sent me talking about you? *'Alec did this.' 'Alec touched me here.' 'I know if I can just get him away from Byron, Alec would love me.'* You didn't even notice her!"

Mace couldn't help but feel sympathy for the long-dead Celia. She knew how easy it was to feel isolated from Alec and Byron when they stared at each other. Even though she'd shared a bed with them, had heard their inner thoughts, she couldn't help but want more. Want to have them look at her the way they looked at each other.

She didn't want to be left behind again.

Byron leaned forward, forcing Alec to shift and giving Mace a clear shot once more. She hesitated, wanting to give them a chance to talk Zran down. He was a brother trying to avenge his sister's death. An evil, deranged, homicidal brother. Still, it wasn't hard to imagine going crazy with grief herself and starting a vengeance rampage if Gar's life had been ended and she thought a bunch of people were to blame. Maybe Alec could tap into that motivation, use his abilities to drain the force out of it and help Zran see reason. She kept a finger on the trigger just in case.

"I'm sorry." Alec's voice was full of emotion as he finally stopped his tapping. "Celia was a brilliant researcher, but there was nothing between us. I didn't . . . There wasn't that connection."

"You were blinded by Byron. You couldn't see how amazing she was. How much she could have done for you if you'd only given her a chance. Byron was controlling you."

"Byron did nothing to me that I didn't ask for. I . . . need Byron in my life."

"Is that why you ran from him?"

The question had both men holding their breath. Mace barely held herself back from running to join them. Gods, they'd each been through so much, they deserved some happiness.

Alec cleared his throat and looked at Byron. "I wanted to make amends. I wanted to be good enough for him."

Zran's mouth twisted, and he spat out his words with renewed venom. "When she heard you'd disappeared, she thought you were coming to find her. She waited for you. And when you never showed up, that's what drove her to end it. You're a twisted, self-centered, murdering fuck who doesn't deserve to live!"

Zran re-aimed his blaster rifle, and time slowed for Mace. In her head she saw the inevitable fallout of the shot. Byron was ahead of Alec enough that he would take the brunt of the blast. But with a rifle at such close proximity, the laser would go clean through him and into Alec. They would both be dead before they hit the floor.

She couldn't let that happen. They loved each other—and she knew they cared for her. Without a further thought, she squeezed the trigger of her blaster. Alec and Byron crouched and rolled away from one another as her shot zipped between them. It sliced through the air and struck the middle of Zran's chest. He staggered back from the force of the blast, openmouthed surprise on his face as his own shot went wild into the ceiling.

Rising to her feet, she kept her blaster focused on Zran. "Hi there. I'm Mace."

Zran fell to his knees, his gaze locked on her. "What?"

"I didn't know your sister, so I can't pretend to understand what she went through. I do know Alec and Byron. I've been lucky enough to become a part of their lives, even if I know it won't be permanent. If Celia hadn't been so selfish, she might have seen that they were meant to be together. Or maybe even realized there's too much love out there to restrict it to two people. I'm sorry she never took the chance to be part of something bigger than herself. But I did, and even if those two fly away tomorrow without me, I'll never regret the time I spent with them, or getting to share even a fraction of their love for each other."

Zran didn't speak. His eyes rolled back into his head, and he collapsed onto the floor.

Byron moved to his side and pressed his fingers against the pulse point in his neck. "He's alive, but he won't be for long if we don't take care of this."

"Pardon me."

All three of them spun around to point their blasters at a man standing in the doorway. He cleared his throat and waved at them to lower their weapons. "My name is Strand. The Admiral indicated you might require assistance with Mr. Zran."

"He'll just come after us again," Alec muttered.

"Not true, Mr. Roiten. The Admiral wanted me to assure you that you will no longer need to worry about your *friend*. He also wanted me to give both Mr. Byron and Mr. Roiten these."

The breath caught in Mace's chest when she saw the two data chips Strand held out for her lovers to take. It couldn't be.

Byron turned the chip over in his hand before he held it up. "What's this?"

Strand smiled politely. "In the old days they were called letters of marque. It tells people you are both under the Admiral's protection and have safe passage in any port in his sphere of influence. If anyone should be foolish enough to hunt you down, or worse, try to kill you, they would quickly find themselves in the Admiral's bad graces."

Alec pocketed the chip. "Thank him for us. I only wish these also worked with Loyalists."

"You'd be surprised at the length of the Admiral's reach." Strand nodded toward Mace. "Ma'am, the Admiral also wanted me to inform you that if you ever wish to take up duty on his vessel, there will always be a vacancy."

Before she could answer, Alec and Byron each had an arm wrapped around her. She smiled grimly. "Please pass along my thanks to the Admiral, but I have a position already."

"I suggest we get back to the ship." Byron pressed a kiss to her temple. "Alec still has work to do."

Strand stepped back to give them room. "Safe travels."

As they headed back toward the *Belle Kurve*, Mace swore she saw the Admiral out of the corner of her eye at the end of the corridor. Gods, she hoped they hadn't made a mistake giving him the necklace.

The trade was worth it, though. She had Alec and Byron both safe and protected now, wherever they decided to go.

When they crossed the threshold back into the docking area, only Ricco stood waiting. The peace Mace had felt evaporated faster than condensation in the desert.

"Faolan?" she asked.

He reluctantly nodded. "You better come with me."

CHAPTER
SIXTEEN

The leather of the seat was warm to the point of comfort, but it did little to soothe Alec as he waited for the latest round of test results to come through. The time they thought they had was slipping away faster than a ship through a dimension gate.

Faolan wasn't going to last much longer. He'd passed out again while Alec, Byron, and Mace were on the *Wyvern*, and he'd been unconscious more often than not ever since.

Every day and night of Alec's past two weeks had been consumed with either running tests or contemplating his relationships with Byron and Mace. Things had changed between them since their run-in with the Admiral and Zran, and he couldn't quite figure out what had happened to make things go wrong.

Or not wrong, but certainly not the way he wanted. It was all *off*.

Mace's little speech was now firmly lodged deep in the center of his brain. *I've been lucky enough to become a part of their lives, even if I know it won't be permanent.* Why would she think they wouldn't want her with them? Sure, he knew he could be withdrawn and moody. And Byron was an arrogant, controlling ass on the best of days. But when the three of them came together, all the pieces seemed to fit. He hadn't realized how centered he'd felt lying in bed with them, a tangle of limbs and sweat-slicked skin, until he'd been without that contact again.

Being without the two of them now? He couldn't even imagine going back to a solitary life. Stifling a yawn, he rubbed his eye with the heel of his hand.

Gods, he hadn't seen his bed in seventy-two hours. And while he wasn't interested in sex—he was too focused on getting Faolan healthy again—he *did* want to lie down and find a bit of peace for a while. *No, there isn't any time.*

The computer was only halfway through its analysis of the latest sample. He'd sent Mace to have a nap a few hours earlier, when she'd fallen asleep sitting up. It had taken Byron carrying her away to get her out of the lab, but he hoped the length of her absence meant she was actually sleeping. And a good thing, too; it was the middle of the night, ship's time. Outside the lab's open door, he didn't hear a sound from the med bay other than the steady *beep, beep, beep* that indicated Faolan's condition was stable.

When he felt a hand on his shoulder, he jumped, half falling out of his chair. "Byron?"

His lover looked down at him, smiled, and gently squeezed his shoulder. "Sorry, I didn't mean to wake you."

"Shit." He blinked, trying to focus. "I didn't mean to fall asleep."

"You're in worse shape than Mace. Why don't you have a rest? You can start again with fresh eyes."

"I can't."

"Alec—"

"Honestly. I need to wait for these results to come through. I hadn't taken into account the impact of environmental factors from a few planets he'd been on. It may have caused any number of the cell mutations, and if I can figure out exactly what those factors are, then I can—"

Byron held up his hands and backed away. "Enough, enough. I get it. The lab *strat* speak will put me into a coma."

Alec smiled. "Sorry."

Falling into the chair Mace normally took, Byron put his feet up and laced his hands behind his neck. "How about I keep you company instead? Then once your results are in, I'll tuck you in to bed with Mace."

Mace. "How did she seem to you? When you put her to bed, I mean?"

Byron lifted his eyebrows. "Tired."

"Beyond that. Does she seem, I don't know, distant to you?" He could tell Byron wasn't quite getting it. "Ever since Zran, it's like she's sad, pulling away from us. I think she's under the impression that once I've cured Faolan we're going to leave."

Byron didn't respond right away. He shifted, letting his hands fall restlessly in his lap. The soft hum of the computers lulled Alec into a relaxed state he hadn't achieved in days. He realized he was finally coming to grips not only with what he'd been a part of at the Loyalist facility, but with his feelings for the people who mattered most to him.

Alec hadn't a clue what Byron wanted now. He was still the head of the guild. A man with responsibilities—even if they were slightly unsavory—that he could take up again with little effort. For the first time since Alec had blasted off the research outpost and refused to look back, he knew he couldn't be away from Byron any longer. What he didn't know was whether Byron still wanted that.

"When this is done," he started slowly, "are you planning to go back to the guild?"

"You sure you'll be able to fix Faolan?"

"No other option but to try." His hands were damp, and he rubbed them against the tops of his thighs. "You didn't answer the question."

"I hadn't thought about it. Would it matter if I did?"

Yes! "It would depend on if you still want to see me. I'm not sure about you, but I don't think I'd exactly fit in with the bounty-hunter crowd."

Byron chuckled. "No. You're too pretty."

"Fuck off." He tried hard to ignore the pounding in his chest. "Seriously, Bry."

"Alec . . ." Byron sighed, closed his eyes, and tipped his head back. "If I had a reason to not go back to the guild, I would take it. It's not like I wanted to be there originally. I just didn't have any other means to look for you. You didn't make it easy, you know."

"I know." Hesitating for only a moment, Alec slid to the floor and pushed Byron's feet down to crawl between his knees. He slid his hands up along Byron's thighs until he reached his hips. "I wasn't running from you as much as from myself. I needed to make sure I was good enough. I couldn't do that knowing I'd caused so much pain and suffering."

"And now?"

It was the first time Alec could ever remember Byron sounding nervous.

"Now I know where I belong. And with whom."

He wasn't sure who moved first, but before Alec realized it, they were kissing. It wasn't the crazy intensity they so often came together with. No, this was a slow burn, a prelude to something bigger. Byron's fingers were tangled in Alec's hair, holding him still as the kiss deepened. Gods, how could he have walked away from this?

Finally pulling back, he opened his eyes to see Byron gazing intently at him.

"Promise me something," Byron whispered.

"Anything."

"Don't run again. I . . . Just don't."

He swallowed past the lump in his throat. "Promise."

"Good. I don't think Mace or I could handle it if you took off. Not again."

Of course Byron would come back to my original concern eventually. "Think she'll stay? With us, I mean."

"I've been spending time with Faolan, giving Gar a break so he can see to the ship. Faolan is under the impression that Mace is not only good for us, but we can give her something she's wanted her whole life."

"What's that?"

"Family. She has it to a point on this ship, but she's never been settled. Faolan thinks if we were to offer, she would join us."

Alec was thankful he was on the floor. He wasn't sure his legs would support him if he were standing. "Do you want that?"

Byron grinned. "My dad may have been a terrible parent, but I did learn one thing by watching how he lived. A man is nothing without a family. Having you *and* Mace, shit, that's just too good an opportunity to pass up. I . . . care too much about both of you to let either one of you leave me."

"Care?"

Byron's gaze didn't waver and his voice was steady. "Love."

Ever since Alec had learned what his research was used for, he'd felt a heavy, silent weight pressing down on him day and night.

When Byron said that single word, the weight evaporated, leaving only relief and gratitude behind.

"I love you too. Both of you. We need to tell Mace. She doesn't realize, and I think she might try to leave if—"

The computer chose that moment to trill at them. Getting up as quickly as he could, he pressed the key combination to display the results.

Byron was by his side, leaning over to read the display. "What does it mean?"

"One second."

"Alec—"

"Shh!"

The chemical breakdown of the poison was there, along with the cell and genetic breakdown of chemicals in Faolan's blood. It took him a second to realize exactly what he was seeing.

"Oh my gods." He scrolled through the test log, scanning each interaction, verifying the results.

Byron growled. "Oh my gods *good*, or oh my gods *bad*?"

"Good. Very good. I might be able to . . ."

If this was accurate, he was pretty sure he had everything he needed here on board the *Belle Kurve*.

"Alec!"

He straightened up, turned to face Byron, and kissed him soundly. "I think I have an antidote."

Mace was hugging herself as she leaned against the wall of Faolan and Gar's bedchamber. It was crowded with everyone jammed in the space, but no one was willing to leave. Doc, Gar, and Alec stood by Faolan, who was lying down in the bed. Byron sat on a chair not far from them, his gaze shifting from Alec to her.

She still couldn't believe Alec had done it, and that after all this time Faolan was going to be okay.

Not yet and not for sure. Patience.

Looking up, she realized Byron was staring at her again. He looked a bit confused, like she'd changed on him and he wasn't sure what to make of her any longer. She wasn't entirely sure what was going on between them either. Maybe he was simply trying to figure out how to tell her they were leaving once Faolan was better. Despite everything that had happened both at the guild safe house and on the *Belle Kurve*, she knew that if the antidote worked, there would be nothing to keep them here.

"Okay." Alec's voice cut through the low chatter. "Faolan, are you ready for this?"

"Now or never." Faolan's smirk held none of its normal zest.

"This isn't going to be pleasant, and it won't work instantly. The antidote is going to feel like fire in your veins as it breaks up the *ryana* in your bloodstream. You're going to feel like your skin is burning and you'll probably throw up anything you have in your system. Or it'll come out the other end."

"Alec." Byron's warning tone had Faolan chuckling.

"It's fine. Better I know what I'm in for. I think once you inject me with this, you should all leave."

"I'm not going anywhere," Gar said, taking Faolan's hand firmly between his. "So don't even start."

"Wouldn't dream of it." Faolan kissed Gar's knuckles.

Doc snorted. "And if you think I'm leaving you alone for even a second, you're dafter than you look."

Alec glanced over his shoulder at Mace and smiled softly. "We'll leave once I inject this. Doc, things will probably get bad in about fifteen minutes. He'll be pretty miserable for at least an hour or two. After that we should start seeing results. Faolan, you'll be weak for days, and a full recovery may take a long time, but we'll know if this has worked within about three hours."

Faolan nodded. "Let's do it."

Mace held her breath as Alec pressed the hyper-needle to Faolan's neck, injecting the dull-red serum into his body. That was it. Everything they'd been trying to figure out for the past six months, done in two seconds. It felt like there should be more to it, but she was nonetheless thankful they actually had a shot now.

No one moved or spoke until, ten minutes later, Faolan let out a low groan.

"Shit," he mumbled, rolling onto his side to pull his knees to his chest. "*Out.*"

Without speaking, Alec and Byron moved at once to Mace's side, giving Gar and Doc room around the bed. Byron slipped an arm around her waist.

"Let's go to the mess hall and get something to eat. They're going to be a while."

Mace let them lead her through the ship, not entirely paying attention as they went. The antidote had to work—Faolan had to get better. The idea of him dying was far more terrifying than she'd wanted to admit to herself. He'd been every bit as much a father to her as her own, giving her a home and looking after her. With him married to Gar, it had felt like her life was finally stable.

It didn't matter that she spent most nights alone with her thoughts. She was a pirate and a member of the best space crew in the sector. She had a comfortable bed, and she got to travel all over the place between the known worlds.

When they arrived at the mess hall and Mace sat down in the chair Byron pulled out for her, she knew the food and drink would be plentiful and good, as it always was. Her life was better than most people living back on her home planet ever dreamed of. Really, she had no reason to want for more.

But she did.

A hand cupped her cheek, and Alec forced her to look up into his concerned gaze. "You okay?"

"Ask me again in a few hours."

"I hate to say it, but if he's feeling the pain, that's a good thing. It means the cure is working. He'll pull through."

"And Alec is never wrong." Byron, falling into the chair opposite them with a thud, slid two mugs across the table. "I thought you could both use a stiff drink."

"Thanks." The moisture on the mug was soothing in her grasp.

Instead of taking his, Alec crouched beside her, sliding one arm around her shoulders while letting the other drape across her lap. "What are your plans once you know Faolan is okay?"

Ah, here it comes. "Oh, you know, I'll probably stay here. While playing research assistant was fun, I'm much better as a pirate. Fewer data forms to fill out."

"You like it here." Byron tapped the table with his finger. "Have you considered doing anything else?"

"Not really. I thought my family was dead when Faolan saved me. This is the only life I've known for a long time."

"It must get lonely." Alec began to trace circles on her thigh. "I mean Faolan has Gar now. Who cares for you at the end of the day?"

Tears threatened to spill. Gods, why the hell were they putting her through this? Dropping her gaze, she let out a small chuckle. She was glad the mess was practically empty at this hour, and the few crew members scarfing down meals seemed oblivious to the drama playing out near them. "I'm good on my own."

"No, you're not." The sharp note in Byron's tone made her look at him. "Mace, you're lonely and miserable. And Alec is not good with words." Reaching over, he smacked Alec on the back of the head.

"What?" Weren't they trying to tell her they were leaving?

"I spoke with Faolan and Gar while you two were still in the lab earlier." Byron scratched his fingers through his short hair. "I especially wanted Faolan to give the okay before he was injected, in case anything happened."

Mace found it hard to breathe. "The okay about what?"

"We asked his permission to stay on the ship." Alec smiled shyly. "We want to stay with you and live on the *Belle Kurve*. If you'll have us."

Unable to stop herself, Mace jerked to her feet and stumbled a few meters away. No, they couldn't want this. They'd finally found each other again. They couldn't possibly want *her*.

"Why?" She didn't even care that her voice sounded raw as she forced the question from her mouth. "I thought you would go off now that you're together."

"We can certainly do that if it's what you want." Byron rose to stand beside Alec. "But make no mistake about it, you would be coming with us."

A shudder passed through her. Both men stared unwavering, and she couldn't help but blush at the intensity of it all. Reaching up, she tucked her short hair behind her ears, a smile twitching on her lips. "Really?"

"Do you think—" Alec took a step closer "—honestly think that after everything we've been through—" and another step "—we would abandon you now?"

"If I'd found Alec back on that planet," Byron said, "we would have fought. I would have dragged his sorry ass back to the guild to keep an eye on him. Hell, we might have even fallen into bed. But I very much doubt things would have ended well. We were both angry and too stubborn to see past it."

"You helped us with that, Macie."

They were now on either side of her, fingers brushing her arms, hands touching her waist. Alec leaned in and pressed his lips against the shell of her ear. "We want us to be three. Do you . . . want that?"

"Yes." The word was little more than a breath, but they both heard her.

Byron leaned in, wrapping his arms around both of them. Trapped in a circle of warmth, Mace knew there was no place else in the universe she would ever belong more. They were hers—her family. While she could never imagine her life without Faolan and Gar in it, they had each other in a way she could never be a part of.

Now she had the same thing.

"Once we know Faolan is okay," Byron said, his voice unusually harsh, "I plan on keeping the two of you busy in our bed for a week. Maybe longer."

Alec laughed softly as Mace burrowed deeper against his chest. "Promises, promises."

"Ones I'm very good at keeping, Alec."

"Good. Mace and I will hold you to them."

The following silence chased away the last few remaining demons in Mace's soul, leaving her at peace. The three of them didn't break apart for a very long time.

SEVENTEEN

Three Weeks Later

Mace heard Alec's moan the second she triggered the door to their quarters. She'd just finished her shift on the bridge and was late coming back. Faolan had finally returned to take the helm, and she'd spent a bit longer than necessary bringing him up-to-date on the events of the past few hours. It had thrilled her beyond words to see him back to his old self.

He'd finally shooed her away. "I've done this before, Macie," Faolan had reminded her, grinning.

Once the antidote had cleared his system of the *ryana* poison, it hadn't taken him long to recover. He was still too thin, and at times he still tired easily, but the old sparkle was finally back.

"I know you have, old man. I just want to make sure you don't crash my ship."

His laughter had chased her off the bridge and carried her back to her new, larger quarters.

Smiling, she stepped inside far enough to allow the door to close behind her. "You two couldn't wait for me?"

Byron had stripped Alec and tied him to their bed, facedown and spread-eagled. Byron stood beside the bed, wearing only his black leather pants and a wide grin.

"Alec was being bad. I thought it best if I taught him a lesson. But now that you're here, you can help."

She smiled when Alec's muffled groan reached her. "You know I'll do whatever you want, Bry."

"Good girl. Now get naked and come here."

She didn't miss a beat, pulling her shirt off over her head, dropping it as she approached Byron. He waited quietly as she kicked off her boots and let her belt and pants fall to the floor. The air in the room was warm—knowing Byron, he'd turned the environmental controls up when he'd planned Alec's discipline.

Byron swiped his thumb across one of her nipples until it stood at attention. He then moved on to the next until it was as hard and she found it difficult to breathe.

"Have you been a good girl, Mace? Should I tie you up and put you next to Alec? Spank your ass until it glows?"

"No." Not tonight at least. She knew this game now, knew what he wanted without him having to tell her.

Dropping to her knees, she pressed her cheek to his thigh and wrapped her hands around his calf. "I've been so good, Bry."

His expression morphed into his stony mask. "Prove it. Take my cock out and suck it."

Rising up so she knelt as high as she could, Mace quickly undid the clasp to his pants, peeling them wide before slipping her fingers inside and freeing his already hard shaft. Her mouth watered at the sight of his red, swollen tip and the scent of his arousal.

Looking up, Mace made sure she had his complete attention before sucking just the head of his cock into her mouth. Byron didn't say anything, but she could tell he was affected by the widening of his eyes and the hard set of his mouth.

She slid down the length of his shaft, taking as much of him in as she could, only stopping when she thought she might choke. Then she tightened the seal of her mouth and sucked hard, pulling back up at an agonizingly slow pace. His hand drifted to the back of her head, fingers tightening in her hair as she continued her sensual assault.

"It's a shame you can't see her, Alec. Gods, her cheeks collapse in, she's sucking me so hard. Her lips are red too. Just the way I know you like them."

Alec groaned, and Mace heard him buck against the mattress.

"He's gagged too. I didn't want to hear him complain earlier, but I think I may have to take it out soon."

Mace pulled away from his cock, moving low so she could lick a path from the base up to the crown. She did it again, only stopping when Byron's hand held her back.

"I think it's time for Alec's punishment. Do you agree?"

This time the pulse that raced through her body made her cunt clench in anticipation. "Whatever you want."

He held out his hand to her. "Oh, it's what I want. And I want you to do it. Come here."

Mace's gaze locked onto the perfection of Alec's flawless ass as Byron led her to the bed. The skin was smooth, leading up to a well-defined back. Her fingers itched to reach out and touch him, squeeze the rounded globes and rake her nails along his skin, marking him. But she knew if she made a move before Byron gave her permission, she'd likely join Alec facedown on the bed.

The silence stretched on, and either it finally got to Alec or he was tired of waiting. Pushing his ass up as high as he could manage, he held it there for them to see before dropping back down onto the bed to grind his cock against the mattress.

"See what I mean?" Byron said, shaking his head. "He's been such a bad boy. Mace, I want you to spank him."

The rush of lust hit her hard and low in her body. Nodding once, she crawled onto the bed to kneel next to Alec's hip. Before she got fully into position, he turned his head to look at her. The black gag in his mouth looked obscene against the white of his cheeks and red of his lips. Sweat beaded across his forehead as he struggled halfheartedly against the ropes binding him.

"You've been bad, haven't you, Alec?" Mace reached out and gently caressed the small of his back, down across his nearest ass cheek. "You know better than to upset Bry, don't you?"

When he didn't respond, Mace quickly placed an open-handed slap on his ass. "Answer me."

Of course he couldn't, not with the gag, but that was part of the fun.

"See what I've been putting up with all morning?" Byron reached around her and gave a slap of his own against Alec's other cheek. "I think you need to teach him there are consequences to his actions."

"How many, do you think?" Mace knew she would never hurt Alec, not seriously, nor would Byron ever tell her to do something they both knew Alec didn't want. Still, she got a bit of a rush every time they played games like this. "Ten?"

"How about ten from each of us. You go first and use your hand. I want him to know who's marking him."

This time Mace didn't give Alec any warning. Careful not to land too many slaps in the same spot, she fired off five hits per cheek. Alec's ass was a nice pink by the time she'd finished. Sliding from the bed, her hand tingling from the contact, she waited for Byron to take over.

She loved watching Byron. Whether it was from years of familiarity or simple intuition, he knew exactly where to touch Alec. Somehow Byron understood how far Alec and Mace could go, even when they didn't. She'd been amazed the first time he'd flipped her over his knee and delivered a *punishment*. Pain had never been a turn-on for her before then—but now she looked forward to Byron's brand of discipline.

"It's my turn now, Alec." Byron took up a spot by Alec's hip, drawing a shiver from his happy victim. "Mace is getting very good at this, but she's not quite as good as me yet. I know exactly what you want, don't I?"

Alec ground down against the mattress once more in response. Byron gave him a warning spank. "You won't get any release if you keep doing that. Now lie still and I might let you come if you're good."

Alec instantly settled, shifting his head to watch Byron. Byron put a hand in Alec's hair and turned him back toward Mace again.

"That's it," Byron cooed. "You look at her the whole time I'm spanking you. If you're very, very good and very lucky, I might let you fuck her before the night is out."

It was Mace's turn to shiver in response. She knew she couldn't say anything, but she hoped Alec interpreted the look on her face as *Please, dear gods, be good.*

Byron straddled Alec's legs, pinning him between his knees. Mace could see the hard line of Byron's erection pushing out from the front of his pants. The tip of his cock was red and leaking, and Mace wished she could suck him into her mouth again. Looking back at Alec, she bit down on her lower lip, suddenly unsure of what to do with her hands.

A sudden, air-splitting *smack* cut through her thoughts.

"One." Byron grinned. "Now that I have everyone's attention. Mace, I want you to play with your nipples while I spank our boy here. I want you so horny you'll have a hard time not coming when I eventually let Alec fuck you."

She couldn't stop her eyes from sliding closed as she reached up and pinched her nipples.

Smack. "Two."

Alec's groan sounded desperate this time. Mace knew it had as much to do with her performance for him as it did the strength of Byron's hits.

"You're such a slut, Roiten." Byron's voice was the lowest she'd ever heard it. "If you could, you'd want to fuck us both at once. Wouldn't you?"

Alec moaned, nodding.

Smack. "Three. See, Mace, he's greedy too." *Smack.* "Four. I wonder if we should give him what he wants, after all. We shouldn't be giving in to his bad behavior like this."

"Maybe." Mace swallowed to try to regain her voice. "Maybe we should torture him a bit longer."

"How, darling?"

"You could . . ." Gods, she couldn't believe she was going to say this. "You could fuck me from behind while we kneel over him. Force him to watch and not touch."

Smack, smack. "Six. I like that plan. Think that will teach you not to be greedy, Alec? Think you'll learn your lesson?"

Alec buried his face straight down into the mattress. *Smack, smack, smack.*

"Yeah, I think that will be good, Mace. We'll do that. One more and we're done, then I'll turn you over and you can watch me fuck Mace."

Byron waited several seconds before landing one final hit to Alec's now-red ass. Mace had been playing with her nipples the entire time and was so damp and aroused she wasn't sure she'd be able to hold off coming the minute Byron pushed inside her. It helped she had some time to try to mentally calm herself down while Byron moved Alec into position.

Byron slid off him and quickly released the ropes holding Alec's feet in place. She was surprised when he didn't untie Alec's hands but instead helped him turn over. The gag couldn't suppress Alec's sharp intake of air the moment his ass touched the mattress. Byron ignored him, instead straightening Alec's legs, pressing them close together.

"Come here, Mace."

Her knees shook as she crossed the short distance back to the bed. Byron pushed his pants to the floor, kicking them free as she reached his side.

"Hands and knees. I want your head to be close to his cock, but no touching yet. Alec, if you try to move, we'll get up and continue our fun in the bathroom without you. Understand?"

Alec nodded enthusiastically, though Mace felt the tremor running through his body as she got close to him.

From this vantage point, she could see Byron had been teasing Alec's body for quite some time. His nipples were red and his chest and neck were littered with love bites. Knowing Byron had marked his lover increased Mace's arousal. Even more so when Byron leaned over her and bit down gently on her shoulder.

"Gods, I wish you could see yourselves like this. So fucking beautiful. *Mine.*"

Large, warm hands braced her hips as Byron moved into position behind her. There was no warning before Byron pushed into her in one smooth motion. Mace gasped, her head falling forward so her hair covered her face. Byron slowly pulled back before slamming in again hard, this time forcing a short cry of pleasure from her.

Byron continued to fuck her with long, smooth strokes, forcing her head lower with each thrust. Unable to resist temptation any longer, Mace stuck out her tongue and ran it over Alec's tip as Byron moved her. Alec squeezed his eyes shut for a second before looking back at her and canting his hips up. It wasn't enough to catch Byron's attention, and for a moment Mace was thrilled at feeling like they'd gotten away with something. Not willing to risk Byron's sensual wrath if he caught them, Mace lifted her head out of reach.

"Fuck, Alec. She's so wet and hot. Her cunt is squeezing the hell out of my cock." He slammed into her three more times in rapid succession. "I know how much you love her pussy. Almost as much as I love fucking your ass."

Mace chuckled at the sight of Alec's lust-filled stare. "I think he'd like that."

"I know something he'd like better."

Without saying anything else, Byron slipped from her body, pushing her forward so her pussy now hovered above Alec's cock. When she tried to lower her body to Alec's, Byron stopped her.

"Not yet."

She was about to ask him why not when his finger gently pushed against her ass. It was her turn to lose focus on the sight before her. Byron had prepared her like this before, but they hadn't gone beyond a couple of fingers. This time she knew what he had in mind, and she wasn't about to stop him.

Byron's hand left her for a second before returning, covered with lube. Her body easily swallowed two of his fingers, and a thrill of pleasure spidered through her body as he twisted his hand. He brushed her clit with his thumb on every pass, taking her dangerously close to the edge.

The pleasure receded for a moment when he worked a third finger into her ass, but within moments she was panting, fucking herself back on his hand.

"Gods, she wants it so bad, Alec. Do you think she can handle it? Me in her ass and you in her cunt? Think we should try it?"

Mace knew this was Byron's way of giving her the opportunity to back out. If she said anything, he would stop, gracefully moving them to another position. No blame, no problems.

There was no way she would stop them, not now. She'd been dreaming about this for weeks now, almost as soon as she'd agreed to let them move in with her on board. Her men—both of them—in her body at once. Not wanting to give either of them a chance to stop, Mace thrust back toward Byron while dipping low enough to scrape her wet pussy across Alec's cock. Both men moaned, and Mace knew she had them.

"Don't move, darling. We're going to get Alec into your pussy first, then I'm going to bury myself in your ass. Just stay relaxed and let me take care of you."

It took little effort to move Alec's cock into position, and Mace slid easily onto him. The sharp intake of air through his nose told her he wasn't going to last long. It was fine; they'd have time for slow later. Right now she wanted to be filled.

Byron guided her up and down on Alec, encouraging her to ride him at the same pace Byron had been fucking her moments before. Alec's cock was so thick, it stimulated her entire slick passage, hitting every sensitive spot deep in her body. It felt like they'd been going at it for an eternity before Byron finally stopped her.

"Gods, don't move." Byron's voice came out in a harsh groan. "Not going to last. You both drive me insane."

Mace relaxed her muscles as much as possible. Even covered in lube, the head of Byron's cock felt huge as he slowly started to push past the outer ring of muscles. Alec held still below her, but she could feel his body wavering between wanting to thrust and not wanting to hurt her by moving.

It took longer than she thought it would, but finally Byron filled her. Sweat broke out in a fine layer, covering every inch of her skin. Byron shifted back an inch or two and slid forward once more. Mace couldn't tell which of them moaned, not that it mattered.

All rational thought fled her mind when Alec started to thrust up as best he could. Byron reached around her body and rubbed her clit with his fingers. Between the spanking she'd given Alec, the aborted blowjob for Byron, the finger-fucking she'd received, and the actual fucking now, they were all on a tightwire.

When Byron ground his fingertips against her clit, it was more than she could handle. Every muscle in her body clenched before a scream was ripped from her throat.

Byron stiffened but continued to fuck her through her orgasm. Alec wasn't as strong. Seconds after her, he thrust one final time and moaned out his release from behind his gag. Hot cum filled her pussy, sending her over into a second, smaller orgasm.

"Fuck, fuck, fuck." Byron's muttered chant made Mace's blood hum.

"Please, Bry. I want to feel you."

The death grip he had on her hips tightened even more as he finally pulsed his release into her ass.

After slowing down, Byron had enough presence of mind to carefully withdraw from her before pulling her down beside Alec. He flopped down on the other side, but after a few seconds they both worked to free Alec from the ropes.

Alec ripped the gag from his mouth the second he was able to, grabbed Mace, and rolled on top of her, smothering her mouth in a searing kiss.

"You . . . are . . . amazing." He peppered her face and throat with kisses, licking the sweat from her skin as he went.

Pausing only for a heartbeat, Alec reached up and brought Byron over to kiss him as well. "I love you both."

Mace couldn't imagine ever feeling happier than she did at that moment. Not one, but two men she adored, who loved her just as much.

Reaching up, she cupped their cheeks and smiled. "You both make me so happy."

"And you've given us so much." Alec licked the tip of her nose. "I don't know what we'd do without you."

"Enough with the sentimental bullshit." Byron shifted to his side and flung a leg and arm over both of them, moving them closer together. "You love us, we love you. If anyone tries to hurt you, I'll kill them slowly. Yes, yes. Now go to sleep so we can fuck again soon."

Mace giggled and pressed her face against Byron's chest while Alec spooned her back. She finally felt like she'd come home.

Explore more of the *Bounty* series:
www.riptidepublishing.com/titles/series/bounty

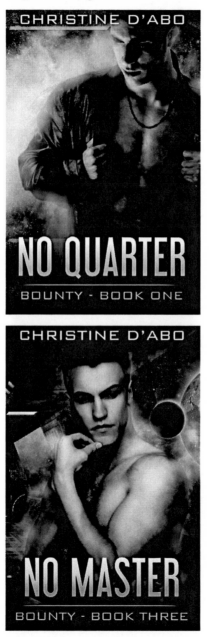

Dear Reader,

Thank you for reading Christine d'Abo's *No Remedy*!

We know your time is precious and you have many, many entertainment options, so it means a lot that you've chosen to spend your time reading. We really hope you enjoyed it.

We'd be honored if you'd consider posting a review—good or bad—on sites like **Amazon, Barnes & Noble, Kobo, Goodreads, Twitter, Facebook, Tumblr,** and your blog or website. We'd also be honored if you told your friends and family about this book. Word of mouth is a book's lifeblood!

For more information on upcoming releases, author interviews, blog tours, contests, giveaways, and more, please sign up for our weekly, spam-free newsletter and visit us around the web:

Newsletter: tinyurl.com/RiptideSignup
Twitter: twitter.com/RiptideBooks
Facebook: facebook.com/RiptidePublishing
Goodreads: tinyurl.com/RiptideOnGoodreads
Tumblr: riptidepublishing.tumblr.com

Thank you so much for Reading the Rainbow!

RiptidePublishing.com

ALSO BY
CHRISTINE D'ABO

Bounty Series
No Quarter
No Master

Rebound Remedy
The Dom Around the Corner

Long Shots Series
Double Shot
A Shot in the Dark
Pulled Long
Calling the Shots
Choose Your Shot: An Interactive Erotic Adventure

Friends and Benefits Series
Sexcapades
Club Wonderland

The Shadow Guild Series
Gilded Hearts
Quicksilver Soul

Taste Test
Facing Dallas
Naughty Nicks
Nailed
Snapped
All Bottled Up

For Christine's full book list, please visit: christinedabo.com

ABOUT THE
AUTHOR

A romance novelist and short story writer, Christine has over thirty publications to her name. She loves to exercise and stops writing just long enough to keep her body in motion too. When she's not pretending to be a ninja in her basement, she's most likely spending time with her family and two dogs.

Website: www.christinedabo.com
Twitter: @Christine_dAbo
Facebook: facebook.com/christine.dabo
Instagram: instagram.com/christine.dabo
Tumblr: christinedabo.tumblr.com

Enjoy more stories like
No Remedy
at RiptidePublishing.com!

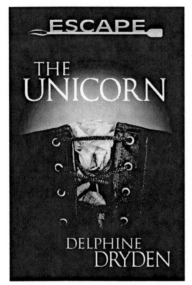

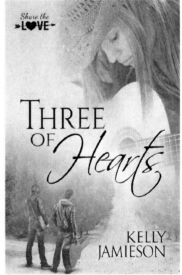

The Unicorn
ISBN: 978-1-62649-372-8

Three of Hearts
ISBN: 978-1-62649-255-4

CPSIA information can be obtained at www.ICGtesting.com
Printed in the USA
LVOW08s1823160516

488465LV00007B/719/P